CAUGHT!

She was going down.

She threw her arms in front of her to break the fall, but something grabbed her across the chest. A warm arm. The action allowed her to regain her footing and stand upright. The arm released her slowly, sliding across her chest and leaving sharp tingles in its wake.

It was Angelford, of course. No one else could possibly be a better witness to her embarrassment.

"What are you doing here?" The words were out before she thought better.

"I will confess after you do."

"It is a good night for stargazing. What is your excuse?"

There was a marked hesitation. "That is mine as well."

She didn't believe it for a second. Her eyes started to adjust. She located another bench and sat.

"What game are you playing?" Angelford asked.

"I have no idea," she replied. It was the truth.

"I give you fair warning," he told her. "You won't like it when I uncover your scheme."

Other **AVON ROMANCES**

Anne Mallory

Masquerading the Marquess

AVON BOOKS
An Imprint of HarperCollinsPublishers

This is a work of fiction. Names, characters, places, and incidents are products of the author's imagination or are used fictitiously and are not to be construed as real. Any resemblance to actual events, locales, organizations, or persons, living or dead, is entirely coincidental.

AVON BOOKS
An Imprint of HarperCollins*Publishers*
10 East 53rd Street
New York, New York 10022-5299

First Avon Books paperback printing: October 2004

Avon Trademark Reg. U.S. Pat. Off. and in Other Countries, Marca Registrada, Hecho en U.S.A.
HarperCollins® is a registered trademark of HarperCollins Publishers Inc.

Printed in the U.S.A.

10 9 8 7 6 5 4 3 2 1

To Mom, for everything,
with love

Special thanks to Selina McLemore

The artist must create a spark before he can make a fire and before art is born, the artist must be ready to be consumed by the fire of his own creation.

—RODIN

Author's Note

Although there were Dalys that worked at the Adelphi Theatre during this time, I have taken liberty with their characters and names.

Also, Robert Cruikshank was a real caricaturist. He was overshadowed by his brother George, but was a well-regarded individual and artist. I have taken liberties with his character as well.

Chapter 1

London, 1823

What was a caricaturist to do when she ran out of material?

Calliope Minton observed the pitch and sway of an aging duke and a newly launched debutante as the two waltzed across the terrazzo floor. She could cast the duke as a tortoise and the young girl as a fresh minnow. No, what about the duke as a long-toothed wolf and the girl as a sheep? Calliope grimaced. The duke and debutante were about as appealing as the ideas floating through her brain.

Calliope was prepared to do something drastic. Even if she had to strip to her shift in the middle of the Killroys' lavish ballroom, at least the ton could discuss something besides the weather.

"Spring certainly has kept its grip on winter. Is it going to be warmer anytime soon?" Miss Sarah Jones asked the small group gathered on the fringe of the Killroys' crowded ballroom.

Clasping her hands to keep from shaking the pretty debutante, Calliope focused on a leafy philodendron in the corner. She had long since decided the foliage was the most interesting thing in attendance.

A mousy girl stepped into view, looking nervous and uncomfortable. Calliope smiled, prompting the girl to straighten her shoulders and tentatively smile in return. Beneath the girls' self-conscious exterior was a warm and intelligent spirit. Next time one of the fashionable girls criticized her, maybe they'd be in for a surprise.

That image was one Calliope dearly wished to publish in the London papers. Too long had the same insipid ladies and feckless gentlemen reigned supreme over the ton. Just once she wanted to see the plain but intelligent girls and lads give back as good as they got. Perhaps if they were to do it en masse . . . She could form a group, create a revolution of sorts. Rise up, normal young people! Break down the social barriers! Overthrow the haughty elite! Calliope's thirst for vengeance against the upper classes took root in the idea. Yes, she could lead them. Overthrow one noble at a time.

Which one first?

Voices rippled through the room, interrupting her thoughts. Lady Killroy motioned for someone to join their group and Calliope froze as she registered the man's jet-black hair and intense onyx eyes.

The too-handsome Marquess of Angelford prowled toward her. Dark locks framed his patrician features, and wealth and privilege clung to him like a winter cloak. He was looking directly at her, his gaze washing over her.

Calliope's heart skipped several beats and she tried to still her racing pulse. Matrons and debutantes preened as Angelford passed. Calliope shifted her feet, caught between irritation and anticipation. The only thing she detested more than his conceit was her own physical response to him.

One noble at a time, a voice in the back of her head said.

He reached their group and acknowledged their hostess, Lady Killroy.

"I am so pleased you could attend our gathering, Lord Angelford," Lady Killroy gushed. Angelford's arrival marked her ball a complete success.

One noble at a time, the voice urged.

"We were discussing the dreadful weather, my lord," Sarah said, "Isn't it wretched?"

"Mmm, yes. We were unable to run the horses last weekend." His rich voice sent warm ripples down Calliope's spine.

Sarah giggled along with Lucinda Fredericks, another pretty young debutante who tried Calliope's patience.

One noble at a time. The voice became more insistent. She plunged into the conversation.

"Considering the inconvenience, I can't believe Aeolus didn't command the winds for you, my lord."

There was a collective gasp. Her once-brave internal voice hesitated and then fled. Calliope wanted to retract the sarcastic comment, but Father Time refused her entreaty. Lady Simpson looked irate. Her fan hammered against her leg.

Calliope could have sworn a fleeting smile crossed Angelford's features, but his expression became even more arrogant. "Perhaps someday he will. Sometimes behavior must be taught." His deep, dark eyes mocked her.

She willed the redness from her cheeks and inclined her head. A discussion of the weather, an internal call to arms and her finest adversary. A disastrous combination. What had she been thinking, to berate him in front of the others? He drove her mad, but she should have waited to discreetly slice him.

The titters from Sarah and Lucinda grated.

"No better than you deserve," Sarah said just loudly enough for Calliope to hear.

Her fingers itched for ink and paper. The mass call to arms once again returned to a personal vendetta. Sarah would lose her smile when she saw the rendition of her vapid look and tart tongue in print, the image of which was already forming in Calliope's mind.

Lady Simpson snapped her ever-present fan closed, interrupting Calliope's thought. "Sometimes a bad apple sneaks past even my watchful gaze, my lord. I do try to be ever vigilant, but from time to time recommendations from some of the gentry are suspect. They tend to be less discerning than those of us with higher standards."

Worry crept into Calliope's mind. She had definitely made a strategic mistake, and probably compromised her position as Lady Simpson's companion. Lord, how she hated society. It was a game she could never win.

Lady Killroy seized the pause, obviously eager not to waste the opportunity of having Angelford at hand. "Yes, it's always hard to find good help. On a more interesting note, Miss Jones was commenting on the new Italian marble being used at the palace. She and Miss Fredericks were recently presented at St. James's."

Sarah took her cue. "Oh, yes. The marble is the loveliest shade of gray. And they found these lovely plants. They looked lovely in the . . ."

Calliope blotted out Sarah's *lovely* voice, which could continue inane conversation for hours. She noticed Angelford's boredom and felt a dash of good humor return at the thought of his being cornered by the two twits all evening.

Lady Simpson and Lady Killroy walked a few steps to the right in an obvious matchmaking attempt. Putting their heads together, unmindful as usual of being overheard by Calliope, Lady Simpson said softly, "Angelford has been out quite frequently this season. I figured his absence this past week meant he had once again disappeared, but his appearance tonight is promising."

"Do you suppose he could be in the market?"

"Anything is possible, though the mamas

haven't picked up the scent. If I had a daughter of marriageable age, I would be battle-ready."

"He's one of the ripest plums in England, although Killroy is of the mind he'll never marry," Lady Killroy said.

Lady Simpson's fan flicked open. "They all do eventually."

"Yes, but there's something different about Angelford. He doesn't chase the ladies of the ton, though I know many who would love to snare him."

"He likes the muslin well enough."

"Yes, well, every man likes their kind."

"Some more than most."

"You don't suppose he will end up like the former Viscount Salisbury?"

"Besotted of his mistress? I tend to think Angelford will be more like the Duke of Kent, he'll come through when duty calls."

The Viscount Salisbury. A shiver traversed Calliope's spine. The biddies never tired of the topic of men who refused to marry proper ladies, but slavishly attended to their mistresses. In their lofty opinion, it was a crime against society.

Calliope tamped the emotions their words caused and once again examined the assemblage. It was the same thing she saw every evening. The debutantes held court in their virginal white dresses, the scantily clad widows and married women flirted brazenly and spun in rainbows of dazzling colors, the dandies pranced in even brighter shades and the ever-present rakes leered at anything in a skirt. They melded together on and around the dance floor, their choreographed movements keeping time with the orchestra's melody and society's rhythm.

The scene was nothing new and Calliope cursed her own folly for her present predicament. It had been two years since she had become a caricaturist and begun satirizing the nobility. Two years since she had started devising elaborate ruses to gain entrance into society's hallowed halls, where she could view the inner workings and shadowed secrets of London's finest.

Drawing caricatures had begun as a lark, but striking back at the nobility had become her passion.

A pink-faced Mr. Terrence Smith appeared at Calliope's elbow with two glasses of lemonade. He puffed from exertion. "I came across as quickly as I could."

The two matrons continued gossiping, although Lady Simpson took a moment to cast a pointed look at Terrence.

"What's wrong, Mr. Smith?" Calliope asked.

A fretful look crossed his unremarkable features. He shoved a glass in her hand. "I thought something might be amiss, Miss Stafford. You looked distraught."

She smiled. He had used her present pseudonym. No one in the hall knew her real name.

"Everything's fine, though I appreciate your concern."

Terrence nodded and scowled at the marquess. Calliope smiled at the reproach by the otherwise timid little man. He was such a dear.

A shrill giggle drew his attention to Lucinda Fredericks. He had developed a *tendre* for the vain debutante who allowed him a single dance each night, and only because her guardian forced her to do so. Calliope found his infatuation incomprehensible. But she supported her friend, which meant she reluctantly left Lucinda out of any damaging drawings.

Terrence was Calliope's only friend among society and as far as the ton was concerned they shared many traits. Everything about Terrence made him fodder for the sharks, from his timidity to his lack of looks and fortune.

Calliope took a sip of the saccharine lemonade and restrained a grimace at its taste. Too much sugar. Again.

Terrence continued to gaze longingly at Lucinda, who glanced at him in irritation before touching Angelford's arm in a coy gesture. It was time to sidetrack her friend. "Mr. Smith, how are you progressing on your book of poetry?"

His drooping face perked up. "Quite well, actually. I have penned several poems this week."

"How wonderful. I'd love to read them."

He shot her an anxious look. "I'm . . . I'm still revising."

Terrence was no different from any other young man of his age and station. He dreamed of fortune, fame and winning Lucinda Frederick's hand. He knew writing would not give him any of those things, so he invested in one harebrained scheme after another.

Calliope assessed his apparel. His outmoded coat showed the ineffectiveness of his ventures.

Lady Simpson's voice sliced through her musings. She was staring at Calliope's drink. "Stop lollygagging, girl, and get me some punch. I'm quite parched."

Calliope reminded herself for the hundredth time that she needed material for her deadline. She bit her tongue and nodded. Her pen would flay Lady Simpson later.

"Lady Simpson, it would be my pleasure to fetch you a lemonade," Terrence said.

"Nonsense. Miss Stafford will do so. That's why I employ her."

Calliope cast Terrence a reassuring look, but he had assumed the dogged look of determination, which sometimes caused him trouble.

Calliope shoved her nearly full cup back to Terrence. "I appreciate the offer, Mr. Smith, but I do need the exercise. It's good for my leg."

Lady Simpson's eyes narrowed as she glared down at Calliope's barely visible slipper. At that moment, Angelford turned in her direction, and he also cast a look downward. He must have been listening to their conversation. Heat spread from Calliope's toes to her head and she excused herself before Lady Simpson could make a disparaging comment or Angelford could add his own.

It was one thing to be criticized by Lady Simpson, quite another to have it come from Angelford. Using her walking cane, she headed for the refreshment area, deftly navigating the dancing couples and groups gathered on the perimeter.

The room was stifling. Calliope surreptitiously pulled her dress from her body, trying to create a breeze under the heavy, coarse material. She could feel moisture gathering along her spine and resisted the urge to waft air down the back of her dress.

But then, imagining the scandalized glances the action would garner, she was tempted to do it. Lady Simpson would surely have a fit, or at the very least a fainting spell. The series of thuds reverberating through the room, as the woman's plumpness inelegantly bounced on the floor, would prove satisfying enough to outweigh the consequences.

Calliope was nearing the end of her time with Lady Simpson, and she was more than ready to find a new post. From the outset, the Simpson position had yielded exceptionally lucrative material. As a companion to one of society's matrons, Calliope attended many of the Season's major social events, giving her access to people and activities she had only dreamed of previously.

Unfortunately, she had underestimated her own exposure.

In her two prior positions she had blended into the background and proceeded unnoticed. Yet those roles had not provided her with the rewards she had come to expect from this post. Lady Simpson had the tongue of a viper and delighted in striking those in her path. Calliope was often tempted to pull out parchment and take notes while Lady Simpson gossiped.

As she had in previous positions, Calliope wore her hair in severe, unflattering styles and clothed herself in drab garments and spectacles. But moving in loftier circles had brought her to the notice of the more acidic debutantes, who viewed her as an easy target on which to practice their cutting wit.

She winced. Her scathing reply a few weeks ago to Cecelia Dort's pointed commentary on fashion had been unwise. Her relationship with Lady Simpson had been in a steady decline ever since Calliope had humiliated the reigning debutante.

A line formed at the refreshment table, and Calliope noticed someone had finally propped open a terrace door. She stole a glance back at Lady Simpson, who was engaged in an animated conversation with the elegantly attired Earl of Flanders. Calliope estimated Lady Simpson would monopolize him for at least fifteen minutes. A short but blessed reprieve.

Calliope edged toward the door, trying to keep as many bodies between Lady Simpson and her as possible. A brief period of solitude was in order. Just a little farther. . . .

Lady Simpson gestured to the terrace and Calliope realigned her body toward the refreshment table. But the earl shook his head, drawing the lady's attention once more, and Calliope crossed the threshold and slipped into the cool spring air. The brisk night enveloped her.

Lanterns were strung loosely across the upper terrace, illuminating it in soft light. Walking near the shadows, she avoided contact with the revelers seeking refuge from the stuffy ballroom. Calliope expelled a breath as she glimpsed a niche near the edge of the veranda. Her emotions and body temperature were still in turmoil. She had managed to keep a serene mask in place until that arrogant man had arrived.

Calliope maneuvered around a small hedge, and delight swept through her at the sight of a small bench nestled in an alcove overflowing with colorful spring flowers. The sweet fragrances of clematis and hydrangea were heavenly compared to the overly perfumed bodies inside. She couldn't imagine a more perfect place. She plopped down on the smooth, cold marble and rubbed her neck.

Calliope tipped her head and winked at the heavens. It was a clear evening and even the heavy London air could not contain the twinkles. The constellations gleamed in the night sky. There was Leo and Draco, and if she strained just a little she could almost see Lyra and—

"I say, what a boring rout this was until you joined us, my lord."

Footsteps approached the hedge of her sanctuary. Calliope frowned at the intrusion. Couldn't someone remotely intelligent have come her way? Sarah Jones's repertoire consisted of ten different sayings, and she had just used one.

When no answer came forth, Calliope leaned forward to peer through the hedge, curious to see if Angelford had accompanied Sarah outside.

"I am so pleased you sought us tonight, my lord. The stuffy set has been selfishly keeping you to themselves at the gatherings lately. How utterly trying for you."

"I enjoy their company."

Calliope whipped her head back and shivered. It was definitely Angelford. His strong, silky voice had imprinted itself on her mind the first time she had heard it.

"You are too kind, my lord. I know you must be quite bored with their endless debate. All of that scientific talk and Greek this, Roman that—it fairly makes my poor head turn."

Calliope shook her head. Angelford's intelligence was obvious, even to a ninny. But he was part of the beau monde, and just as lacking as his peers. The ton was overflowing with well-educated members who held extremely conservative views of the world.

A titter drew her back to their conversation.

"You certainly put her in her place, my lord. Quite skillfully, I must say," cooed Lucinda Fredericks.

"And to whom are you referring?"

"Margaret Stafford, of course. Natty little thing. Always trying to appear better than she is. Why, you should hear some of the things out of her mouth. She's a veritable bluestocking."

Calliope could picture the dainty shiver of disgust Lucinda liked to affect when she found something distasteful.

"She is causing Lady Simpson a fit. Why she was hired in the first place, I'll never understand.

She obviously doesn't know her place," Sarah added.

James nodded mechanically to their drivel. This was almost as bad as the time he and Roth were spying on two French lieutenants and their wives came into the room and talked about fans for an entire hour. The lieutenants had beat a hasty retreat after five minutes, but James and Roth had been forced to keep their hiding places until the women left. So help him, if one of these dimwits mentioned a fan, he was leaving.

Like most women, these two latched on to a topic and drove it to ground. He ignored them and mentally reviewed the Corn Laws. The argument in the House last week had been fierce. If he could just sway the three older earls . . .

Sarah looked at him expectantly and he nodded. Apparently satisfied, her mouth moved again. James returned to his review. He should send Finn to gather information on the dissenters, find out if they would be willing to form a coalition.

Both Sarah and Lucinda were gazing at him expectantly. He nodded again and their brows creased. He replayed the conversation. Sarah had asked about his favorite flavored ice.

"Lemon."

She smiled and laid a hand on his sleeve. They must have finally exhausted the topic of Miss Stafford.

There seemed to be more than a little vindictiveness aimed at her, and it wasn't just due to his pointed remark. He had delivered harsher rebukes to Miss Stafford, not that these two had been privy to them.

Strange, that successfully launched debutantes should feel inferior. Margaret Stafford was a mere lady's companion. Compared to these two, she was a neophyte. She didn't compare in looks or breeding. Indeed, she hardly garnered a second glance. James had the distinct impression that to most people she simply blended into the décor.

But he wasn't most people. He had been trying to shake some spell ever since overhearing Miss Stafford censure Cecilia Dort in support of a debutante Cecilia had been humiliating. He and Miss Stafford had made eye contact and a tingle had prowled his spine. The sensation had become a common occurrence when she was near and was a feeling he neither understood nor enjoyed.

From the outset he had seen spirit, pride and intelligence in those eyes she tried so hard to conceal. And when he had glimpsed her eyes in the ballroom tonight, they had been full of passion. A deep well simmering below the surface, so palpable he could almost taste it.

James felt a powerful need to seek her out and demand to know what she had been thinking at the time. He suppressed a grimace as his father's tortured face flashed in his mind. He couldn't afford his interest in her.

He deliberately riled Miss Stafford each time they came in contact. She had been present at every engagement he had attended for the past few weeks.

A faint rustle sparked his attention, and he

caught a whiff of lavender and a hint of something else. The elusive scent had been vexing him. A reluctant smile curved his lips. Sometimes just thinking about a person could cause her to appear.

"Oh, here comes Lord Pettigrew, this is the waltz I promised him." Sarah looked up and batted her lashes at James. "However, I've saved the last waltz."

James made a noncommittal sound, and Sarah frowned.

Before she could say anything further, Lord Pettigrew and Mr. Terrence Smith approached to claim the two ladies.

"I say, Angelford, did you find the Egyptian scroll I described? Deuced lucky Smith here told me you were looking at a new shipment," Lord Pettigrew said.

James looked at Terrence Smith, a man he couldn't recall having spoken to before. "How did you learn about the shipment?"

Terrence shuffled his feet and cleared his throat. "It is well known you enjoy antiquities, my lord. Someone mentioned the shipment last week. I merely informed Lord Pettigrew when he expressed an interest."

James watched a bead of sweat wind down the younger man's cheek. James inclined his head slightly and turned to Pettigrew. "I will know tomorrow."

"Good, good. Now, my dear, shall we join the others inside?" Pettigrew inelegantly clasped the hand of Sarah Jones to his meaty arm.

She looked at James, her eyes beseeching and

lashes fluttering in a poor imitation of the accomplished flirts. He didn't move a muscle in his face. If he allowed his feelings to show, he doubted the girl would be pleased.

Bowing slightly, he watched the four stroll into the ballroom. Smith was fawning over the Fredericks chit, who in turn was coolly rebuffing his attentions.

"My guardian forces me to dance with you. I don't do it freely."

James shook his head. He wouldn't want to be saddled with either bit of baggage. They would drive any man to Bedlam.

He inspected the terrace. Most of the guests had rejoined the crush inside. He smiled at the predicament of the girl on the other side of the hedge. She could not leave without being seen, and she wasn't aware he already knew of her presence. He pulled a cheroot from his pocket and lit it.

"Miss Stafford, are you spying on me?" James walked around the hedge.

He saw her wide-eyed frozen look, and was pleased at catching her off guard. But all too soon she regained her wits and stiffened her posture, nose in the air.

"It is you, not I, who sneak up on people. Quite bad form."

"Indeed it is. About on par with eavesdropping, I'd say."

She sent him a haughty look. "Eavesdropping connotes intent. I was merely seated here enjoying the air when you three happened by, like ants invading a picnic."

He found himself enjoying the repartee, as usual. "I was taught one should announce one's presence and not skulk in the shadows."

"I'm not surprised to find you've been caught skulking before, Lord Angelford." There was a sparkle in her eyes even as she frowned.

She was never a slowtop. Although her earlier comment in front of the others had been uncommon in its vehemence, it was her habit to verbally abuse him when no one was within earshot.

He smiled. "Miss Stafford, if I didn't know better, I'd say you've missed me."

"Missed you? My lord, I was not even aware you were absent. I'm not even sure we've been properly introduced."

He carefully studied her over his cheroot. On the surface she was no great beauty. In fact, any sparkle was hidden beneath heavy layers of bombazine and netting. She was the exact opposite of the showy women he usually squired about town. Yet something about her drew and held his attention.

It was difficult to discern her features in the evening shadows, but in the ballroom her cap hadn't fully covered hair the color of honey. No fashionable curls hung around her features due to the ruthless hairstyle pulling her skin from her face, but her bone structure was fine. High cheekbones and kissable lips. And unattractive spectacles could not mask bright eyes full of intelligence.

When he had returned her earlier barb, those eyes had contained mortification followed by disdain. He was struck by an unusual twinge of conscience.

He bowed low and plucked a blue-and-purple-tinged flower from a vine covering the hedge. "Miss Stafford, I am pleased to make your acquaintance." He offered her the bloom, but she eyed him suspiciously and didn't accept the token. The flower matched the color of her eyes.

"I am not pleased to make yours, my lord."

He smiled. "Apparently not."

A maid rounded the corner, a tray in her hands. She emitted a squeak as she toppled backward, surprised at finding someone in her way. James grabbed her and the tray before either hit the stones.

"Goodness. I beg your pardon, my lord. I was just collecting stray glasses, and . . ." The maid wrung her hands.

James returned her tray and the maid scurried around the hedge. Miss Stafford sat frowning at him.

"You should probably fetch that drink now, Miss Stafford, or may I call you Margaret?"

She looked outraged. "No, you may not. Good night, my lord."

She rose quickly and, with head held high, walked gracefully across the terrace and into the ballroom. James watched her, extinguished his cheroot and bent to retrieve the soft flower, which he had sacrificed to save the maid and her tray.

He twirled the bloom between his fingers, then picked up Margaret Stafford's forgotten cane, unsure whether to smile or frown.

* * *

Calliope moved into the ballroom and toward the refreshment table. What an irritating man. While reaching for a cup, she was intercepted by the heavy bulk of Lady Simpson.

"Miss Stafford, where have you been?"

She had been on the terrace waiting for the interlopers to leave.

Calliope gathered her wits. "My apologies, Lady Simpson. I grew warm and thought the cool air might be soothing."

"Walking alone in the garden? Really, now, you must endeavor to maintain decorum."

From past experience Calliope found it better to ignore Lady Simpson once she began a tirade. "Yes, my lady. Here is your lemonade."

Lady Simpson sniffed. "When you failed to return, Lord Flanders graciously brought me a cup. I was parched and feeling faint."

Calliope nodded apologetically and set the cup down. "Are you ready to retire?"

Lady Simpson stared at her coldly and raised her voice above the din. "No. However, I do believe it's time you did. Yes, indeed. As others tonight have brought to my attention, it is painfully obvious you are not suited to this position. Your behavior is questionable and your presence disastrous. It is time you find other employment. Unfortunately, it is quite impossible for me to provide you with a good reference, so I will save myself the trouble and not give one at all."

Calliope heard murmurs and snickers. Her eyes skimmed the assembly. A number of people were staring. Some guests appeared to be enjoying the show, some were eyeing her with pity and others looked uncomfortable. Calliope's glance fell on Angelford lounging in the doorway. She tried to read his expression, but he was too far away. No doubt he was pleased with the entertainment unfolding in the ballroom.

Calliope straightened her spine and addressed Lady Simpson. "And it is a good thing, *Georgina,*" Calliope said, drawing out her Christian name. "A reference from you would mean I might be tempted to seek employment from one of your friends, such as Lady Turville. Looking at her muttonchops over dinner every night would probably upset my ability to eat, just as you claimed it upset yours. Or perhaps I would have tried Mrs. Dunleavy's employ. I remember you calling her an ordinary fishmonger. And let's not forget Lady Flanders, a woman you claim dresses and acts like a flagrant strumpet. I would have been plumb fatigued after opening her well-used door for each devotee."

Lady Simpson was sputtering, and her fan mimicked the action as it madly twitched.

Calliope did not falter as weeks of pent up abuse spewed forth. "How kind of you to decide not to recommend me to your friends. What a nuisance to search for a miracle cream to shrink Lady Killroy's nose. I believe you called it piglike?"

Calliope raised her chin. "No, I don't believe a reference from you would do me much good." She started walking and then turned. "By the by, you would make a wonderful lady's maid. Keep it in mind in case fate is unkind."

Calliope swept out of the ballroom. A swath was made for her, people too agog at the verbal interchange to do anything but move out of her way. She marched up the curved staircase and looked toward the green-and-gold-liveried servants. They were staring avidly and showed no sign of movement, so she decided to abandon her cloak.

She exited the Killroy residence and halted at the drive, rubbing her arms. She hadn't given a thought to how she would get home. And she had forgotten her cane on the terrace, blast Angelford. She had no trouble walking most distances unaided, the cane was more a part of her disguise. But her right leg would not hold for the long trek to her real home.

"Miss Stafford! Miss Stafford!"

Terrence raced down the steps, his face etched with anxiety. He skidded to a stop in front of her. "Where will you go? For whom will you work?"

Calliope's shoulders drooped. It was easy enough to disappear and reappear when one used a variety of pseudonyms and attracted little attention, but after tonight she would have a difficult time reentering society in a new guise. "I'm not sure, Mr. Smith. I'll think about that later. Right now I must find a way home."

Terrence cast an uneasy glance toward the mansion's entrance. Any minute the curious would be exiting to see if the spectacle might continue outside.

"Take my carriage. My driver will drop you at your residence." He told her how to identify his carriage and slipped two worn cards from his jacket. One was embossed with a heavy red wax seal, probably the symbol of his father's baronetcy. The other was a calling card. He handed her the latter. "Give this card to my driver and tell him your destination."

The night's events started to weigh on her. She gripped his arm. "Thank you, Terrence."

He looked startled at her use of his given name, but patted her hand. "Send a note around and let me know how you're doing."

She nodded and walked quickly toward the row of carriages parked along the lane. The merged voices of the guests increased in volume, so she stuck to the shadows. She located Terrence's carriage and gave his card to the sleepy driver along with her direction. He asked no questions.

Inside the carriage, Calliope slumped into the well-worn seat and leaned her head against the door as the conveyance moved down the drive.

What a fiasco. Even though a voice in her head cruelly taunted her quick tongue, she placed the responsibility for the disturbance on the Marquess of Angelford. He was undoubtedly the one who had advised Lady Simpson to dismiss her.

One nobleman at a time. The sentiment was sound.

Intent on her thoughts, she missed the thoughtful figure standing in the doorway swinging her forgotten cane lightly in his hand.

Chapter 2

"**C**al, don't you think you've become a bit preoccupied with the Marquess of Angelford?"

Calliope shot Robert Cruikshank, her mentor and caricaturist extraordinaire, a fuming glance and dropped into her soft leather chair. "He provides so much material. How can one not take notice?"

Robert shook his head and ran a hand through his fashionably cut locks. "Three more drawings on the same subject—'The Travails of a Marquess.' It's a bad idea to concentrate on one person, especially a peer who values his privacy."

"I know, but admit it, they are good illustrations."

Robert inspected the drawing in his hand.

"Better than good, they are inspired. Just be careful. Angelford is a powerful lord and isn't accustomed to this type of attention. None of the other artists portray him in such a narrow, unflattering manner."

Robert tossed the sheet to her and leaned back, crossing his shiny Hessians on the edge of her worn mahogany desk.

"At this juncture of your career it would be much easier, as well as safer, to portray those who expect and encourage the notoriety."

Calliope groaned. "They've all been overworked."

Robert shook his head with more than a little irritation. "Cal, that's one thing you need to accept. Everything doesn't need to be new. One of an artist's greatest challenges is to create something exciting from the mundane."

"I understand Robert, really I do. I just think Angelford is an interesting subject." *And he deserves the comeuppance,* she added mentally.

Calliope scanned the image. The marquess was dodging carefully laid traps set by society mamas and debutantes as he scampered after a dozen scantily clad courtesans. Examining the caricature, she felt an odd mixture of satisfaction, anger, sadness and regret. Across the lower right she signed the name *Thomas Landes* with a flourish and slid the sheet back to Robert.

He sighed and carefully placed the sheet on top of the other two caricatures of the marquess. "The publishers are very pleased with your work.

Sales have increased and they are eager for the mysterious Mr. Landes to provide more fodder for their presses. You will notice an increased compensation."

He handed her the banknotes and she noticed the look of pride he tried to conceal. She swelled beneath it.

"Thank you, Robert. You're a dear friend, and I don't know what I'd do without you. I'll have a new selection for you next week, and I promise to choose a different subject." Behind her back she flexed her crossed fingers and promised herself she would indeed try.

His expression turned serious. "See that you do, Cal. I have an uncomfortable feeling about the direction you're taking with the marquess. Most likely these three sketches of Angelford will be published every two weeks, to whet the public's appetite. The others you did of him were much different." He shook his head. "Tongues will wag over these new ones, so be prepared for possible repercussions in the next few months.

"Then again," Robert said, and shrugged in his offhand manner, "since your work is selling well, perhaps you shouldn't take my advice."

Calliope laughed but couldn't hide her nervousness. He looked at her questioningly and lifted his eyebrows. "Out with it."

"Lady Simpson terminated my employment. I need to retire 'Margaret Stafford.' "

"Yes, I know. Even the men at the clubs have been talking about the 'Killroy Incident.' You made Lady Killroy's ball the event of the Season thus far. She is fair to preening from the attention, despite being called porcine."

Some of Calliope's embarrassment must have slipped through her reserve, because Robert reached over and patted her hand. "You should be relieved at this turn of events. If I'm not mistaken, I believe you called Lady Simpson something akin to a harridan quite loudly in front of the entire assemblage.

"Regardless of your feelings for the woman or the fact that the position gave you entrée into the ton, by your own admission you had almost drained her of ideas."

He motioned to a blank sheet of drawing paper. "You really ought to illustrate the occurrence from Margaret's point of view. Other artists are bound to capitalize on the subject, and it would be best to have yourself well represented."

Calliope nodded, opened her top drawer and handed him an already sketched and signed caricature of the event. He took one look at it and roared with laughter.

The picture illustrated a sparrow with a bandaged leg and spectacles applying tar and feathers to a large-mouthed harpy standing in shock. In the background, ornately plumed birds had wide eyes focused on the twosome, and the flock was depicted gathering up bits and pieces of grain on the floor.

"And here is another." She withdrew a second caricature. It was a tribute to Lady Simpson, who wielded a knife as she carved into a roasted pig bearing Lady Killroy's features.

"These are fabulous. The public will love them."

She allowed herself a small smile. Paybacks were quite satisfying. One noble at a time.

"However, it does leave you in rather odd straits." Robert tucked the sketches into his leather satchel. "You may not be able to get a companion position under a different persona. There are limited ways in which one can appear severely dowdy and not be recognized. And you have stressed to me several times the desire for your real identity to remain anonymous."

Yes, anonymity was essential. Calliope knew society. Lady Salisbury had countless friends who would keep her fully abreast of the latest on-dits. And since Margaret Stafford definitely was in the on-dit category at present, Calliope could only breathe a sigh of relief that she had persisted with the disguises.

Robert's hands were crossed in a contemplative fashion as he waited patiently for her response to the dilemma.

Calliope breathed deeply. "Robert, after much consideration, I have decided to view society from a totally different perspective."

His eyebrows rose, but he waited for her to continue.

"However, in order to do so I will need your help finding a man of noble birth who can be completely trustworthy. A nearly impossible request, I know."

She saw more interest gather in his eyes. Robert loved a challenge. "Well, don't keep me in suspense."

"I've decided to become a courtesan."

Robert's face went blank. "A what?"

"A courtesan."

"A courtesan?"

"Yes." Her nerves were already frayed.

He sat up in his chair. "Let me get this straight. You want to be a lady of the night, a bird of paradise, one of the demimonde, fallen?"

Calliope fought to maintain her composure. "Yes, but in name only."

"Ridiculous."

"No, it's a perfect cover."

"Why not a seamstress?"

"Too tedious and limiting."

"Governess?"

"Too restrictive."

"Scullery maid?"

Calliope cringed. "No. Any service position would be skewed to the household I would inhabit."

Robert's face had turned an unbecoming shade of red. Calliope jumped into the brief silence.

"Robert, listen before you negate the idea. I've been mulling this over for days." Calliope examined her ink-stained hands as she reviewed her arguments. "This role will be terrific. I will have access to new haunts and will be able to view the ton from a new perspective. The position will give me insight into the vagaries of society and provide an exceptional opportunity to observe and capitalize on the ton's wilder side. And I stress it will be *in name only*."

Robert paced to the window, his hands clenched at his sides, his protective nature in obvious conflict with the thought of the adventure.

Calliope held her breath. The room was cloaked in silence, and she shifted uncomfortably. Her plush chair, the one extravagant purchase she had allowed herself from her caricature earnings, felt hard.

He had to agree. He had to see this was the best way to proceed. A lady's companion position was closed to her, thanks to her interactions with the infernal Marquess of Angelford. No other position would do. He had to agree.

An eternity passed before she saw Robert's fingers relax. He turned to her, a thoughtful expression on his face. "Your benefactor will need to be completely aware of your position and his role in this undertaking so there is no misunderstanding. In order to meet the appropriate people he will need to be accepted by and have access to the ton."

Calliope allowed herself a tentative gleam of hope. It must have shown in her eyes, because she received a stern look in return. "This role will not be easy, Cal. The rules of this game are quite different from any you have played thus far."

She couldn't stop her head from bobbing in agreement.

He gave her an admonishing look. "I want you to note I feel this is a dangerous idea."

Calliope gave a suitably restrained nod.

He regarded her seriously for a moment and

then regained his usual flippant air, tapping his chin. "As odd as it may be, I happen to know just the person who fulfills the criteria. He would find this charade highly amusing, and despite his rakish appearance he is a gentleman and utterly trustworthy." He paused. "Although he has been out of the country recently, he is well connected and possesses a stinging sense of humor. He would enjoy playing the ton."

Robert walked to the door and touched the handle. Turning back, he said, "I'm going to contact my distant cousin, Stephen, and get back to you by the end of the week. Just remember my cautions."

Calliope exhaled and forced herself to relax. She had passed the first hurdle. Despite any mustered objections, the new role would provide a perfect cover with excellent exposure. The familiar excitement of creating a new persona radiated through her. She was anxious to talk to Deirdre.

A week later, Deirdre Daly rubbed her hands in eager anticipation. "Let me repeat that I think this is a wonderful development. I hated getting you ready for all those boring soirees." Dee grimaced. "What a miserable way to play, no less live."

Calliope grinned at her foster sister as they pillaged Mrs. Daly's dressing room at the Adelphi Theatre. "Yes, it was a truly constraining existence."

But the grin slowly slipped from her face as she mulled the matter further. "Although it is quite advantageous to be one of them. As an outsider looking in, I don't envy some of the poor debutantes who barter themselves each night on the marriage mart."

A bitter note crept into Calliope's voice as the cast of faces who had snubbed her flitted through her head. "However, the ones I feel sorry for are few and far between. Most of the ton is composed of lazy, selfish entities who live off their relatives, contribute very little to society and spend countless hours degrading others."

Deirdre stopped searching through her mother's theater wardrobe and cast her a worried glance. "Callie, is something wrong? Your ranting sounds worse than usual."

Calliope felt weary and older than her twenty-four years. She rubbed her hand over her brow. "No, Dee, I'm fine. I just have a case of opening-night jitters."

Deirdre did not look appeased, but she returned to her task and changed the subject. "I believe you are still on the hook for painting this Saturday. Mr. Franklin still has the ague."

Calliope sighed. For as long as she could remember, she had worked backstage at the Adelphi Theatre, filling in for whoever was absent. Set painting was just one of the many tasks she had undertaken over the years.

"How did I get roped into that again?"

Deirdre wagged her finger at her. "No complaining, remember?"

"I wish I hadn't been so excited when my first caricature sold. Otherwise I never would have told you to remind me not to complain about working backstage."

"Well, you mustn't blame me. I wasn't even in the *Life in London* production. Blame Robert."

But Calliope would never blame Robert for anything. She had met Robert Cruikshank backstage two years ago when the Adelphi produced *Life in London*. Robert had helped illustrate the famous serial by Pierce Egan and had popped in for several of the performances during its over-three-hundred-night run at the Adelphi. One night he had ventured backstage and observed Calliope creating illustrations of the dandies who patronized the rooms of the actresses after each performance. He had been her secret sponsor ever since, toting her caricatures to Ackermann's and returning with her profits. Under his tutelage her caricatures had become increasingly popular.

"I suppose I can fit painting into my schedule. Drawing in the park is never as nice as sitting in the middle of paint fumes all day."

A hatbox fell from a shelf and Deirdre grunted as it hit her shoulder and bounced off. "I'm not going to feel sorry for you, if that's what you're after. At least you won't be practicing dance steps all day with that taskmaster St. Albin." She shuddered as she bent to retrieve the box. "I swear the man has taken lessons from Satan himself."

"Dee!"

Deirdre shot her a look of pure innocence. "I'm only stating the obvious, Callie."

Calliope chuckled and walked toward the closet. "What are you doing in there? I have to meet with Robert's cousin soon and I need an appropriate garment."

Deirdre muttered what sounded like a mild obscenity and then triumphantly held up a flowing piece of material. "Here it is."

"Um, where's the rest of it?"

Deirdre shot her a long-suffering look. "You will look fabulous in this. Now try it on."

Deirdre thrust the dress toward Calliope. The soft silk whispered against her hand, and she fought the urge to stroke the gorgeous fabric against her cheek. It was a lovely shade of turquoise and the material seemed to pool around her.

Deirdre shoved her toward the dressing room and bustled around picking up odds and ends, periodically dismissing and keeping items.

Calliope slowly undressed and slipped on the gown. Deirdre helped her fasten and arrange the material.

"Now, this is excellent."

Calliope frowned. "I repeat, where's the rest of it?"

"Now, none of that. It was your idea to pose as a courtesan, and you certainly can't play the role in your typical clothes. Besides, it's about time we got you into something a little flashier. With all of those drab, dull outfits it's no wonder you didn't pick up an admirer or two."

"Dee, you know how difficult it is in the foreground. Too much attention would've dragged me further into the viper's nest, and made it more difficult to hide our lies."

"Your companion references were well faked. Our contact has been superb in digging up the necessary documents each time. But you did garner your share of attention during the 'grand exit.' "

"And, unfortunately I've brought myself to this."

"This will be a splendid entertainment. You just have to immerse yourself in the role. Mistress to a cousin of a duke and earl, how exciting!"

Calliope frowned at the revealing dress. "Mistress in name only, and I've always been more fond of being in the chorus."

"But now you must be stage front. It's the only way to attract the attention and get the information you need. You've been in the theater business too long not to be able to play the lead role." Deirdre picked up a hairbrush from the dressing table. "So sit down and let me ready you for tonight. A handsome gentleman, a marvelous evening gown, a lovely coiffure, stunning jewelry and a new identity. I quite envy you the adventure."

Calliope laughed and plopped into the proffered chair. "Yes, I seem to remember you were quite willing to go along with all my schemes."

Deirdre pulled the brush through Calliope's hair and fond remembrance lit her eyes. "I was always the one in trouble, however. Mother and Father seemed to think you were the innocent one and I spearheaded the mischief, when really it was the other way around."

There was no antipathy in the statement, only happy memories. The smell of burning assailed Calliope's nostrils. Her breath quickened.

"Lud. The iron is too hot." Deirdre fiddled with the iron and Calliope tried to bring her breathing back under control.

Anything connected to fire always caused her anxiety.

It was so long ago, yet she could still remember the feel of the cinders in her hair. Her home engulfed in flames, her mother's departing form as she ran back inside the inferno. She shut her eyes, trying to block the images. That night had brought her into the care of the Dalys. She had no idea how she managed to make it to their home, but she liked to think it was her mother's spirit guiding her to safety. Her mother had been friends with the acting family, but hadn't visited them often at their house.

In the wee hours of the morning Calliope was discovered huddled on their doorstep, too scared to knock. The Dalys had hustled her into the house and given her warm soup. Then she had been tucked into bed with Deirdre and sung to sleep by Mother Daly. They had been her family ever since.

Little by little Calliope relaxed her tightened muscles and gave herself up to Deirdre's ministrations. Dee expertly pinned her locks and fastened a chestnut wig to her crown. Examining the assorted hues and tints in the containers littering the counter, Deirdre selected shades and placed them next to Calliope's cheek. Once she was satisfied with her selections, she went to work. Deirdre's brows furrowed in concentration as she alternately enhanced Calliope's bone structure and disguised her face. Kohl was painted on her eyelids and a smattering of rouge tinted her cheeks and lips.

"Perfect. The men will be falling all over you. And yet, it won't be you." Deirdre winked wickedly.

Calliope looked in the mirror. Although she saw her own features, she barely recognized the reflection. The odd sensation of freedom overtook her, as it did each time she became someone new. She was a new woman in a new guise, unfettered by the demons of the past. A knock sounded at the door, and before they could respond, it swung open to reveal Robert and a tall blond man with twinkling green eyes.

Robert stopped and his jaw dropped. "Cal?"

Calliope and Deirdre both grinned, and the handsome stranger in dark eveningwear stepped forward. A mixture of emotions crossed his face. His gaze surveyed her with the fond expression of one who had lost and then found an old friend. The warmth in his friendly green eyes sparked a feeling of kinship. His eyes then turned to Deirdre.

"Robert, you failed to mention there were two gorgeous ladies."

Deirdre tossed the man a saucy look. "Callie, I think we should switch roles for the evening. I promise to return with some great material for you."

The stranger winked, and Robert looked like he might gag.

"Please, this is difficult enough as it is. Stephen Chalmers, this is Miss Calliope Minton and Miss Deirdre Daly. Let us not forget the 'Miss' part, shall we?"

"Of course not, cousin. Ladies." He bowed low to each one and shot Robert an unapologetic grin.

Robert ignored him. "Cal, Stephen knows the basics of your situation. I know you will enlighten him later on the particulars. Since tonight is your introduction as a couple, attending the opera should be a safe test to see if you suit one another and if you'd both like to continue this masquerade."

Calliope nodded.

"It's a long ride, so the two of you can decide the specifics of your arrangement." He cleared his throat. "She is to return at a decent hour. Alone." He sent Stephen a warning look, but the blond Adonis blithely brushed it aside.

"Miss Minton, shall we begin?" he inquired as he placed Calliope's hand in his while tossing a last flirtatious wink to Deirdre. He smelled like a forest, fresh pine in the morning. An odd choice of cologne, but refreshing. Most men smelled as cloying as the females.

They exited the theater. At the end of the alley was a splendid carriage harnessed to four dark horses standing at attention. Calliope's palms felt damp as she waded into the still night.

"Are you ready to proceed?" Stephen seemed concerned. He held out a hand to help her inside.

She hesitated but nodded in response. They settled into the carriage and it moved smoothly toward the opera house.

"We are attending *The Barber of Seville*," Stephen said.

"*Il Barbiere i Siviglia* is one of my favorites."

"So you're familiar with the story? Excellent."

"Yes. One has to feel for the sufferings of Bartolo. His jealousy over the beautiful Rosina is comical, but sad to watch."

"I saw it performed at Teatro alla Scala in Milan several years ago with my friend James. A family acquaintance played Figaro and his comic 'Largo al factorum' nearly brought the house down."

"How wonderful. I regret my mother was never able to see it."

Stephen patted her hand. It was an odd reaction, but comforting.

"Other than warning me to be a gentleman and explaining my role in this arrangement, Robert didn't elaborate on the details leading to this ruse. Mind you, I'm delighted to be your escort, but I'm also very curious."

If she truly wanted his help, then she owed it to him to be as honest as possible. "I am a caricaturist, as I'm sure Robert informed you. I recently completed a position as a lady's companion. Quite an awful job, if I do say, but it served its purpose. I thought this role might provide an opportunity to sharpen my skills and vary my acquaintances."

She waited for a negative reaction, but none was forthcoming.

Instead, he said, "A companion to Lady Simpson, correct? I don't envy you the experience."

She searched his unfamiliar features. "How is it I've never seen you in society, Mr. Chalmers?"

"It has been a long time since I have stayed in London more than a few weeks at a time. Too long, really."

Stephen looked to the window and did not elaborate. A short silence ensued, and Calliope pried her nervous fingers from her wrap.

He roused himself and looked at her. "Robert said I must not refer to you as Calliope, although it is quite an ideal name for a woman in your position. Perfectly uncommon."

"I thought Maria would be nice."

"Too plain."

"Cecille?"

"We need something flashy. Something befitting a siren."

She blushed and ran her fingers down the silky blue-green gown.

His eyes lit up. "Esmerelda."

Aghast, Calliope sputtered, "How about Selina?"

"Esmerelda is perfect."

"I'm not an Esmerelda."

He shrugged. "There really is no way around it, since that's what I'll be calling you this evening."

She stared at him, nearly at a loss for words. "You're being difficult."

He grinned unrepentantly. "According to my friends, being difficult is my modus operandi."

What an exasperating man.

Taking pity on her, he sketched his family history and pursuits, telling her he would introduce his friends as they were met. He wasn't titled, but his smooth voice and commanding presence bespoke his heritage. He left gaps in his background, but she made no comment until he was finished.

"Here's what I thought we could do tonight—"

"A woman with a plan. I'm in love."

"Somehow I bet that happens on a frequent basis, Mr. Chalmers." She was quickly becoming comfortable with him, and grateful for the feeling.

He winked, and she continued, "After the last overture I thought we could slip out rather than mill with the others. It will give me time to get my bearings and give you an opportunity to change your mind about this whole scheme."

"I won't change my mind, Miss Minton, but I think it's a sound plan. A quick in and out will titillate the crowd. Make them more curious."

"Exactly. And I should have enough time to determine a direction for my work."

"I haven't yet been able to view your caricatures. What do you illustrate?"

"Society." Calliope was tense. She had assumed Robert would fill him in. After all, Stephen was a member of the ton. What if he wasn't amenable?

"Yes, yes, of course." He waved his hand in dismissal. "Not much else to talk about these days other than social commentary, and nothing else would explain this scheme."

She relaxed and regarded him in amusement.

He leaned forward in his seat. "Whom do you pick on in particular?"

"You'll just have to wait and see."

A flash of surprise crossed his features, and then he sat back and grinned. "Cheeky little thing, aren't you? I just better not see myself pictured at Ackermann's."

She bit back a retort as the carriage pulled to a stop.

Butterflies fluttered in her stomach as Stephen's smile disappeared and a more solemn expression replaced it. "Ready?"

She nodded, and they exited the carriage.

A swarm of people had gathered outside the theater. Milling about the entrance were beggars, pickpockets, prostitutes, courtesans, members of the ton and middle-class men. Each group had a role and every one of them was actively engaging in it. Calliope watched as a pickpocket quickly dipped a hand into the pocket of a man who was soliciting the services of a doxy. A beggar petitioned an inexperienced young man for change. Unable to extricate himself, the young man looked increasingly concerned. The tableau swirled through her consciousness as she prepared herself for her role.

A path opened and they strolled toward the entrance. Calliope observed the demeanor and nuances of the high-paid ladies and adjusted hers accordingly. A practiced flick of the wrist, a brazen flash of the eyes, a skillful movement of the hand across the chest, a sway of the hips. She witnessed subtle flirting and overt invitations. By the time they entered, she was ready to perform.

Calliope took in a deep breath. Esmerelda exhaled.

Stephen smiled appreciatively and gave her waist a reassuring squeeze.

As they meandered through the lobby, Stephen

stopped periodically to chat with acquaintances. The men assessed her with considerable interest, some gawking rudely and others examining her in a speculative, yet friendly manner. She experienced a heady rush of pleasure and power. The reception was better than Calliope had received in any ballroom. The awkwardness of the past faded, and she relaxed.

Stephen guided her toward the stairway, and Calliope caught sight of a fiery-haired beauty, one of the loveliest women she had ever seen. Calliope followed the woman's adoring gaze and looked straight into the midnight eyes of the Marquess of Angelford. He was staring at her intently.

She stumbled slightly and heat raced to her cheeks. Stephen gripped her waist and held her upright, covering the mistake. He sent her a questioning look, but she shook her head. They ascended the stairs and she attempted to regain her composure as they entered his box. Her pleasant feeling of euphoria had evaporated with a single glance from Angelford. She shook off the dark feeling and focused on the task at hand. So what if he was here. Had she really expected never to see him again?

Stephen began sharing humorous stories about several patrons while Calliope made mental notes of their relationships and mannerisms. She unconsciously scanned the boxes for Angelford and then scolded herself when she realized what she was doing. Faces and lorgnettes turned her way, and Calliope found it disconcerting to be scrutinized by the assemblage.

"I find this tableau quite amusing," Stephen said.

She smiled. "Yes, finding caricature ideas is exhilarating when you first begin."

"No, I think you misunderstand. Here I am observing the audience and looking for interesting tidbits about them to share with you, while those below are focused on my beautiful escort and preparing interesting gossip about us. The irony."

He continued to scan the crowd and said as an aside, "I haven't shared our secret. James and Stella don't know our real relationship."

She was about to ask who James and Stella were when she heard someone enter the box. She turned to greet the newcomers and blanched at the familiar dark gaze of Angelford. There were many men named James in the ton, so why did this have to be the one to whom Stephen referred?

The redhead, presumably Stella, entered the box with a bright look on her face. "It's been so long, Stephen."

Stephen stood and kissed her outstretched hand. "Stella, you are stunning as ever."

Stephen grasped the marquess's hand in a familiar manner. "Hullo, James."

James smiled warmly and returned the greeting.

Calliope looked from one to the other. They appeared to be very old, very good friends. She had confessed to the best friend of her nemesis? After she jumped over the railing she was going to hunt Robert down and deliver a good beating.

"James, Stella, this is Esmerelda."

Calliope couldn't help herself and shot Stephen

a quick, dirty look. Her new name sounded even worse when spoken as an introduction than it had in the carriage.

Stephen grinned. The cad had obviously interpreted her thoughts.

Stella smiled, but Angelford's gaze was piercing.

"Stephen has been away so long. Where did the two of you meet?" Stella asked. "I love a good story."

Calliope allowed her lashes to slowly brush her cheekbones, something she had seen other women do, and related the tale they had concocted. "We met in Vauxhall, and it was love at first sight."

Angelford was observing her intently when Stephen said, "Yes, pet, it was something at first sight, definitely."

Angelford turned and glared at Stephen.

The curtain rose and they took their seats. Unfortunately, Calliope was positioned so her leg was brushing Angelford's. She could feel the heat emanating from his leg and tried to surreptitiously move closer to Stephen. Angelford bent away from her, helping Stella arrange her dress, but as he sat back, his legs were even closer. There was nowhere for Calliope to move, so she tried to ignore the flurries in the pit of her stomach.

She folded her clammy hands in her lap. Angelford crossed his ankles and brushed her leg. A flash surged through her and perspiration gathered on her brow.

Calliope again considered how to move out of leg-brushing range without drawing attention. She turned her head slightly and received the full impact of his gaze.

He was smirking.

Anger coursed through her. He had been toying with her the entire time. How typical of a rake to poach on a friend's territory.

She gave him a dark look then fixed her eyes on the stage. Her thoughts were in tumult during the entire first act of the opera.

James's blood pulsed. It was Miss Stafford.

He had known her from the first moment he spied her in the lobby, although he had to credit her for the disguise. It was very good.

Her appearance and hair color were completely changed, but the stormy eyes were the same. She was doing a credible job disguising her voice, although the melodic tones still shot tingles up his spine. Her elusive scent and outraged expression had been the final nails in the coffin of her disguise.

She was an enigma. What game was she playing? What caused her to go from a dowdy lady's companion to a gorgeous courtesan? And what the bloody hell was she doing with Stephen?

The latter was the question foremost on his mind.

Stephen had just returned from a sensitive government assignment and it was uncharacteristic for him to have a mistress. Why had he selected this woman? How had they really met?

James brushed a resigned hand over his left sleeve and straightened his perfectly tailored jacket.

He was going to have to investigate, make some inquiries in the ton.

That meant attending more functions, which he'd never enjoyed. They were trite and endless, even if necessary. Not many people would describe the beau monde as a soothing group, but James had quickly figured how to use them to his advantage. The ton was very much like a continual business negotiation, and James was an excellent businessman. Having to rebuild a fortune made or broke a man in the business world.

A thought nagged at him. He had been attending numerous functions, but had selected only the affairs he knew Lady Simpson would accept, and thus Miss Stafford. The realization made him irritable, so he pushed it aside.

What was she doing here? James had sensed her presence before spotting her in the lobby. When he turned he had expected to see spectacles, cane and dowdy garb. Instead he had seen a barely clad, sparkling beauty, reveling in the attention she attracted.

The sense of connection had grown stronger as she neared, and when she had met his eyes, her identity had been confirmed.

Perhaps she was a spy. At least it would explain his odd reactions to her. It was a cheering notion.

The first act of the opera ended and the assemblage rose. Gentlemen and their escorts began their promenade through the lobby, making connections and showing off their finery. It was business, after all.

Stella spoke to Esmerelda as they excused them-

selves and exited the box. Stephen turned toward
James and leaned back in his chair, casually crossing his ankles to mimic James's posture.

"The ladies will be fine. Now, do you want to
tell me what's going on?"

James shrugged nonchalantly. "Just enjoying
the evening at the opera."

Stephen continued to stare at him. "Mmmm,
yes, that would explain why I felt I was being
warned off my own companion."

James kept his face unchanged, but he mentally chastised himself for the slip. Stephen was
too observant.

"Don't know what you mean."

Stephen's eyes narrowed and James diverted the
conversation. "Isn't it too soon after your return
from the continent to make such an acquisition?
Are you sure she's legitimate?"

Stephen's face abruptly softened and his eyes
twinkled. "Oh, I have nothing to fear from that
quarter."

His expression disgruntled James and made
him uncharacteristically press the subject.
"Something strange is going on. There is something odd about the situation and how you two
met."

"This is a first." Stephen grinned. "The Marquess of Angelford, jealous."

James frowned. "I'm not jealous. I'm concerned
about you."

"As you will."

James's frown deepened and his voice rang with
emphasis. "Believe me, women are not worth the

trouble. Getting foolish over them makes a man weak."

Stephen continued to smile at James, but his voice was directed past him. "My dear, did you find anything interesting?"

James turned to the box entrance and saw the chestnut-haired beauty shooting daggers at him. He hadn't heard her approach and wondered what the hell was wrong with him.

He was off his game.

She had obviously overheard his last remark, and he wondered why he felt a twinge of regret. He had meant every word. What was it about her that made his conscience rear its ugly head?

She turned to Stephen. "I had hoped we could leave. I've had enough of Rossini's opera for the evening, and I think we can find better ways to occupy ourselves." She threw him a saucy look and moved her body invitingly.

James's own body flared, as did his temper, but Stephen was staring at him so he schooled his face into lines of boredom.

Stephen was clearly enjoying James's discomfort.

He rose and took her hand. "Yes, darling, a wonderful idea. Good night, James, and say farewell to Stella for us when she returns."

Stephen drawled the *darling* and each new syllable grated more than the last. They exited the box and left James inside, perturbed.

He willed his body back to normal. His reactions were always unpredictable around her. The only predictable aspect was there would be a reaction.

There was something strange about that girl. He had never been able to resist a puzzle, and he had never encountered one he couldn't solve.

He would expose her secret.

Chapter 3

"I didn't realize you and James were acquainted," Stephen said when they were safely ensconced in the carriage.

"We aren't," Calliope responded. The words came out more tightly than she had planned.

He gave her an assessing look. "I thought our plan was to remain for the second act."

"After the exciting intermission I thought the second act might seem interminable. All of those ideas racing around in my head with no outlet."

Stephen leaned forward. "What are some of your ideas?"

Calliope launched into a description of the various sketches she had planned, successfully distracting his attention from the subject of Angelford. She still hadn't figured out how she was going to tell Stephen that she had slaughtered his best friend in the papers.

Stephen laughed at her opera descriptions and offered suggestions of his own. They tried to one up the other's ideas all the way back to the Adelphi Theatre.

The ride was merry until Stephen said, "Like you, James has a keen eye for observation. Someday I think I'd like to hear the two of you plotting sketches together."

A pounding noise caused the carriage to shudder as lightning split the sky. Calliope tried to laugh at Stephen's comment, but failed. A nervous sound rolled from her throat. Luckily the carriage stopped and she was saved from the conversation.

Stephen threw an old greatcoat over her shoulders and hurried her to the theater's back entrance just as the rain began. "I will come by tomorrow afternoon so we can plan our strategy. Good night, Calliope. It was quite an interesting evening."

She turned and placed her hand on his sleeve as she handed him the coat. "I'm sorry for any rudeness in our abrupt departure from the opera, Mr. Chalmers. Tonight was a bit overwhelming. I truly appreciate your part in this mad scheme. You must let me know when it becomes tiring for you."

Stephen smiled. "You needn't concern yourself with me, Calliope. And please, call me Stephen."

She returned his smile. "Good night, then, Stephen."

He sketched a dashing bow and kissed her hand.

Calliope entered the theater and headed to the dressing room, unnoticed by the busy stagehands. Deirdre breezed into the room a second later. "I want to hear everything! Absolutely everything. How was it? Tell me about the people, your grand entrance, the performance. . . ."

Calliope collapsed into a chair. "I suppose it was a success."

Deirdre's brows drew together in a frown. "Suppose?"

"I believe this new pursuit will serve extremely well if I can keep Stephen Chalmers on my side. Unfortunately, I will encounter many of the same arrogant people."

Deirdre's eyes danced. "Might I remind you that you created the position for that very reason?"

Calliope shot her a dark look. "No, you may not."

She received a knowing glance from Deirdre. "You encountered your deliciously haughty lord, didn't you?"

Calliope scowled. "He's not my lord."

Deirdre rubbed her hands together in glee. "I can't wait to see your next drawing of Angelford. They are some of your best—I can practically taste your feelings."

Calliope stilled. "I will sketch no more of Angelford for a time. Robert warned me against doing so, and I find myself wanting to heed that particular piece of advice. Especially now that there is an added complication, which I'll tell you about in a moment."

Calliope rose and began removing her guise. "Besides, the first of *The Travails* trilogy should be published tomorrow. If Angelford deserves another comeuppance, I can think of the future ones with anticipation."

James glared at the paper.

"What has you so irritable?" Stephen said as he dropped into a wingback chair across from James at White's, a snifter dangling in his hand as he surveyed the club.

James's frown deepened as he glanced at Stephen, whose eyes were suspiciously cheerful. He thought about ignoring his friend, but instead pointed to the sketch and tossed him the paper.

Stephen sipped his brandy and picked up the paper. He scanned the illustration and started choking. The paper bunched in his hand.

James rose and pounded heavily on his back. Stephen gave him a devilish glare, putting James in somewhat better humor. Stephen's color returned to normal and he opened the paper again. James looked over his shoulder at the caricature drawn of him, and then returned to his seat, signaling for another scotch. "It's a ridiculous drawing. I'd like to wring that man's neck."

Stephen continued to study the paper, saying nothing. When he finally looked up, he appeared to be laughing at some hidden joke.

"Stephen, you're getting damn irritating."

Stephen chuckled, causing several heads to turn

their way. "This is too good. This artist has been featuring you?"

James did not know what his friend found so amusing about the situation and gritted his teeth. "Yes."

Stephen glanced back at the drawing, and although he vainly tried to hide it, another smile crossed his face. "How do you define irony? This is certainly an interesting turn of events."

An attendant appeared. James grabbed his drink from the frightened man. "And how is that?"

"The artist who composed the drawing put a great deal of effort and feeling into it, don't you agree?"

James shrugged. When the first illustration appeared, he had known the aspersions were personal. "I suppose."

"Personal grudge, I'd say. What did you do?" Stephen sent him a considering look and took a tentative sip of his brandy. Satisfied, he took a larger swallow.

"Absolutely nothing of which I'm aware. You know I play a discreet role. I'm the epitome of the boring nobleman. I suppose I may want to employ runners to investigate this fellow. He seems a bit too interested in my business and may pose a threat."

Stephen began choking again but recovered quickly and wheezed, "Do you really think that's necessary? No harm has been done, no secrets uncovered."

James smirked. "Can't hold down the drink, old boy? It reminds me of our days at Eton."

Stephen glowered and muttered an expletive.

James grinned, his mood lightening.

Stephen looked at him and sighed. "It appears the individual who created this cartoon sought retribution through the pen. Perhaps you inadvertently insulted the caricaturist. What's his name? Thomas Landes? I doubt you'd find anything physically harmful from the man."

He seemed awfully sure of himself. Suspicion took root. "Is this your work, Stephen?" He pointed at the paper. "Or do you have knowledge of the artist?"

Stephen looked at him in surprised amusement. "You know I have no talent for drawing." He smiled as he gazed at the picture again. "However, I can't say it isn't a grand thought."

James could have cheerfully strangled his friend. "I believe I'll head over to Jackson's. You look like you could use the exercise. Care to join me?"

Stephen continued to grin. "I certainly know better than to box with you when you're in such a foul mood."

"Tell me about your new ladybird."

A shuttered look fell over Stephen's face, and he put the paper on the table. "She is a lady of unusual talents and has an engaging sense of humor. I enjoy her company."

"Did you two really meet in Vauxhall? She reminds me of a lady's companion who circled the ton several weeks ago. You wouldn't happen to be chasing the ton wenches, now, would you?"

Stephen gave him a horrified glance. "I would

as soon chase a lady of the ton as you would marry."

James smiled in satisfaction. "Then I think you'd better save your hide and give up this particular lightskirt. There's something shifty about her."

"I am quite content with the way things are at the moment, but I appreciate your concern." Stephen absently rolled a cigar through his fingers, pausing to smell its aroma. "However, I am curious to know why you're so interested in my lady friend."

The conversation was heading into territory best avoided. "You have recently returned from a serious situation on the continent. Is it wise to give your trust to a new acquaintance?"

Stephen visibly relaxed. "Times are changing, James. Perhaps it's time you let down your walls a bit."

James stiffened and changed the subject.

They fell into a comfortable discussion and the tension diminished. This was Stephen. It was inconceivable that something as trivial as a woman should ever come between them.

"Stephen, I really don't think new clothes are necessary. I have many to choose from in the wardrobe department, and I'm not above making modifications if a garment doesn't suit."

Stephen had been nattering her for the past week about purchasing new clothes. He swung the curricle wide of a large rut in the road and frowned.

"Calliope, it's not just evening gowns you require. There are day dresses, morning dresses, bonnets, turbans, gloves, fans—"

"Yes, yes, I'm well aware of what constitutes fashion." She tried to keep the disgruntlement from her voice.

"In your previous post with Lady Simpson weren't you required to dress for the occasion?"

Calliope shrugged. "Yes, but I could service the same unexceptional frocks and accessories for many occasions. Black, gray and brown are rather easy to use over and over."

He grimaced. "Those obviously won't suffice."

"Where are we headed?"

"Madame Giselle's."

Calliope went rigid. "She is the most exclusive modiste in London."

"And she will make you gowns damn well better than serviceable."

She mentally tallied her savings. She could not afford more than a few gowns from the renowned French émigré. Calliope looked down at the only gown she possessed that passed for a fashionable day dress. Stephen was right, her wardrobe needed updating.

She sighed. Two gowns. She would purchase two outrageously priced gowns and consider it a necessary expense.

They reached Madame Giselle's shop in time to see Lady Simpson and Lady Flanders exit.

"I can't believe the nerve of that woman. I will have Flanders speak to her right away. Refusing us both, the gall!"

Calliope ducked her head as the two angry ladies entered the waiting carriage in front of the shop. It was more of a reflex, because she knew they would never connect Esmerelda to Margaret Stafford.

Calliope grabbed Stephen's arm as the ladies' carriage navigated into the street. "Stephen, Madame Giselle will never outfit me with so much as a bolt."

Stephen grinned. "I'm confident if Giselle knew you were the recent companion of Lady Simpson and ready to take the ton by storm she would instantly lend a hand. Notoriety is good for business."

He assisted her from the curricle and handed the reins to his tiger. They entered the hallowed dressmaker's shop.

Whatever Calliope had expected, this was not it. The shop looked like a storm had been unleashed inside. Bolts of cloth, sketches and measuring implements were strewn about, and several half-finished dresses lay discarded on the floor near a back room. Three harried girls scurried around trying to tidy the endless mess.

"Ah, Monsieur Chalmers, so nice to see you."

Stephen took the hand of a tall, severely dressed woman with upswept hair. "Madame Giselle, your beauty is a light in these dark times."

"Bah, I am not one of those half-wit females you like to chase. Hurry and tell me what you want. The Duchess of Kent was here today, and she thinks she runs the country already. It was a trying enough day ministering to her whims without you and your empty flattery."

Calliope noticed Madame Giselle smoothed her hair and skirt during her caustic reply.

"Madame, I have brought you one of the half-wits." Stephen winked at Calliope. "I wonder if you might have one or two suitable outfits."

Ah, so it was his charm that would win the day. For a moment she had entertained the notion that he had some secret hanging over the seamstress's head. Stephen did some sort of intelligence work for the government, although she hadn't been able to piece together exactly what that entailed.

Madame Giselle's attention shifted to Calliope. She stared at her for a long moment and then circled her, making Calliope feel rather like a rack of beef being inspected. She filed the visual for future use. One caricature idea already. Maybe this trip would pay for itself.

"Yes, I do believe I might have a gown or two for her."

Madame Giselle stared intently. Calliope was sure something had gone unsaid, but she had no idea what it was.

The shop door opened. Madame Giselle's eyes moved past Calliope and lit up. Her hand rose to smooth her hair again, repeating the movement twice this time. Calliope turned to see who had caused the reaction.

Angelford stood in the door looking directly at her, a rakish top hat perched on his head. He maintained eye contact as he removed it.

"Lord Angelford, please come in."

Calliope managed to keep her mouth from gaping at the sweetness in Madame Giselle's voice.

This was the woman half of London feared and the other half groveled at any chance to curry her favor?

"Giselle, I couldn't stay away. You have the best pastries in all of England."

The woman blushed. She actually blushed. The amused irritation caused by Stephen's flattery escalated into a simmer over Angelford's.

"Two of my favorite men. Give me Roth and I'd have the trio complete. Come with me."

She hustled them to the back room and issued sharp commands to the girls to serve tea and cakes.

"I must do a fitting, but please enjoy the refreshments in the interim. What do you require, my lord?"

"A lemon day dress, hold the ornamentals."

Madame Giselle nodded briskly. "It will be delivered tomorrow."

Angelford nodded and helped the gawking assistant with the tea tray before her excited hands could pour it all over him.

Calliope grimaced. Angelford ordering dresses for his mistress was obviously a common occurrence. Madame Giselle hadn't needed a dress size or even a particularly good description of the gown.

"Corinne, come with me. We shall fit Esmerelda."

Calliope blinked. How had the woman known her name?

Stephen waved in dismissal and grabbed a cake. Angelford lifted a cup of tea and watched her.

Madame Giselle ushered her into the fitting area, where Corinne helped Calliope out of her gown. Stripped to her shift, Calliope stood waiting.

Madame Giselle studied her, lips pursed and one finger tapping her lips. "Corinne, the peacock satin. Quickly."

Corinne ran from the room.

"I think we will try darker colors first, yes?" Madame Giselle didn't wait for a response. She turned to the doorway. "Corinne, hurry."

A shadow filled the doorway and Calliope tried to will Corinne to move faster. It was chilly standing nearly naked.

It was not Corinne in the doorway. Calliope's first instinct was to throw her hands in front of her, but obstinacy prevailed and she maintained her stance, jutting her chin forward.

"My lord, you are not allowed in here." Madame Giselle was frowning.

Angelford didn't seem to notice. His gaze lazily scanned Calliope from head to toe, lighting each spot on fire as his eyes dropped. "Try not to spend Stephen's money all in one spot, love."

She placed her hands on her hips. "It's not Stephen's money that you have to worry about being spent. Good day, my lord."

He doffed his hat, smiled and turned. Madame Giselle followed him out. Calliope ran her fingers down the shift as if to lengthen it. She tried to cool her body and mind. He was turning her into a bawdy actress.

Madame Giselle returned, pushing Corinne in front of her. "Please excuse the intrusion, mademoiselle. I don't know what his lordship was thinking."

The next few hours were a whirlwind of pins, fabric, designs and fittings. Calliope was forced to select eveningwear, undergarments and riding habits as well as the requested day dresses. Madame Giselle was adamant she could only gain a sense of a woman's style by looking at every facet of her dress. Calliope finally relaxed and allowed some of her own taste to show through by making suggestions and recommendations.

Calliope decided on a morning dress in vibrant blue and a day dress in deep green. They would suit her courtesan's persona. A bolt of pale violet blue caught her eye.

"I would like the two in the forms we discussed. In addition I would like the violet blue in the classic style, something simple." She couldn't resist the one indulgence for herself, not Esmerelda.

Madame Giselle gave her a measuring look. "Of course, mademoiselle."

"If you could send them to my address, I would be most appreciative. And the bill as well."

"As mademoiselle wishes."

"Thank you, Madame Giselle. Your taste is exquisite and I appreciate the time you have taken with me."

A startled look crossed Madame Giselle's face, quickly replaced with the measuring look. "It has been a pleasure, mademoiselle. I look forward to finishing more garments for you."

There would be no chance of that, but Calliope nodded.

To her relief, Stephen was waiting alone.

"Once more you have made wonderful cakes, Giselle. If you could send ten of each type, words would fail to express my gratitude," he said.

"For you, anything. But I would have made the cakes without your sponsorship. The ingredients were enough."

Stephen nodded and kissed her hand. Calliope knew she had missed something again, but all of the poking and prodding, standing up and sifting through designs she would never be able to afford, had left her physically and mentally exhausted.

Stephen escorted Calliope from the shop and handed her into his curricle as the tiger jumped on the back. "Would you like to attend the races this weekend?"

She looked at him in surprise. "I would love to."

"Wonderful. We will meet James and Stella there."

It was too late to back out, but she could feel her lips twist. "Wonderful," she repeated sourly.

He ignored her sarcasm and pulled into traffic. "Madame Giselle should have at least one of the gowns ready for you tomorrow."

Calliope bounced up the steps to the plain brick townhouse. Sketching in the park was revitalizing. The door was immediately opened and she stepped into the warm, inviting interior. It was like stepping into a forest. Stephen and his plants. Who would have guessed he had a green thumb? An emerald thumb, really. Flora inhabited every section of the house. She had heard more than one maid grumble about living in a jungle.

She placed her sketchpad on the hall table and handed her pelisse to Stephen's butler, Grimmond, currently on loan to her for a few weeks.

Stephen had inherited the small brick townhouse from an uncle. Since his primary residence was more suited to his needs, he used the smaller townhouse to store and display his numerous and assorted collections. A rudimentary staff managed the house, but when it was decided Esmerelda needed a place of her own, the unused townhouse had been the easiest solution. Stephen had put his own butler in charge of imposing order and making a smooth transition. A new staff and inexperienced mistress of the household could be a disastrous combination.

"Miss Daly is in your room, and Mr. Chalmers is in the library. A few parcels arrived from Madame Giselle's an hour ago," Grimmond said in his dry, haughty manner. Calliope wanted to tease the man. He was quite nice when he thought no one was looking, but the presence of two footmen necessitated a display of superiority. She had learned she would receive raised eyebrows and a flat look if she tried anything in front of others.

"Thank you, Grimmond."

Calliope ascended the stairs to see Deirdre first. Bless Madame Giselle, and for more than just the dresses. Adjusting to her new home had been difficult. Calliope had finally gotten a decent night's sleep thanks to Madame Giselle and her army of marauding Huns. She had been so exhausted she couldn't remember anything past placing her head on the still-unfamiliar pillow.

She entered her room. Clothing littered every surface.

"Where did all of this come from? Dee, did you raid the costumes?"

"One of the girls from Madame Giselle's brought them. There are ten dresses here. It's a good thing we are similar in size, because I plan on borrowing quite a few of these."

"There must be some mistake. I ordered three gowns."

"The girl said they were paid in full and the other dresses would be arriving within the week. She wouldn't even accept money for delivering them."

"But who—"

Deirdre wasn't paying any attention. She held up garments for inspection. "Did you order these on two different days? The styles are nearly opposite."

Calliope looked at the two dresses she held aloft. One had obviously been made for Esmerelda, the other for Calliope. A well-executed plan.

"And look at this riding habit. Is Stephen going to teach you to ride?"

"Excuse me for a moment, Dee."

Calliope headed down to the library, her favorite room in her new home. Stephen reclined in front of the fireplace reading. A potted fern sat next to him on the floor. The leaves were oddly shaped, which labeled the plant as one of his experiments.

He looked up from the book. "I heard some of your new garments arrived. How do they look?"

"I can't believe you did this."

"You don't like them?"

"They're lovely. That's not the point. I only needed the three gowns." She could only afford the three gowns.

"You will need more than just those three. If we are to put the proper face on this charade, you must be outfitted in the style I am able to afford. The same argument for you moving into this house applies. Appearances count."

"I will pay you back."

His expression turned serious. "No, you absolutely will not. I can't explain my reasons to you, but if you refuse the gowns it will be one of the greatest blows to my honor anyone could make."

"I don't understand."

"I know, but please trust me."

Calliope nodded for his benefit but resolved to pay him back for the fortune in garments lying in her new bedroom.

She would definitely arrive in Newmarket in style.

"And they're off!"

Shouts and cries greeted the announcement as the gate went up. Prime horseflesh rounded the track. The crowd urged the riders on and the riders drove the beasts forth.

"Come on, Devil's Own!"

"Get in there, Cypress Tale!"

"Knock it loose, Credinburgh's Bane!"

The stands were full of people actively engaged in betting and cheering, seeing and being seen. It was a gorgeous spring day with a crisp breeze and no clouds in the sky. The day reflected the crowd's mood.

Calliope lapped up the excitement. She wished Deirdre had been able to join them, but rehearsals were in full swing for the new show set to open next month, and the weekend trip to Newmarket had been out of the question. Robert was in the crowd somewhere, but was keeping his distance in public.

"Let's look at the horses in the next race," Stephen suggested.

Calliope put her hand on his arm and they joined the crowd of onlookers. The horses fascinated her. She had never learned to ride, and the powerful beasts were captivating on the track. They didn't look nearly so primal when they were being danced in the park with delicate ladies perched sidesaddle.

A gorgeous, spirited black stallion caught her attention.

"I like number five."

Stephen smiled and rolled up the sheet of statistics. "Excellent choice. I believe I will also choose five."

Stephen escorted her back to their seats and left to place their bets. He usually read all of the statistics aloud. Odd he hadn't this time.

"Esmerelda, a pleasure to see you."

Calliope turned in her seat and smiled at Marcus Stewart, who always managed to appear somewhat of a fallen angel with his dark hair and golden eyes. "Good afternoon, Lord Roth. I haven't seen you since the Campton party last week. Are you enjoying the afternoon at the Heath?"

Marcus unrepentantly sank into Stephen's chair. "I am. And how have you fared? Are you winning or will Chalmers be required to pawn his new townhouse?"

Calliope grinned. "I am up twenty pounds."

"Good to hear. Where is the boy, anyway?"

The "boy" was only a few years younger than Marcus.

"He is placing our bets."

"Ah, yes, the feature race of the afternoon. Should be a good one. Which horse did you choose?"

"Number five."

Marcus cocked a brow. "Thor? Speaking of which, I haven't seen that boy either. Where is he?" Calliope didn't hide her confusion as Marcus scrutinized the other spectators. "Would have thought he'd be here to watch Thor." Marcus snorted. "The names he gives his animals. If I didn't know better I'd say he had vanity problems."

"Who?"

"Roth, get out of my chair."

Stephen nudged Marcus with his foot. Marcus winked at her, ignoring her question. "Chalmers never did like competition from the older folk."

Stephen rolled his eyes. "Yes, Grandfather. Now out of my chair."

Marcus took his time unfolding his long legs and standing up. "Ah, there's the other youngling. Think I'll go put a bee in his bonnet, too."

Calliope followed his gaze. Angelford and Stella were strolling through the crowd. Stella was beautiful in a pale yellow day dress. Calliope would have bet all her winnings it was the garment Angelford had ordered from Madame Giselle.

Marcus moved toward them, and Stephen sat down.

"All set. I put all our winnings on number five."

"All our winnings on one horse? All on Thor?"

Stephen looked surprised. "I thought you didn't know the horse."

"I didn't, but Marcus volunteered the name. Said something about the owner and his vanity."

Stephen laughed and hit his knee with one hand. "I wouldn't put it past Roth to say it to his face either."

"Who?"

"The race is beginning!"

Calliope focused on the gate. The gun sounded, the gate opened and eight magnificent beasts surged forth. The riders leaned forward, their bodies moving in unison with the animals. The pack was tight down the stretch, but as they rounded the corner, three horses pulled away. Thor was third. The animals tore around the track, bodies lunging, chests heaving. The crowd mimicked them and an excited man bumped into her, his breath coming out in puffs. "Hang in there, Champion."

Her blood pounded. Thor was moving into second. *Come on, Thor.* Half a track remained. The rider leaned into the movement and Thor burst around the last turn, hammering toward the finish.

"Stay up there, Champion," the man was muttering.

Thor and Champion were neck and neck. Stephen was smiling. The people in the front row were jumping. Thor broke away and soared through the finish. Calliope felt like jumping too. A man swore. A lady fainted. The crowd cheered.

"We won! We won!"

Calliope hugged Stephen. He looked smug. "Knew we would. Always bet on James's horse in an event race. You stay here, I'll go pick up the winnings."

He scurried off. Calliope sighed. Was it hypocritical of her to have cheered for Angelford's horse?

Calliope followed Stephen with her eyes and saw him join Roth and Angelford. Stella was nowhere to be seen.

People were vacating the stands and Calliope resumed her inspection of the crowd. Even learning Thor was Angelford's horse hadn't dimmed her elation. This setting would make a nice backdrop for a number of drawings. She wished she had her sketchpad. She noticed a scurvy-looking man staring at her, but as soon as she made eye contact he moved to the side and melted into the crowd. Strange.

"Here are your winnings." Stephen handed her thirty pounds.

"Thirty pounds? I thought you wagered it all."

"I did. But the odds aren't the best when betting on one of James's horses."

Calliope pocketed the money with a small measure of triumph. She had begun with two pounds, her limit on the day's gambling. As soon as she had doubled her money she had pocketed the original two pounds and gambled her winnings. It had been hard enough to wager the original two.

"I invited some of the others to dine."

"I hope you invited Roth. I don't believe he brought anyone with him."

Stephen nodded. "Roth has been spending most of his time alone, which is unusual. The man used to be quite social."

Calliope took Stephen's arm and they made their way out of the stands. "I also invited James and Stella. The Pettigrews were standing close, so I was forced to extend an invitation to them as well. They accepted."

The earl had established a marked interest in Esmerelda. She had learned the Pettigrews enjoyed varied entertainments, often with other couples. They were yet another sterling example of the ton, the moral center of all Christendom. Pettigrew frequently hinted for her to attend one of their parties. Someday, when she ran out of cartoon ideas, she would accept.

Stephen would probably have a conniption. He was becoming as protective as Robert. He only left her alone in the company of Roth and Angelford.

Stephen knew of her caricatures of Angelford. Yet, he seemed pleased when she and Angelford were together. When confronted, Stephen had merely grinned and said he liked to "watch the sparks fly." Stephen could be irritating sometimes. She could never rely on him not to leave her stranded with the beast.

Stephen stranded her at dinner.

They had been the last ones to enter the dining room and she had been forced to take the last available seat. The one opposite Angelford.

The mood at the rest of the table was light. Everyone had done well at the races. The Pettigrew threesome chattered. Roth appeared entertained by their conversation. Stella and Stephen were embroiled in a lively discussion.

Only she and the man across from her were silent. Angelford sipped his scotch and observed the rest of the table. And her.

He leaned back in his chair, and she felt his boot touch the top of her slipper. He had stretched his legs out, forcing hers to remain tucked under the chair. She leaned back and lashed out, kicking him in the shin. His eyes glittered.

Calliope widened her eyes and made a show of looking under the table. "Oh, how clumsy of me."

Stephen glanced at her. She smiled, and he resumed his conversation with Stella.

Her toes hurt.

"Tell me, Esmerelda, what do you do in your spare time? Do you have any hobbies?"

It was the first thing Angelford had said to her all day.

"I enjoy reading."

She stabbed a piece of the tender beef on her plate and popped it in her mouth. Stephen had already finished his meal, but she had been pushing hers around her plate.

"What do you like to read?"

"Shakespeare."

"*Macbeth?*"

"*Twelfth Night.*"

"Interesting."

She forced another piece of meat into her mouth, hoping he would stop talking. The juicy beef had lost its flavor and tasted like leather.

"And do you enjoy music?"

She chewed slowly and sipped her water. "Mozart, Rossini, Beethoven." She was being rude and didn't care.

"James, I was telling Esmerelda the other day about Milan and La Scala. Do you remember that night?"

The mocking dropped from Angelford's face and he smiled at Stephen, his eyes crinkling in the corners. A genuine smile from the Marquess of Angelford. Calliope was suddenly glad he had never loosed one on her.

"I do, but I'm surprised you remember." Angelford looked at Stella. "Stephen imbibed a bit too much wine. Thought a contessa was a tavern wench. Nearly got his ears boxed."

"She *was* a tavern wench."

"Aren't we all?" Stella joined in the fun. Calliope didn't want to like her, but it was hard not to. Under different circumstances they might have been friends.

"But she was a tavern wench, I tell you. Ask Roth, he was there."

"Ask me what?"

"About the tavern wench masquerading as a contessa," Angelford said.

"Nearly unmanned Stephen, if I recall."

Stephen looked affronted. "Am I the only one here who remembers the evening correctly? The contessa nearly unmanned James. The tavern wench liked me."

"Sorry, boyo. They were not two women, and you were the one on the ground, not me."

Roth nodded agreement.

Stephen glared at him. "Well, if I remember correctly, Roth ended up in a—"

A piece of bread bounced off Stephen's head. "I insist we cease now before the three of us damage what's left of our reputations," Roth said.

Suddenly all three of them were smiling. Calliope remembered Madame Giselle's comment about the trio.

The lighthearted bantering continued, and Calliope found herself swept into the fray.

Calliope strolled out of the Newmarket inn and into the cool night. Her back and right leg ached from the ramrod posture she had maintained throughout dinner. Why couldn't Stephen have invited only Roth? And perhaps Stella sans Angelford?

Dinner had proven to be much more lively after the Milan memories, but it had been too late to help her aching back.

The cloudless day had spilled into the night. The stars shone brilliantly this far from the London haze.

How nice it was to spend time away from the bustle of town. Too bad they would be returning on the morrow.

She walked farther into the small garden outside the inn. One of the benches she had spied earlier would be perfect for stargazing and was close enough to the inn to keep her out of trouble if one of the drunks coming out of the taverns happened by. She skirted a few hedges and peered into the dark recess of the garden. Moving from memory, she neared one of the three benches facing the small fountain in the center. It was a modest garden, and quite perfect for uninterrupted gazing.

She was certain one of the benches was straight ahead, but her eyes hadn't totally adjusted to the dark. She tentatively stuck out a foot and hit stone. Success.

She walked forward and hit an object with her right foot. She stumbled forward and her left foot tangled in the lowered hem of her dress. Damn roots. She hadn't seen them this afternoon.

She was going down.

She threw her arms in front of her to break the fall, but something grabbed her across the chest. A warm arm. The action allowed her to regain her footing and stand upright. The arm released her slowly, sliding across her chest and leaving sharp tingles in its wake.

A long shadowy leg lifted, bent at the knee and

rested on top of the bench. There was no other movement. The mysterious root had been a foot.

"I believe the other two benches are empty."

It was Angelford, of course. No one else could possibly be a better witness to her embarrassment.

"What are you doing here?" The words were out before she thought better of speaking. She could picture his raised brow, but could barely discern his form stretched out on the stone.

"I will confess after you do."

"It is a good night for stargazing. What is your excuse?"

There was a marked hesitation. "That is mine as well."

She didn't believe it for a second. Her eyes started to adjust. She located another bench and sat. "Marvelous. Which constellations have you spotted?"

"Ursa Major, Cassiopeia, Cancer, Leo . . ." He rattled off a dozen and she was glad the darkness hid her dropped jaw.

"I'm still trying to find Hydra. Can you help?" The voice dripped sarcasm.

"Very amusing."

Calliope gazed up into the night, and after a few minutes spotted the multi-headed serpent. "Well, Hercules, if you found Leo and Cancer, just look south. Perhaps you'd have more luck looking for Virgo. It's in the same region." Give him something to think about.

"What game are you playing?"

"I have no idea." It was the truth.

"I give you fair warning. You won't like it when I uncover your scheme. Hercules slew the Hydra."

Calliope drew herself up. Stargazing had lost its appeal. "Hercules also made sure two heads didn't sprout from each one he cut off. Good night, my lord."

She walked through the hedges and back inside the inn. Nightmares of Hercules slaying the Hydra plagued her sleep.

Chapter 4

～◦◦◦～

James tossed the paper to the floor the next evening. A second caricature, this one less flattering than the last.

"What's wrong, James?"

Stella kneaded the muscles in his shoulders. The massage felt good, but he wanted to be tense. Too many things were upsetting him since their return from Newmarket.

"That damn Thomas Landes. I'm going to wring his neck."

Stella gracefully picked up the paper. "Not very fitting. Where does this man get his ideas?"

James threw up his hands. "I've no idea. I instructed Finn to look into the matter. I'll know soon."

She tapped the paper thoughtfully. "Maybe you

should look at the situations depicted. Where are the ideas spawned?"

James had already tried, but the pictures, though brilliantly rendered and emotional in nature, were vague. "Any number of people with an active imagination could have culled these. The drawings don't give me any more clues to the artist's identity."

"You are awfully interested in this artist."

"I've never been under attack before."

Stella hesitated. "James, I know you didn't come here to discuss these terrible drawings. Why don't we finish the business and have an enjoyable dinner?"

She knew. "Stella, I—"

"I know, dear. I've seen the way you look at her. And the way she tries to hide her interest. If she were free of Stephen I would give you my blessing, for I quite like the girl." Stella hesitated again. "I hope you don't mind my bluntness, but something is wrong with the situation."

He waved her on, already in a mild sort of shock.

"She's not . . . she's not one of us. It's not that she doesn't behave like she is, but there's an aura about her. Almost of innocence. I've been wondering if it's an act, perfectly devious if it is—and guaranteed to bring her fortune and fame—but a part of me thinks her innocence is genuine."

James shook his head. "No, Stella, she has ulterior motives. I will discover them."

She smiled, almost sadly. "Yes, James, I know you will. Now let's eat. Afterwards you can buy me the lovely sapphire necklace I've been admiring as a parting gift to soothe your conscience."

The festively decorated ballroom glowed in red and gold and smelled of lit cinnamon. The cheerful guests sauntered the length of the room, mingling and offering their various services. Buyers and sellers alike. It was a merry atmosphere and one was hard put not to smile at some of the antics.

Calliope did just that as she mentally calculated how much cleavage the flamboyant widow on the settee displayed. Could one measure décolletage in acres?

She added another caricature idea to the growing list in her head. Yes, she could do something with the widow's ample bosom. . . .

She felt a strong presence at her side, indicating Stephen had finally returned.

"I'm glad you're here. What term would you use for a harbor that is too tight for a ship to pass through?" she asked.

"Barred shipyard? Shaven haven? Short seaport? Wrestled vessel? Overwhelmed helm? Surpassed mast? Dismayed quay?"

The unexpected voice startled her and she looked up to see Angelford also contemplating the widow.

"You're not Stephen."

He turned his attention to her, an amused expression on his face. "How astute you are this evening."

"I had some questions concerning sailing."

"I see." He lifted an eyebrow.

It was as if cobwebs instantly formed on her tongue and in her brain when he moved within a few steps of her. Calliope stared unseeing at the widow, trying to determine how to salvage the conversation. Otherwise, she wouldn't be able to use the caricature idea after all. Stephen popped into view next to the barely clad woman.

"Stephen's not the most ardent admirer, hmm?"

Angelford had been on active attack since Newmarket the previous week. Each night brought them face-to-face in a new battle.

The surprising moment's kinship over the widow retreated, and Calliope easily fell into temper. She smiled sweetly. "He's ardent when it counts, my lord."

A wisp of a smile flitted across his face. Or maybe she imagined it.

"Good to hear Stephen can hold up. Wouldn't want his prowess to be questioned."

With superhuman effort, she restrained a blush. "*Stephen's* prowess is not in doubt."

The corner of his mouth lifted. "I have a pleasant solution for eliminating doubt."

"Alcohol?"

"No, you strike me as the adventuresome type." At the last few gatherings he had hinted at her being worse than an adventuress. "The kind of lady who would like to try new things. Maybe play different roles?"

She gripped her dress. "Sounds interesting."

"You must find it so liberating, a woman in

your position. Much easier for you to do as you please than, say, someone within the ton."

Calliope plucked a morsel from a passing waiter's tray and took a bite. "Mmm, yes, you can't do nearly as many delicious things."

"How is the devil's cake?"

"Mouthwatering."

"It looks divine from here. Would you like another?"

She leaned into him and traced a finger down his cravat, her lids heavy and her lips slightly apart. "Desperately."

His warm hand secured hers. "Careful what you ask."

The look in his eyes told her to retreat. Retreat quickly. She smiled lazily and withdrew, trying not to give him the advantage. "I'll keep that in mind, my lord."

He stared hard into her eyes and then turned and walked away. She watched him join a group, which included the new Cabinet minister, a rich merchant's daughter and an actress. It was the beauty of these types of entertainments. They allowed class fusion.

She took a deep breath to slow her quickened heart. Angelford was much more dangerous when he played nice. And much more disconcerting.

A gentleman brushed her backside as he passed, an unquestionably intentional caress. Good Lord, if she received one more proposition she would scream. Indecent offers were all part of the act, but chats with Angelford always made her extra sensitive. She had to stop letting him unsettle her.

Stephen walked over. "How are you managing?"

He looked concerned. She must have let her emotions slip through.

"A bit out of patience with some people, but fine otherwise."

His eyes twinkled. "I missed a good fight? Damn, knew I should have rushed over here sooner."

Calliope gave him an exasperated look. "Right. And miss that lovely view above the widow's dress? I doubt it."

Stephen walked the familiar steps to Lord Holt's brick townhouse, feeling more tired than usual, and happier than he had been in a long while. Calliope Minton, alive after all these years. If only they had found her after the fire, how many wrongs could have been righted?

It wasn't too late to mend things. He owed it to his late mentor to try. And Calliope was like the sister he had never had, which made the days and nights filled with activity fun. Their outings were even more amusing when James was present. Stephen had never seen him react to a woman with such intensity.

James seemed to feel it was his to duty to protect Stephen from his own folly. His eyes followed Calliope's progress around the room at every event, and Stephen was pretty sure protection was not foremost in his mind.

James was in serious trouble if he thought to wiggle out unscathed. It was obvious whatever was going on between the two of them would have James gnashing his teeth for a long time. The tension between them set the air on fire. Every time they were within ten paces of each other sparks erupted.

Stephen enjoyed the fireworks.

Yes, the romantic downfall of the Marquess of Angelford would be spectacular. He smiled as the butler opened the door and escorted him to Holt's study.

"Chalmers, good to see you. Wondered when you'd get around to debriefing."

Lord Holt sat in his favorite chair, the leather permanently dented from long use, and gestured for him to be seated.

Stephen looked around and saw nothing had changed since his last visit to his superior. The room had been designed for intimidation. Low light streamed through shuttered windows, highlighting the visitor. On the other hand, Holt, spymaster of the Foreign Office, was cast into dark relief. It was a good visual effect, as it masked his more subtle expressions. The furnishings were dark and designed to put the visitor at a disadvantage.

Stephen sat comfortably in the offered chair. He was no longer the green lad he had been at twenty. The room, best known for the interrogations held there, had become a room like any other.

"The others should arrive shortly, Chalmers. We need to make some quick decisions, especially given the recent data we have gathered," Holt said. He stroked his pointed chin in the familiar rhythm he had adopted long ago. Stroke, stroke. Pause. Stroke, stroke.

Stephen nodded. He had expected a large gathering. Discussing the options and possibilities of the mission from various perspectives was normal. When the five gentlemen arrived, the questions began. Stephen leaned back in his chair and let the answers roll fluently off his tongue. From years of practice, part of his brain detached to appraise the group while the other segment supplied the information the men craved.

Each man present was a member of Holt's elite group, selected because each held a unique position and possessed an important skill. Only Angelford was absent, having been unexpectedly called to another task. But Stephen had filled him in earlier and received his feedback.

Stephen looked worriedly at the duke, who appeared as ill as the gossips claimed. His face was wan and drawn. He was known for his logic and candor, and Stephen hoped he was consulting a doctor about his health.

The earl seated to his left, a wizard at languages, looked distinguished as usual with his sleek black and silver-shot hair, but something in his demeanor had always put Stephen on edge. Involved in numerous cases on the continent, he was the member Stephen knew the least.

Another earl, to his right, was a leader of the ton and a skilled marksman. He had always reminded Stephen of a bulldog, and the image grew stronger the longer he stared at his blunt features and stubborn eyes. Stephen let his gaze slide away.

The earl was a likable fellow of passing clever-
ness. Of the team he seemed the least suited to intelligence work. Yet Holt included him in most
projects.

Continuing to the right was the baron whose
features were as inscrutable as usual in his tanned
face. The shadows concealed the lower portion of
his face, but Stephen would have bet a five
o'clock shadow had already appeared, the bane
of his valet's existence. The baron was a good
friend and Stephen had always admired him for
his ability to mask his emotions, a most useful
tool for a spy.

The only other nontitled gentleman, whom
Stephen referred to as Mr. Righteous, looked
faintly bored with the proceedings, a strange reaction considering the importance of the topic at
hand. The man's pinched features usually looked
to be on the verge of shattering but today appeared less brittle than usual.

Stephen wound down his presentation.

"In Paris, are you sure?" The duke looked ag-
grieved.

Stephen nodded.

"But how would it come to be there?"

"I believe—" Stephen hesitated as he looked at
Holt, who was rolling a ring in his right hand,
while stroking his chin with his left. The insignia
design on the ring was a bird of prey.

Stephen had seen a ring just like it the night
before.

"—it was moved two months ago. We still have
time to eliminate it," Stephen continued, picking

up his line of thought quickly. Dangerous thoughts were racing through his mind.

Discovering Calliope Minton alive, the ring and the spy list, all within a matter of weeks. Stephen didn't believe in coincidences.

The men in the room continued to ask questions and plan strategy, as other questions circled through Stephen's head.

The old but clear memory of his mentor's dying expression came rushing back and he had to fight the need to hurry home. It was imperative he reach his townhouse.

Calliope's maid bustled into the room. "Is there anything else, miss?"

"No, Betsy, thank you. Have the others left?"

"Yes, miss. The footman, Herbert and I are the last to leave." Betsy was bobbing and shifting her feet back and forth as if the floorboards had turned into hot coals.

"Have a good night, Betsy."

"You too, miss." Betsy hesitated in the doorway. "Begging your pardon, miss, but I'd like to thank you for giving us the night off. Some of the others might think you're a tad strange, but I think you're an angel."

Calliope coughed into her handkerchief to hide her smile. "Thank you, Betsy, that means a lot."

"Good night, miss."

Betsy turned and sprinted down the hall. Her footsteps echoed in the empty house. Calliope smiled in triumph. Stephen owed her a lemon ice. He had been so sure Betsy and Johnson, the driver, had a romance. Calliope had put her money on Herbert.

There were two at least who were going to enjoy their free night. Hopefully Grimmond was having a good time too.

Calliope applied the finishing touches on her makeup. Tonight she and Stephen were attending a small party given by an aging roué.

She looked at the ornate clock on her table. There was still quite a bit of time before Stephen would arrive. She picked up her sketchbook and started drawing.

A sketch took shape. Thorny rosebushes hemmed in the background. A garden bench faced sideways. A debutante leaned back against the bench, attempting to get away from a foul-breathed old man leaning toward her. A young dandy had one foot on a globe and was pinching the debutante from behind. She knew exactly how the girl felt. Stephen's laughing presence had saved her on more than one occasion from bloodying a nose.

Some men were more difficult to handle than others. Although she had felt Angelford's stare frequently in the past few days, he had refrained from approaching her outright. It was as if he had decided to end the cat-and-mouse game they had been playing for weeks. She wasn't sure why the thought brought a stab of disappointment. Being away from his overpowering presence made it much easier to formulate sketch ideas. She flipped the page and moved her hand absently across the paper.

Calliope checked the clock again. Little time had passed. Why was she so uneasy? She looked at the new page. She was alone in a ballroom and the walls were closing in. Calliope blinked. Where had the notion originated?

A floorboard creaked. She whipped around, but no one was there. The silence of the house stretched. It was just the house settling, nothing else. Funny how one became so sensitive to noise. The Dalys' house was always teaming with sound. From the younger boys bounding from room to room to the ragamuffin dog scurrying about, someone or something was always raising a fuss.

Stephen's servants usually bustled about, but now the house felt watchful. Calliope shifted in her seat. She would convince Stephen to stay in his room down the hall tonight.

Maybe she should get a spot of tea to calm her nerves. She smiled. Tonight she could brew her own tea without receiving raised eyebrows and darting glances from the servants. Grimmond had nearly had apoplexy the first time she'd fetched her own drink.

Poor Grimmond had been uncomfortable leaving the townhouse. Calliope had almost needed to resort to pushing him out the door and latching it behind him. She had finally hinted he could check on how things were faring at Stephen's primary residence. Grimmond had never complained about his interim role, but she knew he worried about Stephen.

She couldn't wait to find out from Stephen how

much bullying Grimmond had done in the few hours he'd been back.

The rest of the staff thought her a trifle odd; Betsy's well-intentioned appreciation had confirmed Calliope's suspicions. Giving them the night off had only increased their perception of her as peculiar. Peculiar, maybe, but every one of them, bar Grimmond, had disappeared as soon as their shift was complete.

The servants' perceived notions of hierarchy excluded her from joining them. She had scoffed at how the nobility treated their servants. Yet her servants had not allowed her to treat them any differently. She poked her pen into the inkwell. She'd redouble her efforts to win the servants over. She wasn't part of the nobility; the servants would eventually relate to her.

She sighed. She missed the camaraderie of the active theater atmosphere. But loneliness could be kept at bay. The endless parties and ideas were what she had wanted. And they were what she had received.

Calliope looked down at her paper. The walls had gotten closer and there were faces in the windows.

Tea. Go get some tea, you ninny.

The floorboard in her room creaked again, and suddenly the kitchen seemed a long way off.

Calliope gathered her remaining courage and descended the stairs to brew a cup and wait for Stephen.

* * *

The man gazed at the slim shaft of light coming from the townhouse window. The little filly was probably getting ready for a big night out. He spat on the sidewalk, and a snarl curved his lips. Fancy men and their fancy pieces. He had no use for the first, but the latter might make a fun bit of sport when this assignment was over. A wicked gleam lit his eyes. A fun bit, indeed.

Footsteps interrupted his thoughts. A young lad ran up the path toward the house. The man pulled out a baton and held still. The lad moved just past his hiding spot. Thunk. The boy crumpled lifelessly to the ground. The man stepped over the slight body and rifled through the boy's pockets. Picking up an envelope, he ripped it open and scanned the contents.

> *Cal, leave the house immediately. Take the carriage to the Dalys'. I will explain all when I reach you.*
>
> *Stephen*

Good, the man thought. *Very good.* He looked up at the weak but steady stream of light from the window. No rush here. Nothing to tip the gal off. He could take his time dealing with Chalmers and finish here later. He rifled through the rest of the boy's clothes, pocketing some loose bills and a most likely stolen pocket watch, and then he lifted the inert body and melted into the shadows.

*   *   *

Stephen backed against the cold railing. He was outnumbered. The rotten stench of the Thames drifted up to the bridge, but couldn't quite mask the odor of the ruffians surrounding him.

They rushed him, and he managed to lodge a few damaging blows before the sheer number of hands beat him to the ground. Then their feet took over. He felt a heavy object hit the back of his skull and the ground became fuzzy.

"Enough." A tall man advanced to the front. His voice was low and masked like his face and hair. He was obviously in charge.

The attackers backed away, and Stephen gasped for air. He hauled himself up against the bridge railing. The pain in his head was excruciating and his chest seared. His insides felt like collapsed dominoes.

Stephen searched the small, blurred crowd and found no help, only bloodlust.

"Where is the ring?" The tall man asked.

Stephen reached behind him and felt the other side of the railing. He grunted in pain. "Go to hell, traitor."

"Too bad that's your attitude, Chalmers. I believe we could have done business together had you been willing to be more cooperative. However, under the circumstances . . ." The man shrugged, and the gesture confirmed his identity. Stephen had spoken with him no more than five hours earlier.

The puzzle was solved. Stephen finally had answers, but it was too late. He coiled his remaining strength.

The tall man gestured to a burly ruffian wielding a club. "Leonard, you know what to do."

Stephen waited for the thugs to make a swath large enough for the man called Leonard to advance, and then he launched himself over the railing.

"Bloody hell!" he heard from the street above before he plunged into the cold, dark waters of the Thames. His last thought before all went black was a prayer that Calliope had left the townhouse, and that James had received his hastily scrawled message.

Calliope began to worry. It was growing late, and Stephen hadn't arrived or sent a note.

Normally, he was annoyingly punctual, so when he hadn't arrived at nine she had to wave off a feeling of unease. When he hadn't shown by ten she began pacing. When he hadn't arrived by eleven she was ready to go searching.

The mantel clock struck midnight.

Anxiously, she peered through the front window but could see nothing amiss. The street looked empty. The nearly moonless night made it difficult to see. A prickling on the back of her neck made her close the drapes. If she weren't feeling so skittish already, she would have sworn she was being watched.

Things hadn't gone as planned, the man reflected as he watched the pretty face disappear from the window. His employer hadn't been pleased with the outcome. Who would have thought Chalmers would be crazy enough to jump?

The man shrugged. Let the others search for Chalmers in the filthy waters. He alone would find the ring and be rewarded.

A hard, cold-eyed smile crossed his harsh features.

He would find it right after he found out if the lady knew its location. He hoped she did. The spirit he had glimpsed in her would serve him well. Dragging the information out of her slowly would be quite pleasurable.

They didn't call him Curdle for nothing.

Calliope walked to her wardrobe, intent on packing her overnight things and heading to the Dalys'. She sensed something was wrong, could almost taste it in the air. She had a number of things out and ready to pack when she heard another squeak. The creak in the front door hadn't been fixed yet, and she was suddenly glad. Her glance flew around the room and settled on the beautiful gold and mahogany cane she always kept nearby. She grasped it and padded softly to the bedroom door, her stomach clenched tightly. She heard footsteps ascending the stairs. She wiped her cold brow.

A door opened down the hallway and closed half a minute later. Another door was opened and closed. Her door was next.

Calliope raised the heavy rod above her head as the door to her room slowly opened. A man's boot was thrust into the doorway, and the rest of his body followed.

She pulled the cane down with all the strength she could muster, but the rod was easily caught in his hand. She pulled the cane back to jab the intruder in the side, but he yanked her forward.

Calliope found herself hauled unceremoniously against the hard chest of the Marquess of Angelford. He looked down at her, expressionless. Her mouth hung open, she panted slightly. His eyes turned molten and suddenly she was brilliantly aware of every place where his body pressed against her. He continued to melt her with his eyes and for a wild moment she thought he might kiss her. Instead he roughly picked her up and dumped her on the bed.

Her voice came out a little more shrill than usual. "What do you think you're doing? Are you trying to frighten me to death?"

"The next time you want to do harm, might I suggest you employ the second technique first? Sidestepping an unseen jab is more difficult than catching a falling object."

Her heart started to beat at regular intervals again and her initial relief gave way to anger. "And might *I* suggest that simply calling out a greeting or *knocking* at the door, which is the proper way to enter one's house, might save us both the trouble?" She caught her breath and puckered her brow. "Why are you here in the first place?"

He ignored her question and looked around her room. "Going somewhere?"

She resisted the urge to bean him with the cane, not that she would succeed in inflicting any damage to his stone head. "That is none of your business. I repeat, why are you here?"

"Where is Stephen?"

She threw out her hands. "I don't know. He's not here."

Angelford remained silent, but his narrowed eyes continued to scan the room. Her emotions were so riled she couldn't quite separate all the feelings, but she recognized irritation. She jerked the coverlet on the bed. "Not here." She stomped over to the closet and yanked it open. Sarcasm dripped from her voice. "Not here either."

He walked over to a chair and sat. She couldn't credit his gall but decided humoring him a bit might speed up his late, uninvited visit.

"Would you like some tea, my lord? Crumpets, cakes, sandwiches?"

She thought she might have seen the beginnings of a smile, but it was a fleeting impression.

"I need to find Stephen as quickly as possible. Your help would be greatly appreciated." His voice was soft but direct, a voice used to being obeyed.

Calliope was suddenly weary. "My lord, Stephen was supposed to arrive here at nine but hasn't shown. I don't know where he is, and quite frankly I'm worried."

James surveyed the room. "Why are you packing?"

Calliope couldn't explain the irrational drive to leave the house as soon as possible. "It seemed a good idea."

James strode to the window and looked out at the street. "Have you had any other visitors tonight?"

"No, you are the only unwanted guest this evening."

This time she was sure she caught a brief glimpse of a smile.

"Where is your staff?"

"I gave them the evening off."

He frowned. "Then I will leave my man with you. Don't be so foolish again."

He strode from the room, forcing her to run to catch him. "Excuse me? I didn't ask for your assistance or advice. So you can take 'your man' with you."

He ignored her, and she felt like a small dog nipping at the heels of a mastiff. They reached the front hall. A giant of a man with a scar running down the left side of his face stood at the entrance.

"Finn, stay with—" He looked back at her. "—Miss Esmerelda tonight."

She sputtered as he walked out the door.

Calliope looked at the burly man who strongly resembled a tree trunk. "I don't suppose I can convince you to leave?"

Finn's only response was a raised brow.

The weight she had carried since nine o'clock lifted from her shoulders. Damn Angelford. She shook her head. "Well, might as well get you settled. Would you like something to eat?"

Curdle swore.

He had just managed to melt back into the shadows when the carriage arrived. A fancy and a bruiser had gone inside. Only the fancy had come out. He decided to leave the bruiser unchallenged for the lady and the ring. Patience was not his strong suit, but he would not be able to secure help tonight.

There would be another time.

Soon.

James poured two fingers of scotch and settled into his favorite leather chair. He frowned and took a drink. He had been vaguely uneasy all night, sensing something was wrong. He had been at the club halfheartedly taking money from the other card players when Stephen's cryptic note appeared. James's senses had gone on alert.

James had quit the table and headed straight for Stephen's townhouse. The butler had reported that Stephen had left at noon and had not returned.

James then headed to Stephen's second townhouse, the one currently inhabited by that exasperating girl. The frantic look on her features had inflamed his own alarm.

James examined Stephen's note. Unlike his usual small, neat script, the handwriting was large and appeared hastily scrawled:

Come to the house. Matter of utmost urgency.

It was common for Stephen to disappear into the night; as one of England's best spies he was often called to action. But never like this. Not after leaving a note calling to meet. James was worried. The two of them had fought back-to-back day after day as new recruits in the Peninsular Campaign, saved one another on several occasions and developed a sixth sense when something wasn't quite right with the other. Although the last few years had seen them in separate assignments, the sense had never faltered.

Where did the girl fit into this mess? An image of her with her hands on her hips, staring at him defiantly in naught but her shift flashed in his mind. His body responded and he ruthlessly pushed the image aside.

She had shown up with Stephen right after he returned from his last mission. James knew she had haunted the ton as a lady's companion, but why? What secrets did she possess? What did she know?

And where in hell was Stephen?

He hadn't talked to Stephen as much as usual in the past few weeks because of the girl. He was alternately trying to avoid and nettle her and it was hard to do either when Stephen was around. It was a damn inconvenient time to need information from him.

The girl appeared as concerned and agitated as he. She was a hell of an actress if she was directly involved. His instincts told him her distress was real.

James had left Finn with her as much for her protection as to make sure she didn't escape.

Tomorrow he would have answers.

Chapter 5

Calliope woke at daybreak. Gray light sifted around the drapery panels, casting ghostly patterns on the floor and walls. She pulled the heavy damask fabric aside, and peered across the manicured lawn and into the street. The neighborhood was silent. No birds chirped. The street seemed ominously empty.

Determined to reverse the uneasiness of the gloomy morning and her lingering thoughts from the night before, Calliope donned a bright morning dress and warm shawl. She arranged her wig, applied makeup and finished her toilette.

She headed downstairs to check on her new guard. Finn was in the sitting room to the left of the front door, his posture upright and alert, just as she had left him. Somehow Calliope wasn't surprised.

"Good morning, Mr. Finn. Must have been tiring to maintain that position all night."

"Good morning, miss. You're up rather early."

"I don't require much sleep and rather enjoy puttering around in the morning. You look like you could use something with a bit of a warm bite." Calliope nodded to him and left to fix breakfast. The servants had trickled in throughout the late evening and early morning hours, but they had taken her offer to sleep late.

Calliope rubbed her cold hands together. Baking was a treat for her, one she hadn't been able to indulge in since moving into Stephen's townhouse. The servants were suspicious enough without her usurping their duties.

She made her selections easily from the well-stocked larder. She laid a fire in the oven, brightening the room, but as she worked with the dough, an uncomfortable silence permeated the kitchen. Every sound echoed and was magnified.

Calliope forced a whistle, but it was nothing like the melodic tunes that came readily when the sun was shining and the air a cheery temperature. She wished she had invited Finn to join her.

She finished quickly. Relieved to vacate the empty kitchen, she carried a tray of warm scones, jam and hot tea into the sitting room. Finn helped himself. His greedy consumption left little doubt her fare was satisfactory.

"What is your position in the Marquess of Angelford's household, Mr. Finn?"

Finn popped another piece of scone in his

mouth and washed it down with some tea. He was stalling.

"Just the odd job here and there, ma'am."

"What type of odd job?"

"Oh, this and that." He started in on a third scone.

"Your explanation is somewhat vague."

Finn winked. The gesture was odd and softened his scarred and forbidding face. "So are my duties."

The back door opened to the sound of thumping feet and soft voices. Finn set down his cup, rose and stood behind one of Stephen's large plants near the door. There was a rap on the panel.

"Yes?" Calliope asked.

The door slowly opened and Grimmond appeared.

"The staff have returned to their posts, miss. I trust everything went well in our absence? Cook noticed someone had warmed the ovens, and may I say the smell is divine." His gaze encompassed the tray on the table. "Would you care for anything more?"

"Everything is fine, Grimmond, much as I said it would be."

"Very well, miss. I will be in the front parlor should you need me. I will have one of the maids come in a bit later to clear the dishes."

He had seen the two plates but hadn't flickered as much as an eyelash in response. Stephen had confessed their ruse to Grimmond and she was suddenly glad. "Thank you, Grimmond."

He retreated, closing the door behind him.

Finn emerged from behind the door and snatched the last scone. "I will leave as soon as I have a last look around the property, miss."

He patted her on the shoulder before exiting the room. It was an unexpected but reassuring gesture.

The bustle of the servants sounded through the house and Calliope walked to the library, her sanctuary. Soft, luxurious sofas were placed on either side of the fireplace and small tables and comfortable upholstered chairs in deep crimson and green velvet were drawn into the room to accommodate conversation circles. Stephen's multitude of plants enhanced the ambience.

A ray of sunshine peeked through the diamond-paned windows. The street had begun to fill with vendors and early strollers. Soft rays stroked Calliope's cheek as she pressed it against the cool glass. The world once again seemed normal.

Calliope shook her head, feeling foolish about her frightened thoughts from the previous night.

Grimmond appeared in the open doorway. "A card for you, miss."

Calliope accepted the card. "Grimmond, were things well at the other townhouse? Did you speak with Stephen?"

"The house was not up to its usual standard, but the staff has promised to do better. I was unable to speak with Mr. Chalmers."

"He was in residence?"

"Not while I was present. However, he had been there earlier in the day."

Calliope nodded and Grimmond shut the door. She opened the note.

Calliope,

I apologize for missing you last night. I will make it up to you this eve.

Stephen

The words were written in a careless script. He must have been in a hurry.

She didn't know what had occupied him last night, but at the masquerade tonight they would share a good laugh at her misgivings. She smiled softly yet couldn't shrug the lingering unease.

Calliope had been looking forward to the masquerade. The affair was bound to provide countless opportunities for her pen to fly. Stephen had suggested they attend separately, and in the spirit of the event attempt to discern each other's identity.

Perhaps she would even see Angelford. An image of him pulling her into his arms popped into her head. Her skin tingled. Calliope shook her head to clear the thought and sternly reminded herself that she didn't even like the man.

James was ushered into Holt's townhouse as Mr. Ronald Ternberry was exiting.

"Good morning, Angelford," Ternberry said, "I wasn't aware you had scheduled an appointment with Lord Holt today."

"I wasn't under the impression I was required to go through you to visit."

James stepped past Holt's banal secretary, not waiting for a response. Ternberry had an exaggerated notion of his own importance and probably assumed James would consult him next time.

Holt was seated at his desk and rose when James entered his study. The older man didn't appear surprised to see James, although his words belied it.

"Angelford, didn't expect to see you here until our meeting next week."

"Thought I'd stop by to see how the debriefing went yesterday."

"Nothing out of the ordinary. Chalmers said he filled you in on the details this past week."

"Yes, we discussed it the other night, although I would like to have been present at the meeting."

Holt stroked his chin and sat. "I figured as much, but needed you to look into the trouble we are having in the north with the smugglers. Ternberry will send you the notes from Chalmers's debrief."

"Have you put Stephen onto something new?"

Holt nodded. "Chalmers is doing some extended work and Roth is nosing into another matter for me. Otherwise, we're in a bit of a lull."

Lull? If there were ever a lull, Holt would probably shoot himself like Castlereagh had. The man thrived on intrigue and titanic schemes, and where there were none, he created them.

"Stephen didn't mention he was leaving again so soon," James said.

"He wasn't supposed to." Holt smiled.

Holt had been in charge of the unit for fifteen years and was a tight-lipped soul. James was the same way, but found it an annoying trait in others. He didn't expect Holt to elaborate, although if he pushed, Holt would probably relent. But something still didn't feel right. The hesitation held him back from mentioning Stephen's note or pushing the matter.

"Well, then, good day. I will see you next week."

Holt nodded, returning his attention to the papers on his desk as James let himself out.

"How invigorating, I swear the new play has made me a hermit. It's time I had a little fun."

Calliope smiled. Deirdre had been chattering for the past hour.

"I'm glad you are going, Dee. Someday I will get you to quit the stage and collaborate with me."

"La, if it means being squired about by men who look and act like Stephen, count me in."

Calliope chuckled as she slid the final pin into the mass of raven hair piled on top of Deirdre's head.

Stephen had procured an invitation for Deirdre to attend the masquerade as well. Only Robert would be missing from their foursome. Regrettably, he had accepted an invitation to the country for two days of hunting.

It was a shame Robert would not be present. A masquerade made it easy to conceal one's identity, and the four of them would have been able to converse and gallivant quite freely with no one the wiser.

"Mother met Father at a masquerade, you know. It was love at first sight. Or first masked sight, at least." Dee laughed. "He swept her out of there before any of the young bucks claimed her. It was quite a daring feat too." Deirdre's voice rose excitedly as the tale progressed. "Why, he . . ."

Her voice became a pleasant hum in Calliope's head. Calliope didn't need to listen to recite the story back in detail. She had heard it many times. In an acting family, storytelling was a beloved pastime. The more theatrical the yarn, the better.

Calliope's own adventure at the Killroys' ball had proven a hit with the family. The story was deemed a "classic" directly after its first telling. She had been asked to retell it more than once in the last few weeks. The seal of approval, which was given when someone else in the family retold a story, had come just last week when the youngest Daly boy decided to embellish the tale.

". . . and then she slapped him for taking liberties. Ah, but she was really hoping he would take them again. And so he . . ." Deirdre blithely continued.

Calliope arranged Deirdre's mask and perched a jaunty feather in her upswept hair. She glanced critically in the mirror, trying to see if she had missed anything. Deirdre was gowned in green and gold, a devastating combination with her dark hair, dark eyes and fair skin. She looked gorgeous. Calliope couldn't wait for the reaction.

Her own outfit consisted of a smartly cut black and red costume with a domino. Deirdre and she had dressed differently, but with the goal to attract attention together. She was confident they would succeed.

Deirdre heaved a dramatic sigh. Always the performer, she placed a hand upon her chest. ". . . And then they were married. Such a splendid ending to a wonderful tale."

"Marriage is always a nice way to end such tales."

Deirdre tried to hide her face in a powder puff, but Calliope saw the abashed look spread on her face and was immediately contrite. It wasn't Deirdre's fault that Calliope's parents had never married.

She put her arm around Dee. "That was peckish. And it's not a night for peckishness. Let's go set the gentlemen on their ears."

Dee responded with a quick squeeze as they gathered their props and headed downstairs.

"Have a good night, miss. Miss." Grimmond nodded to both of them as they were bustled into the small coach Stephen had provided for when he was unavailable.

Deirdre revived her earlier gaiety and chattered excitedly as the coach swayed over the cobblestones. Her mood was contagious and Calliope felt a curl of anticipation.

They arrived to a flourish of color and noise, waiting excitedly for each carriage to unload its passengers and move on. In turn, they breezed up to the door, handing their invitations to the door attendants, who ushered them into a brightly lit foyer. Tonight there were no grand announcements enumerating the names of the guests. Identities were to remain secret until the moment of revelation much later in the evening. Calliope and Deirdre were encompassed in the din.

They descended the staircase slowly and absorbed the raucous scene. The room was warm and smelled faintly of wine and perfume. Revelers in every shape and size littered the floor. A small group of brightly plumed ladies prattled at the bottom of the steps to the left. A cluster of gaily attired gentlemen leered at them on the right. Couples danced in the center and their bright kaleidoscopes of hues were dazzling as they twirled in rhythmic circles. Across the ballroom, near the patio, huddles of people conversed and drank refreshments while groups of men fondled ladies who were indiscreetly flaunting their wares.

Since tonight's masquerade was being hosted by a group of gentlemen, Calliope thought it should prove to be a lively night. She knew many of the demimonde and some of the more notorious women of the ton were supposed to attend. If the current display was any indication of later events, her pen would fill countless sheets and have a mind of its own in the morning.

Off to the side, James perused the masked guests passively. A few frolickers had discarded their masks, abandoning pretense for drinking and carousing. Others continued their flirtations in disguise. At one time he had loved these debaucheries, but tonight he was on a mission.

The woman in black and red caught his attention. She and another lady in green and gold were chatting with three gentlemen. The pair was striking. They appeared to be good friends and shared glances passed between them.

It was Miss Stafford. He would know her anywhere. She wore a classic gown with a lowered waistline. It was a style she preferred. Evocative without baring anything. The mere hint of her skin was more enticing and provocative than the frilly gowns the women wore that barely kept their assets concealed. If he concentrated, perhaps he could smell her perfume from here.

The other lady took to the dance floor, leaving Miss Stafford with the remaining two admirers. There was still no word from Stephen. Where in the devil was he?

One of the admirers appeared to be getting a bit too free with his hands and James frowned. He found himself walking toward the trio. "Dear lady, would you honor me with this dance?"

She paused and studied him for a moment before acquiescing.

He twirled her onto the dance floor. She fit perfectly in his arms, soft yet strong. In all the times he had seen her at routs, he had never seen her dance. But as he reflected back, no one at those starchy ballrooms would have invited the dowdy Miss Stafford, lady's companion with a cane, to dance.

Her light perfume wrapped around him and squeezed. The thought of anything of hers wrapped around him made his heart beat faster. She relaxed as he pulled her to him and made a circuit about the room.

Calliope was breathless. Angelford twirled her about, and she let herself melt into the movements. She had spotted him across the room earlier, instinctively knowing he would seek her out. The lights in the room became a blur as everything but Angelford receded from view.

She absorbed the spirit of the masquerade and pretended they were two people meeting for the first time. What a dashing suitor. Midnight eyes seared through her and soft lips curved into a smile. Lips like those were definitely . . .

"Are you enjoying yourself tonight, Esmerelda?"

Calliope missed a step. "Lord Angelford, I didn't know you recognized me."

"My dear, I would recognize you in sackcloth."

She didn't answer and he drew her in more closely, branding her everywhere they touched.

"Did you sleep well last night? Finn mentioned you prepared a tasty breakfast." His warm breath tickled her ear as he spun her and leaned closer. "It seems you have many surprising skills."

Heat kindled inside. His fingers trailed up her left arm.

"Have you heard from Stephen?" he asked.

"He said he would meet me here tonight, but I have yet to see him." Her voice was husky.

Angelford nodded thoughtfully.

The waltz ended too quickly and he returned her to her entourage. Bowing low, he kissed her hand and disappeared into the crowd.

Dancing was a heady experience, made all the more so by the proximity of her skillful partner and adversary. His strong lead made dancing easy, even with her tempermental leg.

After that first dance, she was in much demand. For the next two hours she laughed and chatted with nameless, faceless people. She found it novel that the men attended her in much the same manner they did the popular debutantes, only with more provocative suggestions and behavior.

But as the hour grew later and Stephen still hadn't arrived, worry for him overrode the fun.

Calliope declined dances, instead choosing to scan the crowd. Her court, along with Deirdre's, remained loyal, providing beverages and sweets, and reciting outrageous poems and even more outrageous requests.

"My dear, you must allow me to be by your side at the unveiling. Nothing would give me more pleasure," said the man she had identified as Lord Pettigrew.

"May I also offer my services to unveil you?" said Lord Roth, laughter in his voice.

"He's a wastrel, my lady. Just like a baron to have a girl in every shire. I would be a much better choice," intoned a disguised Mr. Ronald Ternberry.

"Ah, but you are a complete boor, Ronnie. The lady needs excitement." Roth's posture was lazy as he nettled Ternberry. She had the distinct impression it was one of his favorite pastimes, and perhaps the real reason he was part of her court.

Other voices were raised in chorus.

"Alas, you are all worthy," Calliope said, "but I have given my pledge to another."

Groans met her statement.

A squat, gravelly-voiced man in a jester costume approached their group with a note. "Mademoiselle, I was told to hand this to you."

She murmured her thanks and opened the note, concealing its contents from the others.

Mademoiselle,

I have discovered information on Stephen's whereabouts. Please meet me in the garden.

Angelford

Why hadn't he just approached her directly? The man was strange and proving to be as secretive as she. The word "please" in the note was unexpected. She shrugged and excused herself from the group. Deirdre was occupied with a charming young man and appeared to be having a grand time, so Calliope signaled that she would return and then headed for the gardens.

A chill hung in the spring air. Calliope shivered and peered into the darkness. Couples were engaged in all sorts of licentious behavior on the terrace. She restrained a blush at one enthusiastic duo and searched for Angelford's all-black attire.

The moon was dim, and she debated the wisdom of heading into the maze of hedges. The lingering unease grew as she looked into the shadowy foliage. Better to stick to the populated areas.

Calliope stepped to the left edge of the terrace. There was no sign of Angelford. She turned to walk back toward the entry when she spied him making his way through the doors.

She waved an arm to flag him, but he looked straight ahead and strode into the hedges. Her brows furrowed in frustration. She sighed and headed into the maze. She caught sight of him, the dim light glinting off his jet-black hair. Calliope opened her mouth to announce her presence when he veered left. What was he doing?

She clenched her jaw, irritated, and quickened her step. She reached the fork and turned left, but there was another branch and no sign of him. She looked down both paths to no avail, and then examined the ground. Fresh footfalls led to the right, so she followed them. She approached another fork some twenty steps in and threw up her hands. He could damn well talk to her in the ballroom.

Calliope smelled ale and dirty clothes a second before a callused hand was clamped over her mouth. An arm encircled her waist and arms, imprisoning her.

"Where is it?" a rough voice demanded.

Calliope struggled against her attacker. His arms were too strong to break free. She kicked backward into his shin with her slipper and bit hard into his hand, causing him to loosen the grip on her mouth.

"Help!" She managed the start of a scream but he quickly clamped his hand back over her mouth using her chin and nose to force her teeth together.

"You'll pay for that," he snarled.

His grip on her nose made Calliope's vision swim. She could not seem to form a coherent thought. Everything dimmed.

She felt a whoosh of air and suddenly the pressure encasing her was gone. She sank to the ground. *Must run.* She awkwardly pushed upward off the rough pebbles. *Which way?* She was unable to distinguish shapes. Firm but gentle hands slid under her arms and lifted her to her feet. A scream rose in her throat.

"Take a deep breath." The soothing tones of Angelford's voice calmed her. "I'm here. Everything will soon be better."

Shadows became shapes, which in turn became objects, and she was finally able to focus on his handsome face. Calliope looked down at the motionless form on the ground and leaned into Angelford, shivering. He tensed, then relaxed.

"Thank you. He appeared from nowhere."

She felt him tense again. "What in hell were you doing out here?"

She pulled away, surprise giving way to anger. "Meeting you."

He scowled. "Meeting me? I'm flattered, but I followed when you left the ballroom."

She frowned and pulled the paper, now crumpled, from her pocket. "I received your message."

He took the note and squinted in the dim moonlight. "I didn't write this."

The attacker stirred and Angelford reached down and thumped him on the head. The man slumped back. A harsh light played on Angelford's face. "I'll see you to your coach. Finn said your servants are back. Make sure you lock your doors tonight. I'll take care of this."

Calliope was too stunned to argue. The excitement of the masquerade was over, and the realization of what might have occurred set in.

He held on to her arm as they reentered the ballroom and steered her to the stairs.

"Wait, my lord, I need to get my, uh, friend."

But Calliope needn't have worried. Deirdre must have observed their progress across the floor and interpreted that there was a problem because she immediately excused herself from her group of admirers amid heavy protests.

"Gentlemen, it has been a lovely time, but I am wanted elsewhere. I bid you adieu."

Deirdre blew kisses to her court and hurried to Calliope.

She sent a questioning look but said nothing. Without a word, Angelford offered an arm to each lady.

It seemed to take an eternity to reach the coach and Calliope tried to steady her shaking hand, which was still draped on Angelford's arm.

He handed them into the carriage. "Have a pleasant night, ladies. I will speak with you soon." His smooth brandy voice washed over Calliope. He bowed and motioned to the driver.

Deirdre sent her another questioning glance, but kept silent as the coach began moving. They encountered no traffic; the majority of guests had elected to remain until the unveiling.

"What's wrong, Callie? What were you doing with Angelford?"

Calliope shook her head. "I don't know, Dee. I don't know. I need to think for a minute."

She looked out the window and saw the black-garbed figure standing on the steps watching the carriage leave. She watched him until they turned the corner and he passed from her vision. A shiver coursed through her.

"Dee, do you think you could stay with me tonight?"

Deirdre looked concerned. "Yes, of course, I will send a note so our parents won't be worried."

Calliope nodded and nestled into the cushions, trying to relax.

Who was the man in the maze? Why had he accosted her? Where was Stephen?

Angelford had saved her from the attacker. She remembered leaning into his warm chest. Her traitorous body had accepted his help. She was beholden to him.

Questions swirled through her mind and collided with intense emotions.

The following morning Deirdre was still attempting to coax answers from her.

"Callie, come home with me. I don't know why you won't tell me what happened last night, but something is obviously wrong." Deirdre looked tired and concerned. "I'm worried about you.

And why didn't Stephen show up? I'm going to give him a piece of my mind next time I see him."

"He must have been detained. Dee, I promise to come by later. There are a few things I need to tend first."

She nudged Deirdre out the door after promising to drop by the family's house. Less than fifteen minutes after Deirdre left, there was a knock at the front door. Calliope looked up as Grimmond walked in.

"Miss, there is a note for you. It was left willy-nilly on the front stoop." A stickler for convention, disapproval laced his voice.

Calliope opened the card as Grimmond walked back out. Sweat broke across her brow and a cold pulse emanated up her body, halting her heart for a beat.

If you wish your family to remain un-harmed, you will deliver the item we seek. The Adelphi is such a lovely theater. It would be a shame, Callie, dear . . .

The letter was unsigned.

Calliope scrawled on a piece of Stephen's stationery, pocketed the threatening note, threw on her pelisse and ran out the door and into the street.

It took a few precious minutes, but she finally managed to catch a hackney. She needed answers and needed them quickly. Only one person seemed to know more about the situation than she. She gave the driver the address and sped off toward the devil's den.

The short trip seemed to take an hour. The driver pulled in front of the huge estate on St. James's Street. She paid the fare and hopped to the ground. She grimaced as she landed on her bad leg. Too late for a cane now.

The hackney took off down the street and she regretted not asking the driver to wait. She looked at the imposing Palladian structure. It epitomized everything she despised. She was alone.

Calliope climbed the stairs and walked nervously to the large door. She took a deep breath and rapped.

A white-haired butler opened the door.

She straightened her shoulders. "I am here to see the Marquess of Angelford. It is a matter of the utmost urgency." She handed him the hastily composed note she had written.

The butler examined the stationery and then surveyed her once again, obviously noting the absence of a coach and attendant. In order to gain time, she had eschewed both. She held her breath; he might refuse her admittance. There was some relief in the thought he might bar her access, but the situation required entry. She lifted her chin and thought, *I belong here,* a technique she used when preparing for her roles and employing one of her many guises.

He opened the door, reluctantly allowing her into the front hall. "Please wait here."

The main hall had three connecting passages. He strode down the one on the left.

As his footsteps echoed in the hallway, she glanced toward the ceiling, reluctantly impressed. The high ceiling and gorgeous banister dominated the entryway. The ceiling was hand-painted with angelic images depicting the heavens.

A curved staircase flowed down and to the right, a small hallway underneath on the left. Intricate marble tiles were arranged artfully in the floor and stairs. A beautiful Aubusson runner curved up the middle of the staircase, and its cousin lay horizontally on the floor. A regal portrait hung on the wall under the curved staircase, and a small Queen Anne desk sat beneath.

The entire scene screamed wealth, and she again experienced the urge to flee.

The butler returned just as she gained control and motioned to her. "Follow me."

She relinquished her pelisse and followed him down the left hall.

James fingered the note and waited.

Templeton, his butler, opened the door. "The stranger on the step, my lord." He then disappeared from view.

James saw her give his butler a disgruntled look before entering the room.

A glance at her disheveled state had him instantly aroused. She looked as if she had just stepped out of bed, thrown on the first thing she could find and then rushed to meet him. Honey-colored hair dripped down her shoulders and a simple lavender morning dress clung to her frame. Satisfaction flowed through him.

She broke his train of thought. "I know my presence is unconventional, but I need information quickly." She gave a tight shrug and moved a bit farther into the room.

He motioned to a chair in front of his desk. She hesitated before slipping into it. "Thank you."

He sat behind his desk, leaned back in the chair, steepled his fingers and waited.

Her brow furrowed, but she said in a rush, "Why did you appear two nights ago? Where is Stephen? Who was the man who attacked me last night? And why is someone sending me threatening notes?"

James dropped his hands and leaned forward. "Threatening notes?"

She hesitated. "I received one this morning. They threatened my family."

He held out his hand. "Let me see it."

She shook her head, and he saw her finger her left pocket. "No, it has personal information. There is no need for you to see it. Suffice to say the note tells me to give them an item or else."

"Do you have this item?"

"I don't know. I don't know what the item is."

"Then why are you here?"

She visibly bristled. "Because you seem to be on my heels the past two days and I believe you are somehow involved in this situation."

"What makes you say that?"

He said it in a nonchalant way and expected her anger. He was not disappointed.

"Forgive me. I'm wasting my time here. Good day, my lord."

"Sit down, Miss Stafford," James ordered in the steely tone that generally caused people to do his bidding.

She turned toward him, a shocked look on her face. "What did you call me?"

He couldn't tamp down the sardonic smile as he gestured toward her. "You forgot to not be yourself today."

A horrified look crossed her face as she grasped at her hair with one hand and her cheek with the other.

"Sit down."

She obeyed this time, but he thought it more from the shock than anything else.

"I have known your identity for quite some time. But I am curious: What turned you from lady's companion to courtesan, Miss Stafford? Surely you were not that down on your luck?"

Her initial shock had obviously subsided somewhat because she shot him an even nastier look than before. She gazed around the room's elegant furnishings. "I doubt someone such as yourself would understand what the peasants of this world have to go through on a daily basis. Please, don't lower my opinion of you any more by asking such inane questions."

His temper flared. "You are a silly girl. I doubt you know what true hardship is."

She seemed to withdraw and sat staring mutely ahead.

He tried to rein in his temper. He had magnificent self-control. Everyone knew it. Why did she always incite him?

He said in a more reasonable tone, "If you want my help, I need to see the note."

She continued to stare at him, not speaking.

"You are involved in a dangerous matter. Give me the damn note."

Her eyes flashed. "I don't want your help. I want answers."

"Sorry, Margaret, you cannot have one without the other."

From the look she was now giving him he wouldn't have been surprised if she launched herself across the desk, fingernails aimed toward his eyes.

"First, I have not given you permission to call me Margaret. Second, you can go to hell, my lord." She grated the "my lord" between her teeth and he wondered if she might choke on it.

As she rose, her deep blue eyes flashed in rage. "Good day, *my lord*."

She turned her back on him and started for the door, wobbling for a second before gaining her footing. James was around the desk in a flash. He firmly took her left arm and escorted her to the door of the study, ignoring her angry gasp. He let go at the door, allowing her to find her own way out.

James pulled the cord moments after she stalked out of the room, and Templeton's face appeared in the doorway scant seconds later. He must have run.

"Have one of the footmen follow the lady and report back to me."

Templeton nodded and closed the door behind him.

James leaned against his desk. He had handled that poorly. Women usually fell over themselves trying vainly to please him. It was quite a novel experience to find one so disagreeable. She hadn't softened any since their first meeting.

Actually she had felt remarkably soft leaning into him last night. James shook his head.

He had been unable to glean any hard information from last night's attacker. After putting the ladies in the coach, he had returned to the maze to interrogate the hoodlum and relieve a bit of frustration. The man admitted under duress that he had been hired by a bloke to do a few jobs. He had received money to scare the girl and inquire about an object. When given the job he had not asked any questions.

After receiving a bit more abuse from a frustrated James, the man revealed he only heard the man's voice once and that further instructions and payoffs were given through a third party, a man named Curdle. The only real information James had gathered about the leader's identity was, "He sounded real uppity, like you."

James had sent Finn to find Curdle. Hopefully, Curdle would lead them to the unknown man and eventually to Stephen.

James unfolded the threatening note, which he had removed from her left pocket. She was hardheaded and stubborn. He needed to discover if she was scheming as well.

*   *   *

Calliope waited until she had closed the door to Stephen's study before audibly giving in to her rage. She didn't feel any better afterward. She collapsed against the door and a wave of despair drowned her anger. She had been living from one emotion to another for the past two days. And she seemed to be making one bad choice after another. Had she hoped he would help her without any information in return?

Calliope walked to the desk and dropped wearily into her chair, putting her head on her arms. She was ready to give in to a well-deserved cry when she heard a rap on the front door. Calliope heard Grimmond greet the interloper and wished she had told him she was unavailable. She would remedy that when he came to inform her of the guest.

The door opened but she didn't look up. "Grimmond, I'm unavailable. Please inform whomever it is to leave a card."

"I'm afraid it's a little too late for that."

Her head popped up as Angelford walked toward her desk.

"I have a proposition for you."

Chapter 6

~~~OO~~~

Calliope rallied her last defenses. She thrust back her head and gazed at him scornfully. "How dare you be so insensitive? Your so-called friend is missing, my lord. There's no funeral for him, yet you poach on his territory."

His eyes narrowed dangerously and a shiver of fear sliced through her. Perhaps she had gone too far.

"I'll make allowances for your state of mind, but make a similar mistake again, and you will not enjoy the consequences."

Angelford didn't wait for her response, but continued in a deceptively mild tone of voice, "Threatening notes? You obviously have something they value. I *propose* we work together to figure out what they want and who they are. With luck it will lead us to Stephen."

He looked her over. "At the very least it would get you out of your present predicament."

Calliope gritted her teeth and enunciated succinctly and deliberately, "I don't want your help anymore. Please leave."

Angelford ignored the demand, deposited himself lazily in a chair in front of her desk and crossed his ankle over his leg.

He was examining her so carefully she began to feel like one of the animals in the menagerie.

"But what about your family at the Adelphi—would they want my help?"

Cold dread descended upon her shoulders. The lilies in the room smelled funereal.

He pulled a paper from his pocket. "I read the note."

She stared at the vellum he held. It was the same note she had received earlier. "How?"

He shrugged unapologetically. "I lifted it from your pocket."

"What do you want?"

"First of all, Margaret Stafford doesn't quite convert to 'Callie,' and neither does Esmerelda. What is your real name?"

Calliope's shoulders stiffened. She wasn't going to give him the satisfaction.

He folded his hands. "Do you really think it would take me long to ascertain your true identity? All I need to do is make a trip to the theater."

"I wouldn't want to inconvenience you. My name is Calliope Minton." She gritted her name out.

"Calliope. Yes, that's more fitting," he said with a relish that confused her.

"Are we finished here, my lord?"

Angelford's tone softened. "I want to find Stephen, regardless of what you may believe. He is a very close friend and I need your assistance. In return, I promise to protect you and yours."

It was one of the reasons she had visited him. She needed his help. She felt her shoulders droop and she nodded. She'd do anything to save her family.

If it were anyone else, she would have sworn a look of relief fleetingly crossed his features. But this was James Trenton, the great Marquess of Angelford. Did anything not go his way?

A lock of hair fell in front of his eyes. He pushed it back. "Let's put aside personal questions for now, shall we, Miss Minton?"

The lock of hair looked like it might disobey. Angelford suddenly seemed a bit more human, a bit less like a gorgeous avenging demon.

Calliope felt some of the tension drain from her muscles. "Yes."

"Good. Pardon me for a minute and I will have Finn set up some security at the Adelphi. Who would be targeted in particular?"

The admission was hard. "The Daly family."

He nodded and walked to the door. Finn must have been standing just outside, because Angelford whispered something around the corner and then shut the door once more.

"Would you like something to drink?" he asked. He was in her study, offering her refreshment?

"Black tea would be wonderful." Calliope crossed her ankles and waited.

Angelford didn't disappoint. He pulled the cord and waited for her butler to appear. "Grimmond? Black tea, please, and Cook's lemon squares."

"Very well, my lord." Grimmond turned and quit the room.

"Do you always demand service in other people's houses?" she asked.

"Ah, but Grimmond has known me since I was in britches."

That would make sense. But even if they hadn't been acquainted, Calliope didn't think any self-respecting butler would ignore him.

"Grimmond is Stephen's personal butler. I'm shocked he moved him here," Angelford said.

"Who did you expect?"

"I expected Johnson. I must assume he was traded to Stephen's primary residence. Actually, it's a blessing Grimmond is here. I'll have a talk with him later today. He will help."

Angelford walked back toward the desk. He was looking intently at the papers scattered in front of her. Her hair stood on end. A sketch was partially visible. All it would take was a mere flick of his wrist and he'd discover her secret.

Her impulse was to snatch the papers aside, but she couldn't seize the drawing without elevating his already high suspicions. Under the circumstances, he would undoubtedly pounce on her the second she fingered them.

Angelford reached the desk. Calliope's calves tensed for flight.

The door opened opportunely and Angelford looked to the entrance. Calliope brushed a blank paper over the sketch. She hid the action by standing and walking to the settee.

To her immense relief Angelford followed and tea was served. They munched on the lemon squares in silence. She convinced herself he wouldn't have taken a seat if he had seen the sketch.

He broke her musings. "I think I know what's going on."

Her head involuntarily jerked up. "You do?"

He nodded.

Her stomach knotted.

"You have lived here for several weeks, correct?" She was flustered, but nodded.

"What do you do to occupy your time?"

"I go to the park frequently. And to the parties, of course."

"So you are out of the house regularly?"

"I suppose. Although we dine here and sometimes spend the evening playing chess or backgammon."

He raised his brows, causing her nerves to jitter. Damn. She was supposed to be a courtesan. She needed to be coy. Calliope prepared some lines, but he didn't give her the chance to utter them.

"When Stephen placed you here, did he bring in many new furnishings?"

Where was he leading her? "No, I believe the staff cleaned only what was here, and of course I brought several items with me."

Angelford frowned. "To your knowledge has Stephen purchased anything recently?"

"No."

"Hmmmm . . ."

Calliope tried to relax. Her concern over her family's safety and Stephen's welfare warred with protecting her true identity. But, Angelford wasn't asking questions as if he knew she was the caricaturist who had vilified him. She fought to control her breathing. Breathe in. Breathe out. She redoubled her efforts to concentrate.

"What we have so far is one missing nobleman, one attempted kidnapping, one threatening note and one unknown object. All of these are connected." He paused. "To you."

A small knot of fear recurled in her stomach.

Angelford reread the threat. "But you aren't the one missing. Stephen is."

He leaned back in his chair and steepled his fingers. "Stephen is definitely a figure in this mystery, but what part does he play?"

Calliope had no answer, so she remained silent.

He ran a hand through his dark hair. She wondered if it felt as silky as it looked. "The whole matter is disjointed. Why attempt a kidnapping one night and then send you a threatening note the next day? It seems a little backwards."

"Maybe due to your interference last night they revised their plan."

"Perhaps." Angelford didn't sound convinced. He leaned forward. "I've analyzed the situation from several angles, but I always return to the object. Whoever the person or persons are, we need to figure out what they are looking for."

"It makes sense, I agree. But what could they be

seeking? What could Stephen or I have that someone wants so badly to go to such lengths?" She
barely owned the clothes on her back. No, she
didn't even own those, they were Stephen's.

He perused her for a long moment before
speaking. "Stephen works for the government. As
a cousin to both a duke and a powerful earl he has
many contacts. He is also an avid collector of art.
The object in question could be an artifact from
his collection or a certificate in his possession."

"Are you implying that Stephen might have
sensitive government documents?" she asked cautiously. "The man last night asked me where 'it'
was. He obviously thought I knew what he was
talking about."

"Do you?"

"No. I thought we'd already discussed this. If I
knew, I definitely wouldn't be sipping tea and
talking to you about it."

He watched her closely for a moment. "It could
be a slip of paper. It could be a sculpture. It could be
anything. So we'll have to start with things familiar to you. And that means here."

Calliope looked around the library. Stephen's
gorgeous low library writing table suddenly appeared like a large puzzle, with its undoubtedly
vast array of unknown hidden compartments and
secret drawers. Large rococo carved mahogany
bookcases and trinkets of all sizes and shapes
loomed. "Like Psyche starting one of Aphrodite's
labors."

The corners of his mouth creased upward at her
muttering. "Since I don't sense any divine inter-

vention, might I suggest we limit ourselves to documents first? If we are unsuccessful here, we can
search his suite upstairs."

Angelford gestured to the bookcases. They held
an extensive library of bound volumes and foreign
knickknacks. "It makes more sense for the item to
be small, otherwise they would have already discovered it."

The thought of assailants in the house left her
cold.

Angelford headed for the desk.

She hurried to intercept him. "These are my papers. Just private correspondence. Nothing out of
the ordinary."

He raised a brow.

Calliope was sure he would demand to see
them, but she called his bluff. "Listen, if you really
suspect me, then go through my things. But until
then, I'd like to keep my correspondence private."

"I have no reason to suspect you of anything
other than feathering your own nest, so for the
time being you can keep your things."

Relief washed through her even as the words
grated. She swept up her papers, afraid he would
change his mind, but she left them stacked on the
desk. It was an act of good faith. The instinctive
act shocked her. She had no reason to trust him.

For several hours they methodically examined
the room, searching the desk's contents, the secret
compartments Angelford was aware of and the
bookcases filled with expensively bound books by
authors such as Chaucer, Molière, Voltaire,

Rousseau, Milton and Pope. They found nothing out of the ordinary.

It was well into the afternoon, and they were looking through Stephen's suite, when Calliope realized they hadn't sniped at one another since starting the search.

Calliope lifted a leather volume off the dresser and smiled appreciatively. "I had hoped to read this. It's the sequel to the novel Stephen is so fond of. I swear he totes that book everywhere."

"The Red Signet?"

"Yes, that's the one."

His gaze was intent. "Do you know where it is?"

"In my room. Stephen thought I might enjoy reading it."

Angelford looked energized.

"Show me."

Calliope led the way to her room.

She entered the beautifully adorned room and lifted the book from the rosewood dresser. Angelford's eyes were brimming with excitement.

"Here, let me see."

Angelford sat on the bed and took the book from her. He felt the spine, then the covers. He paused and then carefully slid his fingers between the two.

"In the past, Stephen has used this book before to stow important documents. It's an innocuous-looking thing."

Slowly he withdrew two folded pieces of paper. Mindless of the impropriety, Calliope perched beside him and leaned over his shoulder. On one paper was the word *Salisbury* and a list of names: *Angelford, Chalmers, Seagrove, Pettigrew, Ternberry, Roth, Holt, Castlereagh, Hampton, Merriweather, Unknown.* The first three—Angelford, Chalmers and Seagrove—had been crossed out. Castlereagh and Merriweather had been crossed off twice.

Salisbury? Calliope's heart missed a beat. Her mind screamed to flee; her heart froze her in place. A little voice urged her to grab the list and run to Bow Street.

She folded her hands together. "Your name is on the list, my lord. As is Stephen's."

"This is Stephen's handwriting. Salisbury . . ." Angelford's voice trailed off.

Calliope gripped her hands tightly together. She wanted to scream, *Salisbury, what?*

"Do you know what the list represents?"

"Many years ago, a mission went sour. A traitor was suspected and a man was murdered. The investigation was dropped under pressure from the Foreign Office because of the turmoil in France and lack of evidence."

Calliope's heart pounded as Angelford continued his explanation. Fortunately, he seemed not to notice the change in her demeanor. He looked lost in thought; his voice had taken on a distant tone. Absently, almost to himself, he said, "Each person listed here had something to do with that mission."

She kept herself from grabbing the list. "What's on the other paper?"

Angelford held it up for her to view. It was an

imprint of a large bird of prey. "It appears to be an image from a seal or ring."

Calliope took the safer, imprinted page, but she was more interested in the list. Years of smoothing her features came in handy. "So we need to determine who the traitor is from the list. Stephen obviously thought you and this Seagrove fellow were in the clear. Castlereagh committed suicide last year. I don't know why this Merriweather fellow also has two marks. Maybe he is dead as well? We need to find the seal or ring that made this print."

He looked at her as if she had grown three eyes. "You have helped a great deal by showing me this book, but this is where we part ways. As soon as Finn gets back, I will leave him with you."

Outrage flowed through her. And determination. Anything to do with Salisbury was her concern. "Absolutely not. No one wrote you a threatening note, as I recall. You need me."

He shook his head. "I have enough information to proceed. You need not put yourself in further danger. You could have been seriously injured last night."

"I beg your pardon. If you plan to go off on your own, then I will be forced to conduct my own investigation. I was planning to do so from the beginning."

"And if you do so, I will have you removed from London." His voice was uncompromising.

She was appalled but resolute. "Since the note does not specify what I am to do with the item in question, another message must be forthcoming. Who do you propose will receive it, if I'm not around?"

That made him pause. Shrewd obsidian eyes studied her.

"In addition, my lord, you don't know for certain that what they are looking for has anything to do with this list or the imprint. You still need me."

Ideas began to take shape in her fractured mind and she seized the moment. "We can say Stephen is on leave. I will circulate and make some discreet inquiries. At the very least it will appear like nothing is amiss. It may cause some confusion and perhaps someone will slip. Perhaps even send another note."

Angelford rose and walked to her dressing table. He picked up the ornate bottle that contained her favorite perfume and ran it beneath his nose. He gazed at it for an eternity. She wasn't sure what she'd do if he said no. Somehow she would conjure a way to conduct her own investigation without Angelford knowing. She had to discover the truth.

He turned and strode stiffly to the door, his usually languid grace absent.

"We will go to Covent Garden this evening."

He disappeared around the frame and she collapsed on the bed, thoughts racing as she heard him murmur a few indiscernible words to Grimmond in the hall. They were to work together after all.

Things were getting more complicated.

Where was Stephen? What the hell had he been

doing investigating Salisbury? A traitor killed Salisbury? Who was threatening her? How was she going to handle Angelford? And how long could she keep her secrets?

"Did she get the note?"

Curdle nodded.

His employer tapped his fingers together. They were as elegant as the rest of him. "Then why is she preparing to go out? One of the maids said she is attending the opera tonight."

Curdle felt his eyes narrow as he looked up at his employer. "It's that swell in the black coach. He's the one who left his man here the other night."

"Angelford?" His employer showed no surprise. "I expected him to poke around after Chalmers's disappearance. He is loyal to a fault, but I didn't think he would get involved with the girl. Strange."

"Do you want me to get rid of him?" Curdle was eager.

"Not yet." His employer continued tapping his fingers. "I know where they are going. I will keep an eye on them tonight."

He continued, "The men could find nothing in either house after countless times searching, so I am positive the girl has the ring. It is the only way Chalmers could possibly know after all these years. Right now she is our best bet. After she produces it . . ." He shrugged. "Then I will let you have her."

A feral expression stole across Curdle's face.

* * *

Shortly after James's departure, Calliope penned a note to Deirdre informing her that the troublesome issue from the night before had been resolved. She didn't want to upset Deirdre or the family yet. She would tell them tomorrow when she had more information. Otherwise their close surveillance would be inhibiting.

Calliope was dressed as Esmerelda when the town coach arrived. She had taken special care with her coiffure and donned a sky-blue diaphanous gown designed to attract male attention. The décolletage was daring and the fabric clung provocatively to her figure. She turned in front of the mirror, satisfied with her appearance. There would be no doubt in the minds of those present that she was looking for new protection.

Calliope descended the staircase. Angelford regarded her closely and then offered his arm. She placed her hand on top.

Grimmond eyed them with interest but merely wished them a good night. Angelford escorted her to the magnificent carriage. The expert workmanship, from the gleaming heraldic arms to the squabs, was apparent.

It was a smart reminder of his position, the difference in their social status, and reason for their tentative relationship.

Calliope arranged her skirts and met his eyes across the carriage. Angelford was an impossibly handsome man, more so in his eveningwear. Dark, almost jet-black hair caressed his patrician face. It wasn't quite fair some people were so blessed in looks and circumstances while others were so poor in everything. The bitter feelings resurfaced, and she struggled to regain control.

"The Opera Company is performing *Don Giovanni* tonight."

"How appropriate under the circumstances," she murmured.

His lips curved slightly. "Are you implying I'm Don Juan and you're Donna Anna?"

She gave him a dark look and changed the subject. "What should I say if people question me about Stephen?"

"Sidestep the questions and let them imagine what they wish. I have every faith in your talent for manipulation."

She ignored the barb for once, too intent on planning. It would be stretching her acting abilities to pretend nothing was amiss when her head was screaming everything was. She could hear Deirdre's voice scoffing at her to quit whining and assume character.

He continued speaking before she could respond, "Don't allow anyone to know our real plan. It needs to remain a secret."

She frowned. She hadn't said anything yet, but she certainly was planning on it when she learned more. "My family and friends will eventually need to be told, especially if more threats are made. If I don't explain the circumstances soon, they will detect I'm being disingenuous."

"I told you they would be protected. If you tip

our hand, I will have to remove you, and be damned with the consequences." He inclined his head faintly. "I have a driver ready to take you from the city immediately."

Anger and something close to relief stirred in her. "You're bluffing. You wouldn't."

His brows lifted in the semidarkness. "Go ahead, my dear, and test me. You'll find yourself in Yorkshire in a heartbeat."

His voice was hard and unyielding again.

She sank back into the velvet seat. "Very well. I shall endeavor to keep all those who care about me in the dark."

"You demonstrate very good sense, Miss Minton."

She bristled. "Do remember not to call me that. My blasted name is Esmerelda."

"It's a dreadful name, you know."

"Blame Stephen if you must. He insisted on using it."

His dark eyes flashed and his face sobered. He looked out the window for the remainder of the trip. They reached the opera house in tense silence.

Calliope emerged from the carriage with his hand wrapped protectively about her arm. She could feel the speculative glances thrown their way.

"Damn vultures," she muttered.

She caught a half smile on his face. "You're not the only focus of this endeavor." He gave her a little squeeze, surprising her. "You will be wonderful."

She was shocked speechless and allowed him to pull her into the theater.

As they ascended the stairs, she automatically moved toward Stephen's box. James guided her farther along. "That is Stephen's box. We are going to mine."

Angelford's box was in the front of the first balcony. The premier seats. She resisted the urge to pinch him as he removed the wrap from her shoulders and settled into a seat across from her. The lorgnettes in the room focused on them and she managed a beatific smile and turned to Angelford. He raised his eyebrows in faint surprise.

"What a wonderful box you have, my lord." Only Angelford would know she was not being genuine.

He smiled. "Only the best, my dear."

She looked around the box. "How did you come by it?"

"The usual way. I inherited it."

"Ah, generations of Angelfords have graced these seats?"

"No, my father bought it while wooing my mother. He was trying to make a good impression."

The tone of his voice had changed slightly but she was too busy examining the new scenery to pay it heed. "Oh, I do love it when men try to buy a woman's affection."

She expected a witty response in return but he didn't answer. She turned to see why. Immediately she wished she could bring to mind his earlier remarks. She replayed what had been said, but could find nothing that would produce his shuttered expression.

Something about his look tugged at her.

"Oh, look, the musicians are arriving. I always love to hear them tune their instruments. The party scene in Act One is very difficult for them." She bent over the rail to motion to the orchestra. "Mozart was very ambitious when he composed this opera. It requires considerable skill for the conductor to coordinate the ensembles of three orchestras onstage and the opera orchestra in the pit."

Calliope caught a glimpse of Robert on the mezzanine level and pulled back inside the box. It was too late to hide. "And soon we will be treated to another performance. Of course, at times one performance vastly surpasses another. And certain composers obviously hold one's attention better. But then, that is to be expected, yes?"

She knew she was babbling, but she continued talking until an amused smile lifted his lips. She gave a small sigh of relief.

"Do you like the opera, my lord?"

He waited a beat and she held her breath.

"Yes, it is quite odd, I know, but I enjoy the performance." He scanned her lazily from head to toe. "Unless something else is occupying my attention."

Heat rushed over her body. He seemed to have recovered from whatever malady had plagued him. His words caused her imagination to run rampant wondering what the box had been used for in the past.

"Do you need a fan? You appear flushed."

She sent him a saucy look. His current attitude

made it easier. "Mmmm, why, yes, my lord. It is rather warm, don't you think?" She ran her tongue lightly over her lips and gently massaged her neck, letting her head fall back slightly.

His face showed no outward effect, but the muscles in his legs tensed.

Angelford was in excellent physical condition. She remembered how he had easily caught the maid and her tray at the Killroys' party and how he had lifted her after the attack in the garden.

She savored her victory until he switched chairs, putting himself next to her. He leaned toward her and stroked her neck. "Maybe we should ease the tension."

Her breath caught in her chest and warmth suffused her lower body. She allowed him to continue the gentle massage and met his eyes. She felt herself being sucked into a vortex as he bent his head. He had the most sensual lips of any man she had ever seen.

Lord Holt slipped into the box, breaking the spell. "Esmerelda, my dear, I didn't know you were going to be at the opera tonight."

Calliope tried to lean back, but James continued stroking her neck, and held her in place.

"Lord Holt, how nice to see you this evening." She tossed a saccharine smile his way as the door opened again. "Lord Roth, what a pleasant surprise." And it was. He was the perfect buffer for Holt, who she always felt was interrogating her, especially when he started stroking his blasted chin. Both men moved forward.

"Angelford," Lord Roth said.

"Angelford," Lord Holt echoed.

Angelford acknowledged the men tersely. Calliope sent a pointed look in his direction.

He looked irritated, but stood. "Excuse me, my dear, I do believe I will leave you to your admirers while I find refreshments."

She began to hold court as he slipped out the door.

James stepped through the crowd. The orchestra was still tuning, and the performance would soon begin. He wanted to be seated before the curtain rose. He wasn't sure what was wrong with him. He had wanted to sock both men in the nose before leaving, but sense had prevailed.

James raked his fingers through his hair. This was merely a role he was playing, albeit a dangerous one. Calliope was an imposter and an unknown quantity. She was the mistress of his best friend.

She was also a woman he wanted badly.

His feelings were always in flux around her. She goaded him when she flirted with Stephen. She amused him with her quick wit while reducing society misses to stammering ninnies. She tantalized him with her perfume. She intrigued him with her various guises and mystified him with her subterfuge. And a protective streak had manifested itself when he glimpsed her face as she exited the carriage.

He didn't like his lack of control one bit.

Stephen. They needed to work together for

him. James needed to keep his emotions in check.

But how far to trust her? She was hiding something, he could feel it. Although he couldn't totally dismiss her as a suspect, she was at the bottom of the list. The threatening note, her actions and her responses held together too well at present.

He grabbed two glasses of wine and scooted back to his box. The atmosphere inside was jovial.

"Good evening to you, Esmerelda. Angelford." Roth rose, and both he and Holt took their leave.

Calliope accepted the proffered glass and smiled. "Thank you."

She was in a congenial mood and, for once, he had no wish to spoil it.

Act One was exceptional, but he was uninterested. He watched Calliope's face as she immersed herself in the unfolding drama. Five minutes into the act she relaxed and he observed the byplay of emotions streaming across her face. Generally she was a closed book, but tonight she seemed to experience the drama onstage wholeheartedly.

At intermission they talked about the elaborate set pieces at Giovanni's castle and the soprano's wonderful performance.

"Truly a talented lady," Calliope said.

He looked at her speculatively. "With a name like Calliope I am surprised you don't sing."

She looked at him with considerable interest. "Do you like the classics, my lord?"

"Not at first. My tutor said I was quite an unruly student in my early days. One day, probably at his wits' end, he handed me Homer's *Odyssey*. I was hooked."

She nodded in understanding. "I love the ancient myths. My mother was an avid reader. She taught me to read and supplied me with books. She always wanted to build a grand library."

He heard the wistful tone in her voice. "What happened?"

A shadow crossed her face. "She never had the opportunity."

It was the first personal remark she had shared and he didn't know how to proceed. "What other things did she like?"

The shadow cleared and a sad expression appeared. "She loved to sing."

Reality interfered with the conversation. People streamed in and out of boxes and the gamesmanship began.

"I believe it is time for Esmerelda to cast some lures," Calliope said, and gave her fake locks a slight toss.

James nodded and escorted her to the lobby. They separated so he could presumably smoke his cheroot on the balcony and she could hold court freely.

Chaos reigned supreme. It seemed the entire opera house had emptied into the lobby. James realized it was always this crowded during intermission, but he was tense thinking about who could be in their midst. He was having difficulty tracking Calliope, and decided to move to the short steps near the pillars flanking the main stairway.

"James!"

He stifled a groan as Lady Flanders cooed his name and headed his way. Penelope was the wife of a man twenty years her senior, and was always dangling for a rendezvous. She never took the hint that James was not interested in dallying with another man's wife.

"James! I see you have a new trinket to add to your collection." She gained his side, rubbing against him, and turned to watch Esmerelda entertain her admirers. "Not quite as voluptuous as your last one. Let me see, was her name Stella?"

James inclined his head and remained silent.

"You know, you really should think about those whose husbands are too interested in other affairs. There is much to be gained from such a relationship." She peeked at him through her lashes, trying to be coy.

"Penelope, I believe Flanders is looking for you." He motioned toward the earl, whom he could see above the crowd.

She made a dismissive motion toward Flanders. "Dear, don't you know you are the prime catch? Dear Harry wouldn't mind trading partners with you for the night, if you would be so inclined."

James was sure her remarks were true. The earl had been a member of the bevy of admirers Esmerelda had drawn over the course of the last few weeks.

"Not tonight, Penelope."

A pout marred her lips when Lord Holt suddenly appeared, terminating further attempts by Penelope.

"Good evening, Lady Flanders. Angelford, may I have a word with you?"

Penelope had no option but to withdraw from the conversation.

Holt waited until she was out of earshot before saying, "I was wondering if you had heard from Chalmers. He should have completed his task by now."

James gave a nonchalant shrug he wasn't feeling. "Stephen is probably enjoying another lady friend. Or two."

Holt nodded and actively scanned the faces in the crowd. "It is hard to determine who to trust anymore. We are trying to ferret out spies in the department. Haven't had this much trouble in the office since the Little General was in the field."

What was Holt about? He was notorious for keeping his cards close to his chest. In fact, the other day hadn't he stated there was nothing afoot? He had made that ludicrous comment about a lull.

Before James could question him further, the trumpets blew, indicating the next act would soon begin. Holt excused himself. James searched for Calliope and was annoyed to find she had moved. He studied the lobby's occupants. She was nowhere in sight. He walked briskly up to his box, but she was not inside and the second act had already begun.

He felt the first inkling of fear.

James turned and saw Terrence Smith, a man he had seen with Calliope at ton functions, standing in the hallway. Smith tried to appear as if he were waiting for someone, but he wasn't doing a very fine job of it.

James decided to ignore him and proceed toward the first floor. He turned the corner leading to the steps and nearly collided with a group of people in the otherwise deserted hall. Calliope was in the center, surrounded by admirers. One man was grabbing her waist, trying to draw her in for a kiss. She raised a knee to unman him, but James was quicker. He sent the man flying neatly into the banister. The man swayed before sagging to the ground. James thought he should be commended on not launching the man over the railing and dirtying the floor below.

"Gentlemen," he said, removing his neckcloth.

The group quickly dispersed, hurried apologies and forgotten meetings spewing from their lips. The man on the ground stumbled after them.

"What were you doing?" James demanded after the men disappeared.

She shot him a malevolent look and attempted to sweep past. He took her by the arm and started to question her again when a couple emerged from a box. He loosened his grip but firmly pulled her toward the stairs and theater exit.

"Release me," she gritted.

He did so only after they had moved into the brisk night air. He motioned her forward, and though she visibly bristled, she stepped inside the ever-ready carriage. Once there she slid less than gracefully into her seat and focused her gaze on the wall. He took the seat across from her.

"Do I have to remind you we were not there for you to actually solicit a new protector?"

She turned and her eyes shot daggers so sharp he had to resist the urge to check himself for wounds.

"No, my lord, I think I am quite capable of figuring that out myself."

"So, what were you doing?"

Her lips tightened and her hands balled in her lap, "I was attempting to gather information concerning our problem and to fend off my so-called new prospects at the same time."

"What did you learn?"

She gave him a fulminating glare. "That men are animals, just like I've always known."

Amusement swept through him, washing away some of the tension. "Dear, you have chosen to deal with males for a living. In a way that brings out our worst manners and qualities, I should add. Did you expect anything else?"

She sighed and dissolved into the seat. "I keep hoping, for some reason."

He frowned but she continued, "I conversed with four people on the list during intermission. Lord Roth, the only gentleman in the bunch, asked far too many questions about Stephen. Mr. Ternberry has developed quite an interest in our relationship. Lord Pettigrew is a lecherous bulldog, and there is something guarded in his eyes. I'm sure he is searching for something. Lord Holt asked enigmatic questions as usual, but none of them were explicitly about Stephen. And there are about ten others who aren't on the list who were extremely nosy and pushy." She ticked them off on her fingers in quick succession.

James was a bit taken aback. "Quite a good start, actually."

She must have heard the surprise in his voice because she shot him a long-suffering look. "You will find I am a decent observer, my lord. I've had a great deal of experience."

James nodded, already thinking about phase two of their plan. "By the way, Terrence Smith was standing near the box. Is he privy to your disguise?"

"No." She paused. "But I found it unnerving to see Terrence at the opera tonight. I don't think he recognized me as Margaret Stafford, but he was one of the few members of the ton with whom I regularly spoke. Put me off my game a little bit to see him."

The last part sidetracked him. "Not too well treated in the ton, were you? Is that the reason you switched venues?"

She didn't look at him, but answered, "You should know, my lord. You were one of the worst."

His conscience reared, but he firmly repressed it. "I still question your purpose in being the dowdy Margaret Stafford. If I had known what a gorgeous mistress I could have made of you, be assured I would have swooped in long before Stephen."

Outrage bloomed on her face and angry spots of color appeared. "You have some nerve. I cannot fathom why I continue to waste my time speaking with you. We can conduct this investigation with limited conversation. In fact, I mean to not talk—" Her voice broke off abruptly as he grabbed her right leg and hoisted it on his lap.

"Stop that. Put my leg down."

He ignored her and pulled off her slipper, massaging the sole of her foot, her ankle and calf.

"This is totally improper. Stop." She reached forward, trying to pull her leg down, but he casually pushed her back into her seat. She sputtered. He smiled.

"Relax, Miss Minton."

She crossed her arms and glared at him.

He continued to massage her foot. The rhythm of the carriage was lulling. He felt the change in her body as she eased into the cushion. He picked up her other foot and gave it the same treatment. She closed her eyes and a slight sigh escaped from her lips.

Her blissful sigh caused him to stop his ministrations. The air was feeling a tad warm. It was time to get control of the situation again.

"Calliope—"

The coach hit a bump and because of the precarious way she was positioned she bounced right off the seat. He leaned forward and caught her before she landed on the floor.

She gave a startled laugh and looked up at him.

He looked into her intense eyes and lowered his lips to hers. All thought of gaining control of the situation was gone.

She tasted like mint and smelled like lavender. Lavender and what else? Without breaking the kiss, he pulled her onto his lap and ran his right hand along the nape of her neck, tugging off her wig. He moved his fingers through her hair, releasing the pins and pulling her closer. She shivered but returned the embrace and kiss wholeheartedly.

He deepened the kiss and was lost.

Chapter 7

~~~⌒⟲⟳⌒~~~

She was lost. All rational thoughts had flown from Calliope's mind the minute their lips touched. The pleasant feeling that had imbued her during the massage turned into a raging inferno. His hands stroked her scalp until her hair tumbled over her shoulders. His fingers trailed down the tendrils, skimming her bodice.

"My god, you're beautiful."

A small but sharp voice in her brain sounded an alarm, but she ignored it. Instead she wrapped her arms around his neck and pulled him closer. James reclined in the seat and drew her on top of him. Heat radiated from him and she was suffused with it.

Her body screamed for more. She pressed her-

159

self against him, pushing him back farther, and
felt his body's hard response. His hands moved to
her legs and began a slow ascent, bunching the
wispy blue material of her dress as they progressed. The heat, oh, the heat. She thought she
might expire from it.

His caress reached her thighs and the coach
slowed.

She lifted her head. There was hunger in his
eyes. Desire and something more. Her breath released in a whoosh. "Oh, lord." Reality came
crashing down on Calliope.

She pushed away from him and awkwardly fell
back to her seat, cursing her folly. What had possessed her to act with such abandon? Head low
and trying to conceal her mortification and regain
a semblance of dignity, she gathered her wig and
several hairpins and straightened her gown. Angelford sat motionless, his face inscrutable, as he
watched her right herself.

The coach stopped and just as Calliope stuck
the last pin in her hair, the door opened.

The footman assisted Calliope from the carriage and she fled toward the townhouse without a
backward glance. Only after she was safely inside
did she peek out the window. The carriage disappeared down the street.

What must he be thinking? What had she been
thinking?

"Cal?"

Calliope let out a small shriek and turned to see
Deirdre staring at her.

"Dee! You nearly scared me to death. What were you thinking?"

"I was thinking that sending a note with a bunch of mishmash doesn't equal a visit. You said you were coming over, need I remind you?"

Calliope smoothed her mussed skirts.

"Oh, Dee, I'm sorry. I got caught up in work after making sure you all were safe."

Dee frowned. "That we were all safe?"

Damn him for not letting her tell the family. "I heard there was a sickness going around. I wanted to make sure that none of you had caught it."

"Sickness? So where did you go tonight?"

"Oh, to the opera."

"And where's Stephen?" Deirdre peeked out the window. Stephen usually came inside after evening events. "Did he explain his absence last night?"

"He sent his apologies for not attending the masquerade and was unable to make it this evening. He sent Angelford to accompany me." Lie upon lie piled upon her already heavy heart.

Deirdre looked her over and a satisfied smile appeared on her face. "Angelford? How interesting. I see you're having fun with this endeavor."

Calliope frowned. "What are you talking about?"

Deirdre's smile increased but she said nothing.

Calliope shrugged and moved toward the stairs, eager to rid herself of the night's raiment. She could hear Deirdre following behind her. Something about the cat-ate-the-cream smile that adorned her sister's face spelled trouble. "Stephen was unavailable and I needed an escort. That's all there is to it."

There was a significant pause before her sister replied, "Yes, and I suppose that explains why your wig is on backwards."

The cheery morning sun sprayed the disaster area with golden light.

Now, where was her hairbrush?

It had been here only a moment ago.

Calliope tossed some of the clothes that littered the floor into the air. No brush. She tried another pile. Still no brush.

Deirdre must have hidden it somewhere before she left.

Grumbling, Calliope got down on her knees and looked under the bed. Empty.

Closet floor? Only clothes.

Well, she might as well dress before he arrived.

Her face felt warm. Of course she should dress before he arrived; that wasn't what she had meant.

Calliope stepped over a pile of garments and reached for an enticing sapphire morning dress, one of the only ones that had been spared in her frenzy. She touched the delicate material and then snapped her hand back as if scalded. The fine-spun cloth fluttered to the floor with the pillaged masses.

No, she had better wear the dowdy gray dress, the one with the really high neck and demure lines.

Before she could change her mind, she stepped into the staid dress.

Now, where was her brush?

A brisk knock resounded through the house and Grimmond's voice at the front door announced the arrival of Angelford. Calliope checked the clock. It had just turned noon, and she had whittled the morning away.

She ran to the mirror for one last check. Her hairbrush was lying on top of the dressing table, mocking her. Calliope snatched it up and dragged it through her locks, wondering for the thousandth time what was wrong with her.

What would he say? She descended the stairs at an admirably calm clip and headed for the library.

Angelford was sitting behind *her* desk. The uncertainty was replaced with irritation.

"Good day, my lord. Please, make yourself right at home."

He looked up and grimaced at her frumpy dress. His eyes then surveyed her face and he paused for a moment, his face as inscrutable as it had been in the carriage the night before. And then he smiled.

"Thank you, Miss Minton. I intend to. Please be seated." He motioned to the guest chair and she resisted the urge to stab him with her letter opener, which was opportunistically placed on the edge of her desk. He must have followed her gaze because he picked up the opener, whispered something that sounded like *touché* and moved it out of reach.

"Your eyes look a bit glazed. Didn't you sleep well?" His voice was low and lazy.

"I slept fine. Why shouldn't I have?"

"I won't apologize for what happened last night in the coach, because I enjoyed our interlude and so did you. My only regret is that the ride was over too fast. One day soon that won't be the case."

All available rejoinders scattered in her head and she blushed.

In the blink of an eye, he switched from seductive lover to businessman. In front of Angelford lay a stack of papers. He selected the top sheet and pushed it toward her. She perused it, noting that it was a duplicate of the list they had found last evening, with additional names added to the bottom.

James reached into his pocket and donned spectacles. "It's the word *Unknown* on that list that bothers me."

Calliope gazed at the spectacles covering his thick lashes and was surprised to see how much more approachable he looked.

"I never knew you needed glasses."

He looked up from the page. "Only for reading. My eyes tend to get tired after looking at the illegible scrawl of most of my acquaintances."

She harrumphed. "I thought that men of your station employed little old men as secretaries so they didn't have to dirty their hands with correspondence."

A faint smile appeared. "Feeling better, are we?"

She crossed her arms.

He shuffled through more papers and alternately pulled out sheets to add to her pile. "Consider this research material. A little background on some of our prime suspects."

She looked at his elegantly rugged profile, then peered at the mound before her, making no move to touch it.

"Well, Miss Minton, if you are not up to the task of reading through a couple of background briefs . . ."

The challenge was apparent in his chiding tone.

"Your backhanded challenges don't work on me, my lord." She belied her words by reaching forward and lifting the pile. He smiled victoriously and she merely raised an eyebrow. "Someone has to be mature around here."

His smile widened and she resisted the urge to hurl the papers. What was it about him that made her want to do him bodily harm?

"Woolgathering?"

She shot him a dark look and began reading a brief on Mr. Merriweather.

"Merriweather died three years ago. An untimely death, so we may want to inspect him more closely. I thought we should leave no stone unturned," he said.

Calliope agreed absently, something on the sheet catching her attention. "Why would a part-time wrecker get involved with the French?"

He looked up with interest. "Well, it's like this. . . ."

They continued discussing the documents into the late afternoon. They were making only a small dent in the piles and they still needed to go over Stephen's extensive collecting and business interests.

Calliope swallowed a yawn. She needed to stretch, but there was so much more to do and she had vowed to be the last to quit.

James stood. "Why don't we take some air? Do us both some good. Do you like Gunter's?"

Her interest perked and she looked up. "Yes, I love ices."

"Good. Grab a wrap and let's go."

"I'll be back shortly," Calliope called as she sprinted up the stairs. She quickly changed out of the unflattering dress, donned a light blue day dress that was draped over a chair and added a light gray pelisse. Makeup and wig in place, she skipped down the stairs to where James was waiting in the entryway. He looked at her wig in distaste, but offered her his arm.

They set off at a quick pace toward Berkeley Square in James's curricle. The light breeze felt cool on her cheeks and she was glad she had chosen to wear the pelisse. It was not the fashionable hour to be out, but there were a number of vehicles whose occupants paused to converse. Calliope sighed inwardly as she forced herself to flirt and dissemble with the various men they encountered.

After what seemed an inordinately long period of time, they arrived at Gunter's Tea Shop, on the east side of the square. James stopped the bays under a spreading maple tree across the street. As Calliope stood, James put a restraining hand on her arm.

"There's no need to rise, my dear."

Calliope sank back into the seat, embarrassed for forgetting etiquette. In the past she had strolled into Gunter's to buy an ice, whereas the beau monde did not find this necessary. Ices were brought to them. It was considered de rigueur.

The square was busy as usual. Vehicles of all styles and speeds occupied the lanes. Participants were sightseeing or vying to be seen. Gossiping matrons in slowly plodding chaises were passed by young bucks in high-seated phaetons weaving precariously through the traffic. Smartly dressed couples lounging in landaus yielded to spirited horsemen who raced irreverently down the path. It was a wonderful spectator sport.

In the midst of the frenzy, waiters dodged in and out of the traffic. Calliope typically liked to watch them wend their way. But it didn't seem as enjoyable when one of them was risking life and limb for her. She watched their waiter start across the lane. A phaeton shot past and the waiter pulled back to avoid the collision. He darted forward and encountered an older high-flyer phaeton as it rocked by, its driver trying to prevent it from tipping. It barely missed him. The waiter sidestepped an ancient landau and catapulted to their side as a curricle blazed by.

James uncurled her left hand from her skirt. His gaze had been focused on the waiter, and had never glanced her way during the perilous crossing, but somehow he had sensed her concern. She scarcely heard him order and then the waiter was off again. She somehow managed to keep her eyes open as she watched him cross the street and reenter the shop.

James looked at her in amusement. "One would think you had never been here before."

Her head shot up. "I don't see the problem with getting out and ordering ourselves."

He waggled a finger and touched the tip of her nose. "Much better for my consequence this way."

She had to smile. "I'm not sure that it needs any more tending, my lord."

James raised a haughty eyebrow. "One's consequence always needs tending."

She laughed. "I'll bet you put all the others to shame."

"I believe in being the best at everything I do."

"Well, I'll admit you excel at being a pain in the—"

"Here you are, my lady."

Calliope glanced at the waiter standing beside the carriage in surprise. He had already returned with two ices.

"Thank you."

She averted her eyes as he barreled back across traffic. James muttered about sneering women and the merits of buying them treats. Calliope ignored him and spooned a mouthful of ice.

"I swear this is ambrosia. It's heavenly."

James had stopped muttering and was heartily digging into his own ice. "It's not bad."

She waved a spoonful of the divine concoction.

"Not bad? That is like saying that the pyramids are not bad or that the Sistine Chapel is not bad, or that a symphony by Mozart is not bad, or—" She caught his grin and pointed the spoon at him. "In any case, you take my meaning."

She punctuated the statement by plummeting the spoon to her mouth. It made it halfway in. The other half caused ice cream to dribble down her cheek.

She giggled.

He looked at her and laughed.

She tried to lick the ice cream off.

He stopped laughing. He pulled out his handkerchief and dabbled gently at her lips. "I could think of a better way to clean it off."

His eyes suddenly made her pelisse useless.

"Maybe we should go to Hookham's and see if there are any books on seals or signets?" Calliope said as she studied her ice.

"Coward."

"Maybe."

"Esmerelda. Angelford. How good to see you both."

Robert Cruikshank rolled up next to them. His greeting belied his expression.

"Good day, Mr. Cruikshank. Nice weather we are having," Calliope said with a forced smile. Robert looked irritated.

"Yes, it is. I was hoping to see Mr. Chalmers. Have you seen him about?"

"Oh, he is gallivanting in the country for a few days. You know how Stephen is."

Robert sent her an admonishing glance, but was unable to continue because a team of grays was eager to move beyond. He nodded a polite farewell.

James watched Robert's retreating figure. "I had forgotten that he knows Stephen well. We'll need to add his name to the list."

Startled, Calliope turned to him. "Why would Robert be on our list?"

He cocked an eyebrow. "Robert?"

"Mr. Cruikshank. He is a distant relation of Stephen's." She added hastily.

"Very distant. Hmmm . . ."

"There is no need to discuss him further, he is not a suspect."

James's eyes narrowed. "No? You seem awfully sure of yourself. I wonder why."

"Trust me, he isn't."

"Yes, well, let's go to Hookham's as you suggested."

Calliope was relieved to be moving again and away from any conversation concerning Robert.

They had spent an hour in Hookham's searching through books but had discovered nothing new. The sun was dipping in the sky as they rolled down the street toward her townhouse. The trees and plants were in bloom, flowers perking their heads up here and there. It was pleasant.

James stopped the bays in front of the house. "I'm famished. An ice and a few biscuits do not count as a meal."

She looked up and felt her stomach gurgle its agreement.

"I have something in mind. I'll gather our papers and speak to Grimmond," he continued.

"What are you thinking?"

"We'll go to my townhouse."

A gust of uncertainty swept Calliope. "I'm not sure that is such a good idea. . . ."

He looked at her in amusement. "I think your 'virtue' will be kept intact in a house full of my servants."

She mumbled under her breath.

"Besides, my chef, Louis, is an absolute genius in the kitchen. Wellington was trying to steal him out from under my nose last month."

As he exited the curricle, he elaborated on the fabulous dishes and pastries that his chef routinely prepared.

By the time he returned with the papers, she was ready to grab the reins from him and urge the bays to greater speed, her mouth watering with anticipation from his delicious descriptions.

They arrived at his townhouse on St. James's Street a scant ten minutes later and her hunger threatened to overcome her.

He surveyed her with amusement as she ascended the steps ahead of him. "I think I'll go first, if you don't mind. You might eat Templeton otherwise, and I would really despair if I lost my butler. Remind me to feed you regularly from now on."

She was too hungry to think straight, but her

brain registered that the personal remark implied future events.

Templeton met them at the door and removed her pelisse.

"Templeton, we need dinner to be served as quickly as possible."

Templeton nodded in his austere way and headed through the narrow hallway beneath the stairs.

This was only the second time Calliope had been in his townhouse and she studied the gorgeous ceiling. "I must say that I love the ceiling. It's quite exquisitely detailed."

A shuttered look came over his features. "My mother had it commissioned before she died."

Calliope touched his arm. "I am very sorry for your loss."

"It was a lifetime ago." He walked toward the dining area.

The spacious room contained a huge table. Calliope imagined that if two people were to sit at either end they would need to yell to hear the other. A snort escaped at the thought.

"Something wrong?"

She shook her head. "No, just thinking about how one would converse from the opposite ends of the table."

He smiled faintly. "With great difficulty. We usually sat at one end. But I had a stickler of an aunt who demanded we dine formally. It was always amusing when she visited."

Dinner was served and Calliope devoured the succulent pheasant as James related amusing anecdotes about his extended family and friends. She noticed he did not mention his parents. She recognized many of the names and filed the information away, almost unconsciously, for future use.

Calliope stifled a clumsy yawn and James suggested they retire to the study.

Following him, she found herself immersed in a room with dark wood, reds and royal blues. She hadn't paid attention to the furnishings the previous morning. It was a very manly room, no hint of a feminine touch anywhere. A sleek, ginger feline was curled in the nook of the sofa, head tucked under its arm. It glanced up and assessed her. James stroked it absentmindedly as he passed. It continued to stare at her.

She approached cautiously, and the cat did not seem to have any intention of moving. She extended her hand for the cat to sniff. Its nose twitched delicately at her fingertips and licked her finger pad. Calliope lightly stroked its chin. Satisfied, the cat stretched back into the corner and closed its eyes.

She looked up to find James observing the display with a small smile. "Gideon is a good judge of character. It is unusual for someone to receive a token of his affection so quickly."

She glanced at the sleeping furball and was about to comment when Templeton entered. "My lord, this note was just delivered. Would you like tea served?"

James nodded and took the note. Templeton strode out of the room.

James scanned the note. A satisfied expression crossed his features.

"How do you feel about attending a house party this weekend?"

She looked up in surprise. "House party?"

"Yes, Pettigrew is hosting one at his estate just outside of London. Since he's on our list, it would give us the perfect opportunity to have a look through his . . . things."

Her eyebrows lifted. "His things?"

"You are starting to sound like a parrot, Miss Minton. I am sure that Ternberry and Roth will also be in attendance. It is quite a good opportunity."

His parrot comment struck a discordant note and she said a bit tartly, "And what if Stephen's house is broken into and the object we are so desperate to find is taken?"

A glint of amusement lit his eyes. "We can only hope someone does try to break into Stephen's house. Several of my acquaintances will stay in the townhouse while you are gone."

"Oh, and how long will we be at Pettigrew's?"

His shoulders moved in a lazy gesture. "Through the weekend."

A delicate shiver caught her.

He retrieved two pieces of parchment and wrote two notes. Templeton appeared a moment later with tea.

"See that these are delivered," James told the butler, who nodded and departed with the notes.

Calliope unsuccessfully tried to stifle another yawn.

"Maybe we should cut the evening short tonight. My driver will see you safely home. Everything will be ready when you arrive. There will be sufficient time for us to plan our strategy on the journey to Pettigrew's."

Calliope rose to leave and he grasped her right hand and pulled her forward. Their eyes held. His forefinger stroked her palm.

"I will pick you up tomorrow." He leaned down and placed a gentle kiss on the inside of her wrist. "Sleep well, my dear."

She hurried out of the room like the Fates were nipping at her heels.

James stared at the entryway ceiling after she left. He usually avoided looking at it whenever possible. The pain had dulled over the years but he could still feel the emptiness that remained.

He remembered the glow on his mother's face when the ceiling had been finished. She had been so thrilled with the way it had turned out. His father had given the painter more money than initially negotiated. Any amount of money was worth his marchioness's delight.

His vibrant mother passed away a scant two months later. The doctor had said she contracted a lung disease. James knew then, at the age of twelve, that her illness was a result of the chill she had developed on their last outing. If only he had not requested that last picnic, she might still be alive.

His father had agreed. The day his mother was locked in the family crypt was the last day his father had spoken to him. In whispered tones James overheard the servants saying he looked too much like his dear mother for his father to stomach.

And just at the age when James had needed his father the most, he was completely out of reach.

Unreciprocated love was a bitter thing.

James recalled the last evening he had allowed himself to cry. He had been in bed when he'd heard his father screaming in anger. James had come running, only to duck as a spray of glass crested the top of the staircase. He had cowered at the railing, peering through the uprights, hidden from his father's view. But James had a clear view of the tableau.

The gathered servants had scattered in all directions. His father had gone into a frenzy, threatening to tear the ceiling down. He had hurled two more crystal goblets at it, but no damage was done. He had then crumpled to the floor and cried for what seemed like hours. Unbeknownst to the older man, only a stone's throw away, his young son had cried with him. Cried for his father and for himself.

His father drank enough to forget his enraged promises concerning the ceiling, but James had not forgotten. He couldn't recall ever seeing his father sober again. His father's gambling exploits became legendary and he was rarely in residence at the London townhouse.

The marquess finally joined his beloved wife a year later, leaving his only offspring with a ruined empire and the assured knowledge he would never fall in love. Never succumb to weakness.

James broodingly stared at the half-full glass of scotch in his hand. He abruptly placed it on the Queen Anne table and left the room.

* * *

Deirdre and Robert walked into Calliope's sitting room an hour after she returned to the townhouse. Robert looked determined. He was undoubtedly there to discuss her dealings with Angelford and had decided to bring reinforcements.

"When did you acquire such a burly staff?" Deirdre queried.

Two of Angelford's footmen had ridden home with Calliope and were now installed in her household. They looked more like pugilists than servants. "They are temporary replacements for Stephen's footmen. Charlie contracted pneumonia and Fred twisted his ankle. I believe the new men are relatives."

She pulled out a portmanteau and started packing, trying to avoid their sharp eyes.

"Where are you off to?" Robert demanded.

"I am attending a house party at Lord Pettigrew's estate."

Calliope looked over in time to see Deirdre's brows shoot skyward. Deirdre and Robert exchanged a glance. "House party?"

Calliope fastened a determined look on her face. "Yes. I have never been to one, and this is a wonderful opportunity."

Robert looked at her disapprovingly. "I will talk to Stephen. He's gone too far this time. You cannot go."

Calliope lifted her chin. "I can and I will."

She pulled a day dress out of her closet. "Furthermore, I'm not going with Stephen because he's away on business. I'm going with the Marquess of Angelford."

She heard Deirdre gasp and Robert exclaim, "What?"

Calliope didn't meet their eyes. "Stephen gave me permission to be escorted by the marquess. He is perfectly harmless." Calliope choked the last out with some difficulty.

Robert touched her arm, forcing her to look at him. "To say that Angelford is perfectly harmless is paramount to saying a lion is a tabby cat. You don't know what he's capable of, Calliope. He behaves politely in society, but I have it on good authority that he's not one to toy with. Besides, I thought you couldn't stand Angelford. Remember all those caricatures you've drawn of him? The insults, the cuts, your displeasure at his behavior?"

She met his eyes firmly. "I told you, I'm going to a house party to observe. It's an opportunity to do my job better. That is all, Robert, nothing more. I have nothing to worry about from Angelford. Now, if you two will excuse me, I need to pack."

She caught the hurt expression in Robert's eyes and the bewildered look in Dee's. Guilt clenched at her gut, and she struggled with her conscience. Deceiving her friends went against her principles, but there was nothing she could do about it at the moment. Stephen's life might be in jeopardy and she had to carry on with the plan.

She softened her eyes and put her hand over Robert's. "Stephen will be back soon and everything will return to normal. Please, believe me. Just trust my judgment in this."

Confusion warred in his face and he turned and exited the room without another word.

Deirdre remained a minute longer, her expression registering hurt and concern. "Cal?"

The deeper question was implicit.

There was an uncomfortable pause and Calliope was at a loss for words. She dashed a hand through her hair. "Dee, I can't tell you now. Just trust me, please?" She looked up at Deirdre pleadingly, but her sister continued to look concerned.

"Be careful Cal. See that you don't get burned."

Deirdre shook her head and followed Robert out of the house.

Calliope walked to the window and watched her friends leave. She hated shutting them out.

Deirdre's assessment was correct, as usual. The fire was feeling a bit too warm.

Robert spotted the man in the smokiest section of the tavern. The ramshackle building was located in one of the worst parts of London. He didn't enjoy meeting here. Calliope's face flashed in his mind. It was to her that he owed the pleasure of the night's surroundings. He was still simmering over the conversation hours before. He longed to go back and shake some sense into her.

Robert sat across from the man. "Do you have it?"

The man shook his head. "No."

Damn. He had heard Stephen say that it would

be there. Now it was too late to ask for more information. "Does she have it?"

"Pretty sure."

"Do you think she will give it to me?"

"She ain't gonna give it to you. Woulda probably given it to the blond bloke. He was over there quite regular-like."

Robert contained his impatience. Stephen was no help now.

"Yes, I know. But he is unavailable."

"I tried getting in there the other day, just to take a peek around, mind you, in case you folks wanted me to try other means to obtain it."

Robert frowned. "Don't do that again. We need to figure out how to get it without raising her suspicions."

The man took a swig of ale and waited.

"Listen up," Robert said as an idea began to take shape. "Here's what I want you to do."

Chapter 8

Finn entered the study around ten o'clock. James had spent a long, restless night. Since dawn he had unsuccessfully attempted to assemble the bits and pieces he and Calliope had uncovered. The trail remained cold.

"My lord, I haven't found that Curdle fellow yet. Jaws are clamped tight."

"Some good news to start the day. Just what I needed."

Finn gave him an admonishing look. He was one of the few allowed the privilege. "Now, my lord. Things have progressed slowly before. Just need to give people the proper incentive and a little rope to hang themselves."

"I prefer sooner rather than later. Anything else to report, Finn?"

"Well, I do have some information on the other matter you asked me to look into."

James's interest perked. "The caricaturist? What can you tell me about him?"

"Not much yet. Only that Robert Cruikshank takes the drawings to Ackermann's and then collects the fees."

"Cruikshank? I just saw him yesterday. He's a caricaturist in his own right."

"I figured you'd want me to dig into his background so I went ahead. His staff is discreet so I didn't get any ready information from them. But I did learn that he has a predictable routine from which he varies only slightly. On the surface, nothing appears amiss. He enjoys the tables, but not overly so. He frequents the Adelphi Theatre and is often seen in the company of Miss Deirdre Daly."

"Very interesting."

Finn nodded. "Do you want me to keep closer tabs on him? I figured the Curdle job had greater priority, so I haven't done so yet."

"Your instincts were correct, as usual. Stay on Curdle."

Finn nodded. "By the way, were you aware that Robert Cruikshank is also a distant relative of Mr. Chalmers? His great-grandmother was the first cousin of Mr. Chalmers's great-grandmother. A loose connection, but one nonetheless."

James smiled sardonically. "That it is. I think I'll pay the illustrious Mr. Cruikshank a visit."

Finn provided directions to Robert Cruikshank's residence.

The illustrator seemed to be quite visible lately. Perhaps an early morning meeting would shed some light. And give James the advantage.

An hour later James presented his card to a wiry old butler.

Cruikshank appeared shortly and guided James to his study. "My lord, to what do I owe this pleasure?"

His expression looked anything but pleased.

James decided to skip the pleasantries and get right to the point. "What do you know about Thomas Landes?"

"Landes is a young caricaturist who is gaining popularity." His response was uttered in a matter-of-fact voice.

"I'd like to speak with him. Where can I find him?"

"Why ask me? You should try Ackermann's." Robert Cruikshank looked unruffled. "Or perhaps you should take out an ad?"

"I'd rather you tell me his location and save me the unnecessary time and effort."

"Although I would love to be of assistance, my lord, it is not within my power to do so."

"It was confirmed by a reliable source that you supply all of the sketches to Ackermann's. So I find it remarkable that you don't know where or how to contact Landes. Perhaps you are he?"

Cruikshank perused him for a moment and then smiled. "Perhaps."

"I will find out sooner or later, Cruikshank. It's only a matter of time. I would be more inclined to be generous if my energy and resources were saved."

Cruikshank looked relaxed, but James noticed he was gripping the chair arms.

The man was nervous. And he had deliberately allowed suspicion to rest on himself. James vetoed the notion that Cruikshank was Landes. He had to be protecting someone close to him. His brother? No, George was fanatical about signing his work. Besides, if rumors were true, Robert wouldn't go to any great lengths for him.

"It would make matters easier if the man were to contact me. He would be better off doing so soon, before I send an outlay of runners to find him," James said.

"I'll keep that in mind, should I happen to cross paths with Mr. Landes."

"Excellent."

"Good day, my lord."

James let himself out of the townhouse.

He would have one of his footmen follow Cruikshank. The trail would lead to Landes, Stephen or both.

James escorted Calliope to the carriage promptly at one in the afternoon and climbed in after her. He signaled to the two men standing in the doorway of the townhouse and they returned the gesture.

A wave of satisfaction swept through him. The wheels were in motion and the plan was set in action. The carriage began rolling steadily toward its destination.

He glanced across the seat. Calliope's eyes were guarded, her movements anxious.

"It's been confirmed that nearly every member on our list will be at Pettigrew's this weekend. It should prove to be an interesting time. The Pettigrews are infamous for their extravagance."

She clasped her hands and nodded.

"We will arrive and rest before dinner. After dinner there will likely be entertainment. Tomorrow will be filled with lawn games and parlor activities. The festivities will provide an excellent opportunity to converse with the women and listen to any new gossip concerning the men."

She nodded again, continuing to peer out the window. They passed out of the city and James inhaled the fresh country smell. The sky was a bit bluer and the air practically caressed his lungs. He missed his Yorkshire estate and country life.

"There will be a dance tomorrow night, and Sunday after brunch we will leave," he said.

Discussing the weekend activities seemed to be making her knuckles whiter, so he switched topics.

"What do they call the shade of your gown? Mint? Celadon? Pistachio?"

She looked at him in surprise. "Uh, just mint, I suppose."

He nodded. "I think you would do well to wear a darker shade to enhance your coloring. Emerald, maybe."

Her brows drew together. "I don't recall asking your opinion. I believe this color is perfectly suitable."

He waved a hand in a negligent fashion. "You

really should take my advice in these matters. I have more experience, I can assure you."

A spark lit in her eyes and she crossed her arms. "How have the scores of women been able to stand you, my lord?"

He shot her a lazy look and leaned back in his seat. "Just ask one, my dear."

Her lips compressed and she turned to gaze at the flowering countryside. Her hands were no longer clenched.

A number of carriages arrived at the Pettigrews' estate within minutes of each other.

"Angelford, my dear! So wonderful to see you," cooed Penelope Flanders as she sashayed across the slate tiles on the front portico. "The weekend will be so much more enjoyable with you in attendance."

James forced a smile and took her offered hand. "Lady Flanders, you look lovely as usual. Is your husband with you this weekend?"

She preened. "He will be arriving tomorrow evening. He has important business to attend and insisted I come ahead and enjoy myself."

James felt Calliope's eyes sear a hole in his back.

"Well, then we shall see you tonight," he could not resist answering.

Penelope glanced at Calliope and dismissed her. "Delightful," she said, eyeing him with relish before strolling into the house.

James smiled at Calliope and tucked her hand under his arm, doubting she would willingly do so.

"Angelford, my dear. My husband's away and I'm ripe for the plucking," Calliope mimicked.

"A woman of your worldly nature, Miss Minton. You sound amazingly like an outraged virgin."

Interestingly enough, sometimes she acted like one too.

Calliope was spared a response as Lord Pettigrew descended the stairs to warmly welcome them.

"Angelford, good of you to come. Esmerelda, my dear, it's always a pleasure to see you." He raised her hand to his lips and held it a second longer than was proper.

She smiled becomingly and a flash of irritation swept through James.

"The roads are deplorable this time of the year. You must be tired from your ride. Please make yourselves comfortable and let the servants know if there is anything you require. Dinner will be served at eight. I look forward to seeing you there."

Pettigrew exemplified the word *leer*.

He motioned for a servant to assist them to their rooms. James had been to the estate before, but he observed the look of wonder pass over Calliope's face as they entered.

The estate was impressive. It had been in the Pettigrew family for seven generations and the family collection of antiques was notable. The Pettigrews had not experienced the downturn in finances that many wealthy English families had faced during one generation or another.

James's family had been so blessed until his father's downfall. It had been up to James to repair the broken finances. But he had always known he would succeed. Always been sure he wouldn't be forced to sell any of the family heirlooms. So he continued to take the display of wealth as second nature. He had never chosen to look at it any other way.

But Calliope's posture caused him to pause. As she gazed around at the trappings of wealth, her first expression was one of awe, quickly replaced by anger.

She caught him looking at her and an indifferent mask fell into place, but too late.

The servants guided them to rooms across from one another in the west corridor of the second floor. He excused himself, leaving her to rest while he entered his room. It was a large room with Oriental silks and dark mahogany furniture. He had a similarly styled room in his main country estate. He wondered what Calliope would say about his forty-room Yorkshire manor. He felt fairly certain she would not be pleased.

Calliope glanced at the clock. The hour had passed quickly. She pressed her cheek into the pillow and gazed at the fancy mantelpiece. It was entirely covered in gilt. Small angels were trapped in the corners and held there with the heavy gold. The frills in one room alone would feed a small village.

What was she doing here?

Trying to find Stephen. Interrogating people.

Searching rooms. Keeping a firm distance from Angelford.

Not necessarily in that order.

She shoved her face more firmly in the pillow and groaned. Flipping back the covers, she rolled until her legs fell off the bed and her feet touched the cold floor. She pushed herself upright and tiptoed to the settee.

Calliope put her feet up on the settee and pulled her day dress over the top. Betsy would be in soon to help her prepare for the evening. Funny how one became used to the assistance. Calliope grimaced.

Betsy tapped on the door and entered. "What a lovely house, miss. The country is so different from the city."

Betsy's eyes glowed. Was poor Herbert, the footman, already being replaced?

"Anything interesting belowstairs, Betsy?"

"Indeed, miss," she said as she entered the closet and withdrew a red evening gown. "I have heard the most unusual things about the Pettigrews and their parties. Supposedly this is not one of their more wild weekends. Tame entertainments are planned."

Calliope hid her grin at Betsy's disappointment. "Why do you suppose that is?"

"Servants don't know, miss. They say Lord Pettigrew's been awfully preoccupied with some government hubbub lately and has been curtailing boisterous types of entertainment. They say Lady Pettigrew is bored." Betsy shook her head and helped her into the gown. "Never a good thing, a bored noble."

"This is Lady Pettigrew's birthday weekend and they haven't planned anything above mild?"

Betsy nodded sadly and her disappointment reflected Calliope's own. She had been expecting at least some caricature material from this trip. Lord Pettigrew had been promising especially lurid activities for weeks. Not that she would participate, but she had planned to actively observe and document.

What had made the Pettigrews change their plans?

Betsy went to work on her hair. "Don't worry too much, miss. The maids are hoping for some extra activity, in any case. Seeing as there are still quite a few of the notorious in attendance, we should be able to have an exciting weekend."

Calliope looked at Betsy's eyes in the mirror. Poor Herbert.

Betsy chattered while she worked and finally stuck the last pin in her hair. "Too bad you don't go with your own hair, miss. It's much nicer."

"This is my hair, Betsy."

Betsy sighed. "Yes, miss."

Betsy, as gossip-hungry as she was, wouldn't say anything. She wanted the position more than anything. It was too big a step up for her. Moreover, Calliope genuinely liked Betsy and she thought the feeling was mutual.

However, Calliope wished she could dispense with the wig as well. It itched. She surveyed herself critically. The brown wig had been styled artfully so ringlets fell around her face and the ample expanse of skin that her Turkey red gown af-

forded. The gown's gold satin trim and accompa-
nying long lace scarf accented the beautiful color
and style.

This was one of her more daring gowns. Although the gown she was saving for tomorrow
was definitely Madame Giselle's masterpiece. But
this one would do nicely, since the purpose of
wearing the dress was to keep all eyes away from
her face as she took measure of the house.

There was a knock and James entered her
room. Betsy hiked her skirts and ducked through
the open doorway.

Calliope cocked an eyebrow at his impertinence
but swished forward to greet him. His eyes swept
her and his expression left her satisfied the gown
would do its trick.

"Forget what I said earlier in the coach about
your taste in clothes."

Her stomach did a little flip. She placed her
hand on his outstretched arm, and they exited the
room. The gold picture frames winked in the can-
dlelight as they walked down the hall and descended the stairs.

"Just be your charming self and remember not
to venture away from me. We will only observe
tonight, agreed?"

She nodded and they reached the dining room,
where other guests were milling about waiting for
dinner.

"My dear Esmerelda."

Calliope turned to see Lord Pettigrew ambling
forward, hindered by his large girth.

She pasted a smile on her face and extended her

hand to the earl. "My lord, you are looking very dapper this evening."

He beamed. "Saw this style at the races last week, and with all our success that day I took it as an omen and thought I might try it."

"Well, it suits you," she flattered. "Will you keep your horse running?"

"Thunder Peak is an excellent piece, but I believe I will put him to stud this year. He should make me a nice profit." He gave her a meaningful glance. "Suitable enough even for extravagant purchases."

She gave him an inviting smile but bristled at the implication. She offered a noncommittal, "Mmm, yes."

James escorted her to the table as dinner was announced. She found herself seated between James and Mr. Ronald Ternberry. Lord Roth was seated across the table.

Ternberry's expression was pinched as he surveyed the table. "There are to be charades later. How trite."

Although Ternberry was on their list, Calliope couldn't picture him doing anything as remotely exciting as committing a crime.

Roth seemed to delight in Ternberry's boorishness. "Ronnie, there is to be a musicale too. I hope you regale us with your spring larklike voice."

Calliope smothered a smile. Roth was a rogue. "Oh, yes, Mr. Ternberry, I look forward to hearing you sing."

Roth smiled at her approvingly and turned back to monitor "Ronnie's" reaction.

Ternberry sniffed delicately as if he were appeasing mere mortals with his magnificence. "Well, I do have a passing voice, my dear, although I don't often perform for others. I may do you the honor after dinner."

"Afterwards we can do charades. I really hope I get to choose my own." Roth dropped the statement innocently and took a drink of his wine.

Ternberry's brows drew together. It was obvious he was unsure what Roth's statement implied. Calliope sipped from her wine goblet, hoping to conceal her mirth.

"Won't it be fun?" Roth shot her a wicked glance and Calliope gave in and laughed. James was conversing with a lady on his left, but turned at the sound. The first course was served and the servants moved between them. Light chatter flowed around the table during the next courses. Dessert was served and the conversation at their end of the table shifted to politics.

"Making a tidy profit these days. Yes, I do say," Ternberry said.

Roth eyed him sharply. "Feels good to keep those Corn Laws intact, doesn't it?"

"Yes, yes, it does. A good landowner must make an ample income."

"Of course, Mr. Ternberry. A good coat must be purchased no matter the price of grain." Calliope sugarcoated the words, trying to keep her voice neutral.

"Yes, right. Good sense you have, Esmerelda."

"So Ternberry, you don't mind that your workers are unable to afford the cost of the grain they themselves reap?"

Calliope glanced at James in surprise. She hadn't known he was listening.

"Part of being a landowner, Angelford. You know that. We have rights."

"We have votes, you mean," James said.

"Since only large landowners can vote." Roth casually threw in the statement.

James fiddled idly with his knife. "There are rumors of reform bills in the works. Something about having a minimum yearly income, something under fifty pounds, to gain voting privileges."

Ternberry recoiled. "Rubbish! Common riffraff deciding the fate of our nation?"

"Isn't it their nation also?" James said.

Ternberry sniffed. "Second-class citizens. What to propose next, women being allowed to vote?"

James put his hand over Calliope's, loosening her grip on the cutlery.

"I do think there are many ladies in England who might be more sympathetic and a good deal better equipped at decision making than the members of the current House," Roth said.

Ternberry turned an ugly shade of purple. "Criticizing the government borders on treason, Roth."

Roth popped an apple slice into his mouth and surveyed the guests. "Let's see them come and arrest me."

Calliope was concerned Ternberry might explode on the spot, but after his insulting remarks she wasn't feeling congenial toward him and made no attempt to smooth things over.

"Speaking of which, I was wondering, how did you find your last inspection of Newgate?" James asked Roth.

James and Roth began an animated discussion of prison conditions, none of which was proper for dining room conversation. But the entire table was talking and no one was paying them much attention. Ternberry stewed in his seat.

Calliope reined in her surprise. She had expected Ternberry to be a staunch Tory. But Roth and James had turned her thoughts upside down. They were talking as if they were Whigs or Reformers.

She hadn't been aware of either of them dabbling in the political sphere, so she couldn't be sure where their hats lay. She had just assumed they were conformists. Weren't all nobles conformists? Even those who professed otherwise?

Lord and Lady Pettigrew rose. "We are going to hold an informal musicale. It is Lady Pettigrew's wish that everyone participate."

Some good-natured grumbling followed the statement, and a few of the gentlemen griped about cigars, but men and women allowed themselves to be pressed into service as the group adjourned to the conservatory.

A couple of women with passable voices sang. A lord with a deep bass was delightful. And then Ternberry rose for his turn. He had a decent tenor but he liked to hit a higher note than was particularly suited to his voice. It caused a wince from

Calliope every time and she shared a grin with Roth. He had obviously known what to expect.

"Esmerelda, please favor us with a selection," Pettigrew boomed.

She could decline, but listening to the others had brought forth the familiar itch.

"I'd be delighted to accompany you, Esmerelda," Roth announced, stunning more than one person in attendance.

Roth sat at the pianoforte. "What's it to be?"

"Do you know, 'A Bluebird's Love'?"

Roth looked at her strangely for a moment and then nodded. Calliope was actually surprised he knew the piece. It was an obscure song, but it had been her mother's favorite.

He plunked the opening bars and she began. Calliope had a strong mezzo-soprano voice, and she immersed herself in the song and forgot about the audience. She was transported back in time and place to when she was a very young girl singing in the little music room with her mother. She remembered her mother twirling and smiling and her father playing the pianoforte.

It had been a long time since she had inserted her father into a happy memory.

Roth played the last bar, drawing Calliope back to reality.

There was a brief silence and Calliope wondered if she had committed a faux pas. Monstrous applause drowned her imaginings. Roth winked at her and they returned to their seats.

"I say, that was well done!"

"Wonderful!"

Everyone was smiling except Lady Flanders, who was scowling; and Angelford, who wore an unreadable expression. Numerous selections followed until the last volunteer's spindly voice hit the final note.

The guests moved to their chosen destinations. Charades were taking place in the drawing room; cards and dice were set up in the gaming rooms. James was busy talking to Roth and Calliope took the opportunity to excuse herself. She headed toward the ladies' retiring room.

She reached an intersection in the hallway and started to turn left when she heard loud voices. Cautiously she peered around the corner and observed Ternberry and Pettigrew exiting a room halfway down the corridor. They were engaged in a heated argument.

"That is not how one handles these matters."

"I have more experience in these situations. Give me the document and I'll—"

A servant rushed to Pettigrew, interrupting Ternberry, and gave him a slip of paper. Pettigrew glanced at the missive and Calliope heard him swear. He motioned for Ternberry to follow. They were heading straight toward her. She slipped into an alcove, hoping they wouldn't glance her way.

"Ternberry, rejoin the guests. This cannot wait. We will continue the discussion when I return."

Their footsteps faded and she peered down the empty corridor.

It was too good an opportunity to miss.

She strolled toward the room the men had vacated. She heard no footfalls, but forced herself to tread slowly. If she were questioned about her presence, she could claim ignorance.

She cast a quick glance behind, but she was still alone. She touched the door handle and heard a click as the door swung open.

The room was dim; the only light streamed from a small oil lamp on the desk. An unlit fireplace was in the corner, a full-length Oriental screen to its side. The screen seemed totally out of place in the otherwise English décor.

Calliope closed the door and moved toward the desk. Papers were scattered about its surface, as if a frustrated hand had smeared them. Glancing at the mantel clock, she sifted through the pile. She would allow herself five minutes. Staying in the room any longer would be foolish.

She paused and scanned the paper under her left hand. It looked like a contract from the Foreign Office. She flipped the page over, looking for the nature of the agreement.

The door handle clicked. She dropped the paper and dove behind the screen.

For an interminable moment there was total silence in the room. The hairs on the back of her neck were the only sign that a person advanced. Her breath held as she felt the presence stop on the other side of the Oriental cover.

A hand shot out and grabbed her by the arm. Harsh features and a menacing hand chopping toward her face were the only things her mind registered.

The raised hand stopped mere centimeters from her neck and she heard a muttered curse.

"What are you doing here?" Calliope hissed, staring into the familiar dark features and trying to regain her equilibrium.

James gave her a sharp look and motioned for silence as he shoved her back, squishing them both behind the delicate panels. He pushed her to the ground and crouched next to her.

She heard the door open, then a clumsy, hesitant footfall cross the floor.

Rustling papers, muffled curses and the intense beating of her heart were the only sounds in the room. She chanced a look upward at James. He was absolutely still, his eyes trained on the side of the screen.

There was a click of the door, then a solid thunk, as if someone's head met the edge of the desk. Calliope winced for the other intruder and was rewarded with a waist-tightening squeeze from James. Did he think she couldn't keep quiet?

A fourth person entered the room and Calliope resisted the urge to peek around the screen. This was becoming absurd. Besides, there were no more available hiding places.

"Where did I put that?" The low growl indicated Pettigrew was the fourth person. Papers were shuffled and he doused the light and then he strode back out.

A bump and curse indicated the other prowler had extricated himself from the desk. The person fumbled around, knocking papers and something made of glass to the floor. The tinkling sound reverberated through the room. The intruder must have been looking for the lamp and found it.

He beat a hasty retreat, not bothering to clean his mess in the darkened room. The door closed softly.

Calliope released her breath and stared up at James in the shadows. His fingers slid up and down her arm rhythmically. He was trying to soothe her. It was making her arms tingle.

"What are you—"

The hand tightened on her arm and he swung her toward him. She was locked to his chest. Her recently restored breathing sped up again.

"What the devil were you thinking? I thought I told you we were just going to observe tonight."

She raised an eyebrow, and wondered where she found the spirit. "Yes, you did, which doesn't explain your skulking about."

"We'll discuss this later. Let's see if we can clean up and then get out of here. There's entirely too much traffic in this room."

James grabbed her hand and pulled her around the screen. He somehow managed to locate a candle and light it. The lamp had indeed been the casualty of the other intruder.

James swore. "We can't do anything about the lamp. Let's go."

Calliope glanced at the desktop, but the agreement and other papers were gone. James extinguished the candle, and led her into the deserted hallway and up the stairs.

Chapter 9

James didn't release her hand until they were safely inside her room. He was unsure what he wanted to do more—kiss her or shake her.

"Won't we be missed?" she asked.

He shrugged and removed his coat, laying it across the paisley silk armchair.

She frowned. "Well, then shouldn't we go back?"

He glanced around the cheerful and inviting room. Yellows and muted blues mixed together to create a relaxing atmosphere. It was interesting that despite her flare for the spectacularly vivid colors when she was Esmerelda, this soft feminine room suited Calliope.

"The guests are already thinking exactly what we want them to think. Why should they question my being with you?" He moved slowly toward her.

"I'm with an alluring woman who has charmed every man in the house. No one will be surprised by my desire to have you to myself for several hours. In fact, they would question my masculinity and sanity if it were otherwise."

He stopped in front of her, a fingertip starting at the base of her throat and spiraling slowly downward until it rested on the top edge of her dress. She colored, an alluring reaction for a courtesan.

"Your voice is beautiful. You had everyone in the room captivated. I am surprised you haven't made a career as a singer." He said it in an offhand manner, before adding, "Where did you learn to sing so well?"

She turned and walked to the back of the chair, putting it between them. "From my mother."

James stuck his hands in his pockets. "You mentioned her at Covent Garden. Did she have a trained voice?"

She looked at him speculatively. She didn't speak for a few seconds, as if reaching a decision. "My mother was Lillian Minton."

"Lillian Minton, the opera singer?"

Calliope nodded as she absently picked at the fabric on the back of the armchair.

Carefully stored pieces of random information coalesced in the deep recesses of his brain. Not only had Lillian Minton been one of the preeminent opera divas and great beauties of her time, but she had also been the permanent and very public mistress of . . . "Lillian Minton, the Viscount Salisbury's mistress?"

Calliope's eyes narrowed. They glittered in the firelight. "Yes."

James frowned. Something niggled the back of his mind. Hadn't Salisbury's daughter died in the same blaze as the mother? He remembered the only time he had seen the man drunk.

They had been at White's and Salisbury had cried out, "Nothing worse than losing someone you love. Lost my only child and the woman I loved." James had always remembered the look of pain on the viscount's face. At the age of twenty-one it had served as a powerful reminder of what love did to people.

"I recall Lillian Minton and her child died in a house fire. If my memory serves me, she had only one child," he said cautiously, carefully noting the expression on Calliope's face.

"I'm surprised you would even know she had a child," Calliope remarked dismissively.

"It was important news for many weeks that the noted diva and mistress of the viscount had perished with their only child in a fire. I remember well. I knew Salisbury. He was a father figure to many of us and was so distraught it affected us all."

Calliope looked at him sharply, her fingers clawing into the chair's fabric. "How wonderful for you. Can we go back to the party now?"

"No, not until I have some answers. What game are you playing, Calliope? Why do you claim to be Salisbury's daughter?"

"No game," she enunciated clearly. "I am his daughter."

"Salisbury had one daughter and he believed his only child to be dead. He would have known if she were still alive. He would have moved heaven and earth."

She shrugged, but her jaw was set and her shoulders were rigid. "He knew I survived the fire, and he chose not to acknowledge me."

Chose not to acknowledge her? Salisbury? The man who had kept Stephen and he, hotheaded and straight from Oxford, out of trouble?

"Salisbury was an honorable and generous man. The man was inconsolable about the loss of Lillian and his daughter. After their deaths he threw himself into his work with an abandon verging on obsession. He took the most dangerous cases and placed himself in harm's way on more than one occasion."

Pain washed her features. "Then he was a fine actor and fooled all of you."

"Why should I believe your story and doubt the word of a man whose reputation is unblemished? Stephen was one of Salisbury's closest confidants. Do you think he was fooled by the viscount?"

"Stephen knew Salisbury?"

"He knew him very well. Stephen was present when Salisbury was killed."

He saw her eyes glisten as she quickly lowered her head. There had to be more to the story than met the eye. He couldn't credit Salisbury for being duplicitous, and instinct said she was telling the truth. At least, the truth from her point of view.

James cursed inwardly and his voice turned gruff. "Does Stephen know your real name?"

Calliope nodded, head down.

"Did you ever talk to him about Salisbury?"

She gave a quick jerk of her head in the negative and he received a glimpse of emotional upheaval.

Was it coincidental that Stephen was squiring Calliope Minton about town and had set her up in his townhouse? There was obviously more to their relationship than he had divulged to James. What was Stephen doing with Salisbury's daughter? And how did she fit into the equation?

Question after question was raised and supplanted by another.

Calliope's haunted expression was distressing. He wanted to erase it. "I believe you. Now believe me, Calliope. Salisbury didn't know you were alive. He was devastated by your loss."

"James, he had to know. I limped to his townhouse the night of the fire and was threatened and thrown out." Her voice was bitter. "I thought I had nowhere else to turn. I was thirteen."

"You went to Salisbury's townhouse that evening?"

"Yes, although I'd never been inside before. My fa—" she stopped herself and then continued. "Salisbury visited us each week at our home. But when Mama and I strolled by his townhouse, she sighed too often for me to not be aware of the reason."

"I can't believe he would have thrown you out."

"His mother did a nice job of it for him. She screeched in no uncertain terms I was unwelcome." Calliope scooted around the chair in her anger, her limp showing itself slightly. "She stated Salisbury knew of the fire and was glad to be rid of us. That we were naught but a trial. She even threatened to send me to Newgate for stealing. How she would have accomplished that, I'm not sure. But I believed her at the time."

Pieces started to come together. "So you went to the townhouse and spoke to Lady Salisbury? She threatened you, and then she turned you out? Where did you go?"

Calliope didn't answer.

"Why did you believe her?"

Calliope looked directly at James, her eyes full of anger and pain. "She made it very clear I was not wanted there. I'll never forget her eyes when she told me my mother would burn in hell if I ever returned. I couldn't sleep for months worrying about my mother's soul."

"Calliope, Lady Salisbury was notorious for being unpleasant when anything stood between herself and her son. Salisbury undoubtedly knew the animosity she held toward your mother and you, and throughout the years he probably tried to keep you separate from her enmity."

"I am sure you are right, my lord. But it's in the past and it matters little. May we leave now?" The cool, guarded look was sliding over her features once more.

"Let's get a few things straight here." He pushed her into the chair and plunked his hands down on the side arms. She looked up at him, tight-lipped.

"Why didn't you tell me your connection to Salisbury when we found the list?"

"I didn't know you well enough. I had no idea how you would react to the information. I couldn't take the risk that you wouldn't let me participate. I need to find out what happened to the man who abandoned me."

"Your father lived in hell nearly every day for the rest of his life grieving for you. Would he have done that if he knew you were alive?" He nearly shouted.

James saw the tremor go through her.

He relaxed his pose and gently lifted her chin. "Why didn't you try to speak directly to Salisbury at some point after your altercation with Lady Salisbury?"

A painfully bitter look crossed her features. "I planned on confronting him. Plotted exactly what I'd say. He was never in the country and I wanted to do it face-to-face. He died before I had the chance." She paused and drew in a ragged breath. "I thought I had plenty of time."

"I'm very sorry, Calliope."

She drew herself up. "Spare me your pity. A wonderful family adopted and loved me. I've done a lot better than I might have. I have no regrets."

Challenge and pride made her rigid in the seat. In that moment he truly believed she was Salisbury's daughter.

A clock struck eleven.

He straightened and allowed her to rise. "There are definitely some misunderstandings that need to be cleared, but it's obvious you won't accept them from me. When Stephen reappears, he will help."

He saw her wobble slightly as she headed toward the dressing table. She had mentioned limping to the Salisbury estate the night of the fire. He wondered if the house fire had been the cause of the slight limp that was noticeable only when she was visibly stressed.

James let her compose herself for a few tense minutes before changing the subject. There were too many unanswered questions in his mind. It seemed unbelievable she had met Stephen upon his return and become his mistress so quickly. There were too many ties to the past.

"The name Calliope suits you. Your mother was one of the most adored opera singers in Europe. She was amazingly talented."

An acidic look crossed her face in the mirror. "Yes, and she had scores of illustrious admirers, wealthy, successful, high-placed men and women, but was still considered beneath the social strata that adored her."

James paused. "You really hate us, don't you?"

She vigorously stroked the red silk dress. He couldn't see her eyes when she responded. "Not all of you, just most."

He didn't ask if he was included in that group.

He lightened his tone. "Why do you frequent the ton in so many guises? Are you a masochist? Or do you have an ulterior motive to wreak havoc?"

"Enough of this." She turned and moved toward the door. Her movements were jerky. "We're here to find information that will help us locate Stephen."

"I'll let it drop for now, Calliope, but rest assured we'll discuss it another time."

She gave him a disgruntled look and changed the subject again. "Other than Pettigrew, who do you think was in the room with us?"

"Whoever it was, he didn't sound particularly adept, wouldn't you agree?"

There was a slight easing in her tense features, and she nodded.

"We have to assume Pettigrew took whatever he was after, so we are going to have to continue our search later tonight. Together."

She lifted an eyebrow, her features relaxing more.

He continued, "That way we can explain ourselves if we are caught. We'll just say we weren't able to reach our own rooms in time."

He held out his arm and felt the slight shiver run through her as they made contact. It caused an equal reaction in him.

This whole debacle was becoming increasingly tangled. Arm in arm, they headed back to the party.

They neared the card room, where most of the male guests were playing high-stakes games. Calliope ran an imaginary hand over her features, smoothing them into her practiced mask. She tried to do the same with her emotions, but had less success.

Fear and trauma after losing her mother had kept her from confronting Salisbury. With time, both emotions had lessened and the desire to see him and confront him had grown. The opportunity had been snatched away with his untimely death.

Calliope had mourned his death. She had rationalized that her feelings had sprung from the inability to seek her own small justice, but she had always known that in a locked-up place in her heart she had mourned for the smiling man who'd always read her favorite stories aloud.

Her feelings for her father were as jumbled as her feelings for the man on whose arm she had placed her hand.

Lady Flanders rose from the table that included Roth, Ternberry and Pettigrew. She gave Calliope a superior look and swept out of the room.

Roth smiled at Calliope. "Esmerelda, come join us. Oh, you too, Angelford." Roth waved a hand toward James as if to indicate that he was a poor second choice.

They were playing whist.

Roth was partnering Pettigrew. Ternberry gave a snort of disgust and he too rose. "Cheating sons of—"

Roth lifted an eyebrow and Ternberry took himself off quickly.

"Well, then, looks like we have two empty seats," Roth said.

"What do you say to one game, my dear? Would you be willing to be my partner for a quick win before we retire to other pursuits?" James said confidently as he held the seat for Calliope.

Calliope was glad he had committed them for a single game. Whist was addictive and they needed to continue their search.

Roth won the draw. He shuffled the cards expertly, offered James a cut and dealt each player thirteen cards. His thirteenth card, a ten of diamonds, lay face up to indicate trump. Play began and each player tested the others' skills through subsequent hands.

Calliope was unsurprised to find Angelford an excellent player. He was aggressive at all the appropriate times and had an uncanny knack for correctly assessing her hand. The irritating man was enjoying himself as he scooped up the last trick. He gathered the cards and shuffled.

"Pettigrew, did you find the Egyptian scroll satisfactory?"

Pettigrew grimaced at the score. James and Calliope needed only one more point for game.

"What? Oh, yes. It was exactly what I was looking for."

James smoothly handed the cards to Pettigrew for a cut. "Are you searching for anything else?"

Pettigrew fumbled nervously but completed the cut. James began dealing without glancing at Pettigrew and Calliope noticed a bead of moisture forming on Pettigrew's forehead. Roth seemed oblivious to the undercurrents; he merely sat sipping his wine.

"No, at present I am not in the market for anything else." The bead of moisture slipped down the side of Pettigrew's face.

James picked up his cards. "I heard there are some avid buyers right now. I was wondering if you knew anything."

Roth lazily scanned his cards and then threw out a spade lead. "Do you have anything for sale, Angelford? Something of interest?"

"I may."

Calliope watched Pettigrew's pale face as he scooped up the trick he had played off with a heart. Roth, on the other hand, appeared totally at ease. Pettigrew was out of his league on several counts.

Roth nodded and led another spade. "You may find someone interested at the ministry. I hear there is an inquiry into lost objects."

James played his card and Pettigrew threw a spade.

"Well, I say, I do believe I have accidentally revoked, which gives you two the game. Absent-minded of me. My apologies, Roth. I do believe I will check on my other guests."

Pettigrew excused himself and quickly exited the room.

Roth idly played with the remaining cards in his hand. "If I may offer some advice, I suggest you—"

Lady Flanders breezed back into the room and ran a finger suggestively down the front of Roth's tailored coat. "Roth, darling, what are you still doing here? Come join the others."

She sent a coolly appraising look to Calliope

and assumed a lofty stance. "Leave Angelford to his pursuits, odd as they may be."

It was obvious she would not leave until Roth followed. Roth sent Calliope an amused glance. "As you can see, everyone has a motive. Until later."

He placed Lady Flanders's wandering hand on his arm and followed in the footsteps of Pettigrew.

James looked thoughtfully at the retreating couple.

"Where is her husband?" Calliope muttered.

James smiled. His eyes lit with mischief and her breath caught. He was devastating when he smiled.

"Penelope and Flanders don't keep a tight rein on each other. He no doubt is enjoying the company of his latest peccadillo. Each has an insatiable appetite for variety and numbers, much like the Pettigrews. I must say she has damnable timing, however."

"I wonder what Roth was going to say."

"I don't know, but maybe we should begin our search in his room."

Curdle crept silently down the long hall, hesitating every so often as he heard voices.

Things were becoming increasingly more difficult. And he didn't like this latest turn of events.

Someone had spilled his guts and now Angelford's hellhound was nipping closely at his heels. It had taken all of Curdle's considerable talent to elude the man these past few nights.

He would have a long talk with his employer about this inconvenience.

Curdle cracked his knuckles menacingly and proceeded to his employer's room.

Task accomplished.

Confirmation given.

At last his reward was close at hand.

"I never expected Roth to be so fastidious. Appearance is one thing, one's personal space another."

James closed the door silently behind them and they returned to Calliope's room to fetch her wrap. During the search of Roth's room, they had gained nothing but confirmation that the man was single-minded in all of his habits.

Calliope opened her door. "He is very mysterious, is he not?"

James frowned. "I don't think Roth is all that—"

He bumped into her back. She had stopped dead in the doorway.

"James, something is wrong. Someone has been here."

He moved around her and searched the armoire and under the bed, the only two available hiding places in the room. "Are you certain it was not just your maid tidying things?"

"No, it's not that."

"Is anything missing?"

Calliope was already looking through her things. "No, I don't believe so, it's more a feeling."

She was staring anxiously at the door and window.

"We'll both stay here or in my room."

Relief and alarm warred on her face. "Perhaps I'm just a bit edgy because of Pettigrew's study."

"If anyone sees me leaving your room in the morning, it will lend credence to our relationship. As long as no one sees me on the sofa, that is. Now, here's your shawl, let's try Pettigrew's chambers."

The suite was as far away from their rooms as one could get in the huge manor. For the first time James grudgingly found himself admitting he was glad Calliope had accompanied him. If they were caught, their presence in any part of the house could be easily explained away as a lovers' game.

They were in and out of his rooms quickly. Pettigrew's rooms proved as fruitless as Roth's. By the time they left his suite it was three o'clock in the morning. Because it was necessary to keep track of the guests, James and Calliope kept making appearances downstairs. The party was still in swing, but they noted several of the guests had retired.

"It's going to be more difficult to conduct a search when we don't know which rooms contain guests," James said.

They passed the card room, where a heated game was being played. Mr. Ternberry was wiping his brow. He appeared to be losing heavily.

"Ternberry is well known for his tenacity at trying to win his money back. Usually an unwise decision. So let's search his room next. He will be preoccupied for at least an hour or two."

Calliope nodded and they headed toward the west wing where Ternberry's room was located.

A laughing couple came down the hall and

James put an arm around Calliope, pulling her close. He tipped her chin up and their lips met. A soft sound of surprise was swallowed as her body melted against his. The couple passed, but James didn't stop. He couldn't.

Calliope's hands snaked their way around his neck and she was leaning against him. He didn't know who was hungrier, or why were they standing in the hallway when their rooms were just down the hall.

She tasted just like she smelled . . . a hint of lavender.

A door slammed closed and reality intruded. The thought was like a cold bucket of water.

James broke the kiss and looked down at Calliope. Her eyes were wide and her mouth slightly open. Hell, he wanted to kiss her again, but they had dallied too long and time was running short.

"One of these times we won't be interrupted, I promise."

James pulled her along in her slightly dazed state. Ternberry's door was locked.

He withdrew a thin piece of metal from his pocket and worked on the mechanism. It clicked and a remarkably composed Calliope looked at him with a raised eyebrow.

They entered the room and found a mess. It was the opposite of Roth's spartan and well-organized room. There was a certain irony in the situation, since the two men's attitudes garnered contradictory impressions.

"This is going to take a while."

James had to agree. There were piles of papers

on the floor and they agreed it was the best place to start. Paper after paper was discarded. Sifting through the papers together on the floor was uncomfortable. After that kiss, all James wanted to do was drag her back to her room.

Calliope finally held up a sheet of paper in triumph. "This is it, I recognize this sheet from Pettigrew's study."

They bent their heads together. Unfortunately for James, her hair and skin smelled like the scent always surrounding her.

Forcing his traitorous mind back to the paper, he read the pertinent part aloud: " 'Something needs to be done about the Stephen Chalmers situation. Look into it right away and take the necessary action.' " It was unsigned, but a recognizable seal was embossed in the corner.

An icy stab flew through James. "This is from the Foreign Office."

What was this contract doing in Ternberry's room?

Calliope looked at him. "What does it mean?"

"It could mean anything. It's too cryptic."

She frowned in disappointment and picked up another sheet of paper.

"Looks like a birth certificate."

James took the offered sheet. It was a birth certificate for Edmund Henry Samuel Crane. The date listed was 1802. "That's Holt's son."

The clock struck four.

"Come, the time is late and we can't risk discovery." He replaced the sheets and scattered the pile to resemble its former mess.

James grabbed Calliope's hand and when she didn't protest, he pulled her to the door. Peeking outside, he pulled back as a scantily clad woman ran from one room to another, knocking softly on the door. Another glance showed a man buttoning his trousers as he sauntered to a room a few doors away.

Calliope was attempting to peer over his shoulder but he held her back, breathing a sigh of relief when the traffic in the hallway momentarily halted. He locked the door and tugged her outside. They ran down the few steps to her room and fell inside.

Calliope started laughing uncontrollably. "It's like musical doors around here."

James felt a tug at his own lips. "Yes, house parties can be like that. Luckily we don't have to play that game."

Calliope's laughter died as she saw the expression on his face. A fire slowly built. "No, I think that might be a bad idea. I believe we both should retire now. We can talk in the morning."

He didn't move for a moment and she held her breath thinking he might ignore the entreaty. A part of her wished he would. She tried to tamp the thought down but it wouldn't desist.

He moved toward her, toward the bed. Her breathing became erratic.

"My lord, no. . . ." Her voice came out breathy and foreign to her ears.

James reached for her and she felt herself swaying toward him, tipping her chin back to look in his eyes. He rubbed his thumb across her lips, and then bent down, two inches, one inch. She rose slightly off the floor. His hand traveled down her arm. Her eyes started to close.

Air. It was the only thing touching her. She opened her eyes and saw his retreating back, the extra blanket that had been covering the bed in his hand.

Calliope's jaw sagged slightly.

"I will leave at daybreak. The servants will be up and about and you will be perfectly safe."

He dropped onto the settee, his long legs hanging off the end. It had to be uncomfortable, but he didn't make a peep.

She was outraged. Calliope stomped to the wardrobe and withdrew her nightclothes.

She looked over at him, but his back was to her.

She changed her clothes with difficulty, not ringing for Betsy. She watched to see if he peeked. He didn't. And there was no offer of help.

Calliope's teeth gnashed together. She should be relieved. Instead, she was confused and irritated. And she couldn't explain any of it.

Slipping under the covers, she stared at the ceiling.

She was still staring at the ceiling when he rose and quietly left the room at dawn, as promised.

Chapter 10

W hat a terrible night.

Every muscle in his body ached. Between the lumps in the settee and his overactive libido, he was certain he hadn't slept a wink. Calliope had set the terms of their relationship and he had abided by them. Yet she had slammed the wardrobe and acted like a mad bee that had lost its honey. He knew she had slept as poorly as he— her breathing had never gained the even wave of someone comfortably settled. Sometimes he didn't understand the fairer sex.

James threw the blanket on the floor and rose from the uncomfortable settee. Calliope finally appeared to be asleep. She was a small lump under the bedcovers. How to deal with her? She was the most skittish courtesan he had ever met. She acted like an outraged virgin, a category of women that he avoided like the plague. He wondered if she was even aware of the mixed signals she sent.

He had never needed to woo any woman, yet sometimes he felt that was precisely what he was doing with her.

James exited the room and quietly but firmly locked the door. He trudged across the hall to his room. His valet, Rogers, was waiting.

"I'm not in the mood for a long, drawn-out affair, Rogers. Let's try to keep this to a minimum."

Rogers sniffed. He had probably spent an inordinate amount of time brushing James's trousers and polishing his boots. Rogers liked to be appreciated, but James wasn't in the mood.

After sending Rogers off in a snit, James walked down to breakfast trying to divine the workings of the female mind. Fortunately, Roth was the only one at the table.

"Good god, Angelford, you look awful. Wouldn't have expected such a scowl after seeing you retire with Esmerelda." Roth looked positively cheerful. "I anticipated an expression of the cat stealing the canary, not such a woebegotten air."

James sent him a withering look and snatched a plate from a waiting servant, who scurried off.

He helped himself to the delicacies at the sideboard. "Did you tup the countess without trouble?"

Roth's grin widened as he poked a sausage on his plate. "I did not, much to the dismay of Lady Flanders, who was hoping to enjoy an early celebration in honor of Lady Pettigrew's birthday. Supposedly she's inexhaustible. And while that's an admirable trait, her other attributes don't entice me into spending the requisite time."

James smiled. "I'm quite sure she was irritated, since she appeared ready to have you unwrap and sample her overly abundant charms." Roth was a font of information and James decided to use Roth's knowledge to his advantage. "By the way, speaking of birthdays and gifts, Holt was talking about taking Edmund out for some debauchery now that he's older. Can't recall how old the lad is, but seems Holt thinks it will be amusing, what with his birthday approaching soon."

"Boy will be twenty. Time to join up, just like we did."

Two ladies sauntered in for an early breakfast, giving James no time to glean additional information from Roth. Considering Roth a suspect didn't help his investigation. His instincts told him Roth had nothing to do with Stephen's disappearance or Salisbury's death, but he was unable to rule him out yet.

Roth had always been deep cover and one of the country's best agents. The betrayal of Salisbury screamed deep cover, and lately Roth had been acting more cryptic than usual. There had been a subtle, yet unmistakable withdrawal from public events. It was actually surprising he had shown up at Pettigrew's. As soon as this investigation was over, James planned on having a long chat with his inscrutable friend and colleague.

But for now, he had the information he required. Roth's unerring memory never mixed up facts. If he said Edmund was going to be twenty, then the birth certificate in Ternberry's room didn't make sense. According to the document, he was twenty-one.

Why would Ternberry possess a birth certificate for Holt's son? True, he was Holt's secretary, but if what James suspected was true, Holt wouldn't entrust the certificate to anyone. In fact, the information might be something that Holt was willing to guard to the death.

Things were looking worse.

Calliope breezed into the room looking superb in a lemon morning gown. Swirls of delicate white lace edged the cuffs and hem, making her appear as light as a fairy.

"Roth, how lovely to see you this fine morning."

She didn't so much as glance in James's direction. She looked relaxed and refreshed and showered attention on Roth, ignoring James.

"What a beautiful weekend for Lady Pettigrew's birthday. I'm certain the celebration she has planned will be creative. As birthdays go, I was thinking of attending Edmund Crane's birthday celebration next week. That dashing boy will have the ladies at his feet. Why, he's nearly what, twenty-one?"

Roth sent James a quizzical look. "Twenty, I believe."

James was ready to throttle her. Roth donned a thoughtful expression as Calliope rattled off some of the incessant banter that she used as part of her Esmerelda guise. She continued a diatribe about the ladies of the ton, regaling him with anecdotes and the latest gossip. But Roth was no fool. Social intrigue was second nature to him.

"By the by, have you seen Ternberry this morning? I remembered something I must tell him," she said.

"My dear, Ternberry would scoff at getting up before noon. There is to be a hunt and croquet later. He will likely rouse in time to ride."

"Oh, good. Well, I will leave you two gentlemen to your breakfast and see if Lady Pettigrew has stirred."

She breezed out of the room. Roth raised his brows at James. "Well, she certainly has energy and spirit this morning. What happened to you?"

James scowled and pushed his untouched plate aside. He didn't reply as he rose to follow her. He was going to wring her beautiful neck.

A swirl of lemon skirts rounded the landing at the top of the stairs.

She was heading to her room.

He took the stairs two at a time. He heard a door close as he gained the top step. She had been moving quickly. Reaching her door, he knocked. There was no answer. A door opened down the hall and he heard a lady titter. He gritted his teeth. "Let me in."

Still no answer. "I swear I am going to—"

The door opened and Calliope stood, panic-stricken, tears in her eyes.

He stepped inside and closed the door. Softening his voice he said, "What's wrong?"

She pointed to the bed. He followed her gaze

and saw a slashed Adelphi Theatre playbill.

She threw herself into his arms. "I locked my door this morning while at breakfast. It was on the bed when I returned. I'm so relieved you stayed here last night."

James was suddenly glad for the uncomfortable, sleepless night.

"It's merely a threat. Someone's trying to scare you. If anything had happened to the Dalys, I'd already know." He rubbed her arms. "Lock the door after me. Check to see if anything is missing. I'll be back soon. If anyone enters the room before I return, scream."

James walked a few paces down the hall and knocked on Ternberry's door. There was no answer. He turned the knob and was surprised it opened. The room was completely empty.

James headed for Pettigrew's study.

Pettigrew motioned for him to enter. "Morning, Angelford, I expect you spent a pleasant evening. Delightful girl, Esmerelda. And quite talented?" The last was said as a question and Pettigrew had raised a brow.

"It was quite a night." James inclined his head. "I was hoping to speak with Ternberry this morning. Do you know where I might find him?"

"There was an urgent summons directing him to return to London. His valet relayed the message. Didn't even see him myself."

James swore internally, but kept his face calm. "Too bad, I'll speak with him back in town. I heard there is a twist to the hunt. I'm quite looking forward to it."

"Good, good. Should be just the thing. The wife has plenty of entertainment planned for the day."

James finished the small talk and returned to Calliope's room. He knocked on the door. "I'm back."

As she opened the door, the panicked look was still in evidence. "What are we going to do?"

We. Something warm washed through him. "Do you have a riding habit?"

She nodded.

"Good. I'll wait in the hall while you change into your riding gear, and then escort you downstairs. We're going to eat breakfast and converse with the other guests as if nothing unpleasant has occurred. You aren't to stray from my side."

She nodded again. She must be terrified, to have agreed to that.

Betsy arrived minutes later to assist her. She changed quickly. The riding habit fit her well. All of those buttons would make the thing damn hard to remove. James caught hold of his thoughts and escorted her downstairs. Roth had left the breakfast room. They served themselves and sat down. He was much hungrier than he'd been earlier and quickly devoured the sausage and biscuits. Calliope was pushing the food around her plate.

"Eat your eggs or you aren't leaving this house."

A defiant light appeared in her eyes but she ate the eggs. Some of her spirit was returning.

Many of the guests were up and about by the time they pushed away from the table and headed toward the stables.

Guests milled about the yard, some conversing and others waiting for their horses to be saddled. James and Calliope walked into the stable and over to the stalls holding the two horses James had brought from London.

"This is Apollo and the mare is Damsel."

"Apollo?" She smirked over some secret thought as she brushed a hand along Damsel's smooth neck.

He was about to demand to know what she was thinking when she turned the full force of her smile on him. He forgot what day it was.

"Are you participating in the hunt today?"

Yes, that was why he had come here, he remembered now. "Do you know how to ride?"

"No. I never thought I'd actually use the riding habit." Her voice was wistful.

James pointed to a stable lad. "Saddle these two horses."

The lad jumped up and ran to the tack room.

Calliope chewed on her lip. "I don't know if this is a good idea, James. I don't mind staying at the house. It'll be safe in the common rooms." The same warm feeling rushed through him at her use of his name.

"Where's your sense of adventure? And how are we ever going to win the hunt if you aren't on horseback?"

She grinned widely.

The lad had the horses saddled and in the yard quickly. James helped Calliope into the saddle.

"It's rather higher than I thought."

She sat awkwardly with her legs to the left side and almost slid off the horse.

James observed her for a moment and then looked to the stable lad. The lad nodded.

James grabbed Calliope and pulled her down. The lad led Damsel back into the stable.

"I know I can do better." Her voice was laced with disappointment. She thought he had changed his mind.

The lad reemerged minutes later with a different saddle cinched on Damsel's back. James hauled her back onto the horse. Calliope looked disgruntled. "A little communication would be a good thing."

James dismissed the lad. "One of the keys to riding sidesaddle is the saddle itself. Needs to fit both the rider and the horse. The last saddle was too small for you. You have lovely long legs."

Calliope blushed and inspected the saddle beneath her. She looked to the left and right, and then patted the horse's head.

"Don't lean. Sit up straight. Don't sit back. Balance on the center. Good."

Calliope looked like a marionette, jerking back and forth as he gave commands. She gave him an irritated glance, but the color was high in her cheeks and the horse was already interpreting her movements, excited to be off.

"If we were alone, I'd teach you to ride astride. However, some of the ladies would probably slip off their horses into a faint, so you are stuck sidesaddle for today." He grinned.

A light appeared in her eye and James had the odd feeling she was trying to record his exact words.

James gave her rudimentary instructions on controlling her mount and she started to look more comfortable, her back straight, her right foot relaxed. She looked natural in the saddle.

They walked across the yard and he steered her to a path leading into the sun-dappled woods.

"This is my favorite trail on Pettigrew's estate. It's a roundabout way to get to the lake. We can meander and maybe do some cantering so you can get the feel for Damsel's stride."

He looked back. Her eyes were big and she had a dazed smile on her face. It pleased him.

It was a canopy trail, the sunlight mildly pierced the trees here and there, but the feel of the forest was all-encompassing. Unidentified foliage was dripping from every corner. Stephen was the green thumb, the one who always explained the assorted flora. . . .

"Oh, look!"

He pushed aside the direction of his thoughts and turned to see her pointing at a leggy fox scampering into the trees. Hadn't she ever been out of the city?

They rode for a while in silence, enjoying the trail. As the path widened, she nudged Damsel and shot past him, laughing in delight. She looked like a woodland fairy. He wished she didn't have the damn wig on, or the bonnet perched on top. The thought of her hair loose and flowing freely down her back was enough to make him shift uncomfortably on Apollo.

The trail was wide enough for two and he caught up and rode alongside her. The path led across a bubbling brook and through an open field. He pointed to different animals and birds, their legs brushing, her happily bemused expression invoking feelings he thought long dead.

Their ride ended at the lake. All of the trails eventually wound to the lake. Guests were gathering for the games. He could see people walking from the house to join them, although they were far enough away to be unidentifiable.

Lady Flanders cantered over. She was a skillful rider and always made the most of her riding habit, matching it to her mount and tack. James found he preferred Calliope's lack of affectation and pure enjoyment.

"Angelford. I was disappointed in you last night. Perhaps you will be up for more entertainment tonight?"

"Perhaps."

She smiled and opened her mouth to say more when their host interrupted.

"Ladies and gentlemen, please gather 'round."

Pettigrew was in the gazebo motioning for everyone to join him.

"Lady Pettigrew has developed a twist for today's hunt. It is to be a treasure hunt so that the ladies can participate. You will receive your first clue here. In groups of two, you will unravel the clue and proceed to the station revealed in the puzzle. At each station you will be required to successfully complete a task before receiving your next clue. Detailed maps of the grounds will be given to each pair."

"This sounds like fun." Calliope smiled at him.

Lady Flanders looked down her nose. "I would have much preferred the original fox hunt, but since the Pettigrews are bound and determined to play these little games, I think it only proper we form teams. Angelford, you and I—"

"Penelope, I believe your husband is motioning to you."

Her lips tightened, and she turned to see Flanders indeed motioning from the other side of the gazebo. She gave James a determined smile. "I will talk to you at the finish line, dear."

Calliope muttered but her face remained excited as Pettigrew pointed to the croquet sets on the lawn. "One person from each team will play. Once your ball passes through each of the wickets, you and your partner will gain possession of your first clue."

James played for their team, and Calliope cheered loudly as he finished first. Pettigrew handed Calliope a packet of instructions as soon as James's ball cleared the last wicket.

"Angelford, Esmerelda, here is your map and first clue. Have a good time and try not to lose your way." Pettigrew winked suggestively.

Calliope read the clue aloud. "It's a riddle, James. 'Crumble and fall, prayers of old. Find the flame, fight the cold.'"

"The old abbey. Let's go."

She sprinted to Damsel. James hoisted her into the saddle and they were off. They raced to the abbey hidden in a copse of trees, dismounted and hurried inside the collapsing façade. Two servants awaited them. One smiled and lit a candle. "My lord, one of you will need to balance on the log while not spilling a drop of wax from this taper. Otherwise you must begin anew."

"I'll do it," Calliope volunteered.

She gingerly took the candle and mounted an ancient ceiling beam that had fallen to the floor. Moving one foot after another, she gracefully crossed the beam. As she reached the other side, a smile wreathed her face. "Done!"

The servant nodded and handed them a sheet of paper. Another pair of participants ran into the abbey as James and Calliope rushed to their horses.

"Another riddle," Calliope said, bouncing up and down. " 'The sweet bloom of a maiden fair. Pluck one for your lady's hair.' "

"Lady Pettigrew's rose garden."

They set off. A series of six additional stops led them to the maze, the kitchens, the stable, a copse of trees in the shape of a hand, the carriage house and the conservatory. The last clue sent them galloping back to the lake. Calliope was so eager to be the first team back that her wig was in danger of falling off. She had thrown herself aggressively into the challenges. And she had acquitted herself adequately as a new horsewoman, if a bit enthusiastic.

"Hurry up, you're slowing us down," Calliope yelled over her shoulder.

James threw his head back and laughed. He hadn't had this much fun in, well, forever.

They galloped back to the lake but other couples were already milling about. One couple was arguing with Pettigrew.

"We lost it on the way—you can't penalize us for that!"

"How many servants were at the maze station?"

"Two."

"Wrong, three."

The couple stalked away from Pettigrew, muttering under their breath.

"Ah, Angelford and Esmerelda. Do you have your clues?"

They dismounted and left the horses with the others that were grazing. Pettigrew hadn't mentioned keeping the clues, but Calliope had retained each one, refusing to toss them on the ground.

Calliope handed them to Pettigrew, who examined each before proclaiming, "You are the winners. A few other teams tried to claim the title without actually completing the course." Pettigrew scowled at the other couples. "Congratulations, here is your prize. Ah, it looks like the second- and third-place finishers are right behind you. Please excuse me, I need to get their prizes."

He handed them two boxes. Calliope opened the first and her mouth dropped. James peeked over her shoulder and saw a ruby necklace. She opened the other box to find matching earrings.

She sputtered. "What . . . how . . ."

James raised an eyebrow. "A courtesan

wouldn't be impressed with those baubles, my dear."

Her mouth snapped shut and she closed the boxes.

"Yes, they are pretty little things." Her voice had turned haughty. He grinned at her and she looked disgruntled.

The rest of the participants slowly drifted back and everyone was enjoying the sandwiches and wine brought by the servants. The guests were chatting and sitting by the lake.

Roth wandered over. "Heard you two won."

James cocked an eyebrow. "Expected some competition from you, but didn't come across you once on the course."

Roth looked unperturbed. "Lady Willoughby and I stayed close to the lake. We decided to forgo the hunt."

Calliope tugged on James's coat. "If you don't mind, I think I'm ready to go back. My legs feel like they've been molded around a banister."

James and Roth both smiled. "I think I'll ride back with you," Roth said. James followed as they walked to fetch their mounts. A number of people were milling near the horses and examining the animals. One man touched Apollo's forelock. Apollo nickered and moved away. James tamped his irritation.

Calliope gathered Damsel's reins and led her to James for a boost. He lifted her, and as she smoothed her skirts, Damsel fidgeted and tossed her neck.

Calliope leaned forward to soothe the restless

horse and Damsel went wild. James reached forward to grab the reins, but horse and rider were off. Damsel was jerking and Calliope was hanging on for dear life, form forgotten. James vaulted onto Apollo and raced after her. Roth did likewise. Damsel galloped into the trees, yanking left, then right. James and Roth entered the copse seconds behind.

Damsel slowed and thrashed wildly. If he could just get a little closer . . .

Calliope flew from Damsel's back, landing roughly at the base of a giant oak. Damsel threw her head back and galloped down the path.

James jumped off Apollo and ran to Calliope's still form. Terror and despair coursed through his body. He had lost more than one friend in riding accidents. What had he been thinking, letting her ride? Roth dismounted and joined him at her side. James felt her head and she groaned. Relief washed over him as he pictured a totally different outcome.

Roth stood up. "I'll get the horse." He remounted and rode into the trees.

"Ow, stop that." Her eyes opened and she frowned.

"What happened?" James asked.

"That wasn't my most graceful exit."

"Are you hurt?"

"I would have been, sooner rather than later, I think. Why did Damsel react that way? I thought she liked me." Calliope looked more hurt by the horse's betrayal than by landing on the ground.

She sat up and winced. "I think I might rest a bit, if you don't mind."

Mind? She wasn't going to be given a choice. "Do you think you can stand?"

She nodded. He picked her up and gently put her on her feet.

"I can walk. I'm just a little bruised. I think my confidence is a bit bruised as well."

James let her walk around, seeing nothing broken, and then picked her up and set her on Apollo's back.

Roth returned with a grim look on his face. "Check the saddle."

James didn't need to uncinch the saddle. He followed the trail of blood to the burrs that had been shoved underneath the leather. Someone would know an inexperienced rider was sure to lean forward trying to find her seat. The culprit would not even have to remove the saddle for the damage to be done. Rage filled him. Calliope could have died.

"Could have been done anytime at the lake. The question is, why?" Roth asked.

"What are you two talking about?" Calliope inquired.

Roth looked from one to the other. James wished he knew what the man was thinking. He was always so bloody hard to read.

"Fine, keep your secrets, but gentlemen, do you think we can head back now?" Her voice was dulled by pain.

James mounted behind her, his rage simmering

beneath the surface. He enveloped her in his arms and she immediately relaxed against him.

Pettigrew and a few of the other guests burst into the trees. They had to bring their horses up short before colliding with them.

"What happened? Is Esmerelda all right?" Pettigrew looked concerned.

"Yes, a bit shaken but otherwise unharmed. We are returning to the house."

"Of course. I'll come with you. Can't leave an injured guest."

They rode back to the stables. James kept up a quick pace, holding Calliope carefully in his arms, and trying to avoid Pettigrew's questions.

They arrived at the stables. James lowered Calliope into Roth's arms, jumped down and reached for Damsel's reins. Pettigrew dismounted and hurried over. He saw the blood and investigated the saddle.

"Tanner!"

The head groom ran out of the stable. "Yes, my lord?"

"What is the meaning of this? Who put the saddle on this horse? Someone is not doing his job properly!" Pettigrew continued to yell at the groom. "One of my guests could have been killed! I will have someone's head. Yours if no one else's!"

Pettigrew was overdoing the outrage. He could have been convincing with a bit less fervor. He stomped off to the manor.

James walked over to the abashed groom. "I know you and your staff didn't have anything to do with the accident. I will speak with Pettigrew. Here is my card. If you or anyone else is turned out as a result of this incident, go to this address and ask for Stubbins. If you could take care of Damsel's injuries, I'd appreciate it."

"Thank you, my lord." The groom's eyes regained a spark of life. He wiped a hand over his brow, took Damsel's and Apollo's reins and hurried inside.

Calliope was leaning against Roth. She looked at James strangely, and nodded approvingly. James gently lifted her and carried her into the house.

Calliope rested a cold cheek against his shoulder. Roth was keeping up with the quick pace he had set.

"Roth, would you send Esmerelda's maid, Betsy, to her room with some hot tea and a warming pan?"

He nodded. "Think I'll have a talk with Pettigrew too."

James frowned and nodded in return. There was nothing he could do about Roth now. He'd have to talk with him later.

"Lord Pettigrew certainly seemed upset," Calliope mumbled against his chest.

"Yes, we'll have to keep a closer eye on him."

She tilted her head back, her face only inches from his. "Wasn't he just expressing concern as a host?"

"Shh. We'll talk when we reach your room."

She tucked her head into his shoulder. Her body was beginning to feel warmer. That was a good sign.

He unlocked her room and set her down on the bed. "Remove your riding habit. You'll feel better after a nap."

She frowned. "No, I'm going to have tea. You just sent Roth for some."

"Change your clothes and get under the covers, or I'll do it for you."

Her face assumed the disgruntled look she was so fond of, but she must have read his intent, because she hurriedly changed while James walked to the window overlooking one of the gardens. He could see her out of the corner of his eye.

Someone knocked at the door.

"Enter."

Calliope's maid placed the tea tray on the table and lit a fire in the fireplace. James's body was heating the room better than a fire, but the added heat couldn't hurt.

The maid left and Calliope padded to the tray. Her feet were bare.

"Get in bed." His voice was a bit raw.

She looked like she was going to argue but padded to the bed and crawled under the covers, militantly thumping her hands down on the soft coverlet.

James poured two cups of tea and brought one to her. He sat on the edge of the bed, forcing her to scoot inward or be crushed. She gave him a dark look and took the cup.

"Did you see anyone near Damsel? Someone put burrs under her saddle," he said.

Calliope put the cup down and her gaze turned

thoughtful. "There were men poking Apollo right before we remounted."

James nodded. "I wasn't paying as close attention as I should have." He had been watching Calliope and soaking up her pleasure.

"What should we do?"

"I don't think there is much we can do at this point. I will have a look around the lake, but whoever did this is probably long gone. And the evidence with him."

"Come back as soon as you are finished."

He nodded. "I will send your maid back up. She will keep people away."

He walked out and Calliope's maid was walking toward him with Roth. Yes, Roth knew a bit too much, as usual.

James gave the maid strict instructions and she disappeared inside.

Roth studied him, waiting.

"I'm going to the lake. Would you like to join me?"

Roth nodded and they walked back to the stables.

Only after they entered the trail to the lake did Roth speak. "You have secrets. I have secrets. Esmerelda seems to have many. Let's only speak of today. Something foul is afoot. Be careful."

He could trust Roth. He felt it. He should tell him the entire tale. But something held him back.

"Agreed. You didn't happen to see anyone around the horses before we left, did you?"

Roth nodded. "Half of the party ventured past, including servants. Even Lady Flanders. I don't have to warn you not to underestimate her."

"No, you don't."

They discussed the rest of the members of the party until they reached the lake. Most of the guests had joined in one of the other afternoon pursuits.

A movement caught his attention. A small man stood far off in the trees. The hairs on James's neck started tingling. The man hadn't the look of a servant. Roth was staring at the man as well. They rode to the spot but the man had disappeared. It was the same copse of trees into which Damsel had dashed.

Searching the grounds turned up nothing and they returned to the house two hours later.

James headed for Calliope's room. Roth put a hand on his arm.

"James, don't overlook anyone." James nodded and Roth turned and strode down the hall.

The maid let him in and he instructed her to return in a few hours. Calliope was sleeping, one hand curled under her chin. He pulled up a chair and sat down to wait until dinner.

The maid had left some old papers for him to read. He flipped through one. He had already read this paper some weeks before. A caricature popped from the page. He remembered this set of cartoons clearly. They were illustrated by Thomas Landes and James had kept track of the artist's work.

The first one depicted a debutante, who bore a striking resemblance to Sarah Jones, talking to a wilting fern as several gentlemen tiptoed away. Her vacant expression and uplifted nose prevented her from seeing her escaping prey.

The second was of a debutante with large blond curls—probably Cecelia Dort. A rag was tied around her mouth, preventing her from speaking. These were some of Landes's tamer drawings. The man had a cruel streak at times.

Some of his recent ones had been political in nature. Landes must have been in attendance at Parliament to be able to accurately detail those. James would have to pay close attention to the gentlemen present during the next session.

Had Calliope seen these? He'd show them to her when she woke. She would probably enjoy the one of Cecelia.

He shook his head but couldn't stop grinning. He remembered the shocked look on Cecelia's face when Calliope verbally hammered her. What a spirited nymph Calliope was.

She had been a wood sprite today, bouncing in the saddle and having a great time. Her laughing face would linger in his mind for some time. He couldn't remember ever having more fun with a woman. With practice she would make a fine horsewoman.

He sobered as he tried to force a piece of the puzzle into a spot too small for it to fit. It made sense for someone to be after Calliope. Her connection to Salisbury drew her in tightly.

But the lake area had been crowded. Why would someone risk being unmasked? The act smacked of desperation.

Who had put the burrs under the saddle, and why?

Chapter 11

∽⦿∾

Calliope woke slowly. A cheery, sizzling fire had been lit in the hearth. The room was warm and cozy. She snuggled deeper into the covers, reluctant to leave the cocoon. She opened one eye and the deepened shadows pronounced it early evening. Perhaps she could linger here all night.

She buried her cheek in the pillow and saw a movement in the shadows. Someone was beside the bed. She let out a gasp and half rose. Familiar eyes met hers and mixed emotions warred inside her.

James was sitting in a chair next to the bed. She leaned back into the pillow and sighed. It seemed she was going to have to get out of bed.

"What are you doing here?" she asked softly.

He lifted a shoulder. "Your maid should be up any moment with dinner."

"You just arrived, then?" Frankly, she was astonished he had cared enough to sit with her for even a few moments.

He lifted a shoulder again, not answering her.

Calliope scooted against the headboard. The action hurt more than she cared to admit. She rubbed her neck. Her muscles were sore, she was probably covered in bruises, but she didn't think there would be any lasting damage.

"How are you feeling?"

"Like I threw myself from a charging horse."

James smiled.

Betsy bustled in and set a dinner tray before her. Another servant followed and placed a tray in front of James. Betsy fluffed her pillows and with a gesture from James left the room.

"Ordering my servants around again?" She stabbed a juicy slice of roast, swirling it in the dark au jus.

He didn't answer and she forked a potato. "Why aren't you eating with everyone downstairs?"

"The view is better up here."

Calliope tucked the covers around her bare knee, which had snuck out while the tray had been seated. Her gown had crept up while she slept.

James smiled and cut a piece of beef. The crackling fire cast dancing shadows on the walls and across the planes of his face. His unfashionably long hair fell forward as he regarded his plate. He looked like a pirate, albeit an entirely too handsome one.

One potato after another disappeared from his

plate. The meat followed. Calliope took a bite of the roast and had to force herself not to push the food around the plate.

James finished quickly and sat back, studying her. "Eat. Or do you need my assistance?"

"I'm sore, not an invalid." Perhaps if she showed her leg again he would leave her lack of appetite alone. Or give her that look that heated her to her toes.

There was a knock on the door and Betsy poked her head around the frame. "Lord Pettigrew wishes to know if you will be attending the festivities tonight, miss."

James looked at Calliope, allowing her the decision.

"Yes, Betsy. Please tell Lord Pettigrew we'll be down shortly, and then return to help me dress."

"Very good, miss."

"Since you refused my offer to feed you, I would be delighted to assist you in dressing," James said, a glint in his eyes.

Her heart quickened. "Betsy would be despondent."

"You're not very sporting." He shook his head in mock despair, stood and opened the door. "I'll see you in a bit."

Calliope put her tray to the side and tentatively stretched each leg and rotated her waist. Her muscles strained. She repeated the motions, extending farther and feeling better each successive time.

Her body was still slightly sore. But the nap and stretching had gone far in removing the pain.

Betsy bustled in and helped her prepare for the evening.

It took some time, but Calliope was pleased with the result. She touched the shimmering indigo gown embroidered with white. Madame Giselle had created something more than dramatic. The iridescent bodice was pushed into a display of creamy flesh. Yet it had a touch of innocence too. The embroidered lining along the top simultaneously suggested and concealed.

Calliope ran her white-gloved hands down the skirt, trying to calm her nerves. So the dress was slightly outrageous. That was her persona. She had gone beyond the point of entertaining missish notions.

Her own hair strained beneath the wig, wanting above all else to be free. The wig was styled in an upswept tangle of curls. Small tendrils fell loosely about her face.

There was a knock and James entered the room. She walked forward to join him and he brought a gloved hand to his lips. His eyes were hot. His warm breath scorched her skin through the glove and tingles radiated from the spot.

"Are you ready to join the festivities below?" He smiled and she started to feel a bit wicked in her dress.

"Yes." She felt slightly breathless.

She slid an arm through his and pressed against his side. He tightened his arm.

They descended to the ballroom, where most of the guests had already gathered and were chatting and laughing with more abandon then the previous night. Spirits flowed freely and the mood was relaxed and a bit racy. Women stood closer to the men and the men's hands were freer in their placement.

The ballroom was large and the lighting was low. Lady Pettigrew had created an intimate setting and the guests were having no trouble absorbing the mood.

A set was forming and the orchestra began to play. Calliope and James skirted the edge of the floor, chatting briefly with different couples before joining Roth and Lady Willoughby, who were standing off to the side.

Calliope liked Lady Willoughby. She was a lady in the true sense. Her bearing was proud, but kindness shone in her eyes. She was not unattractive, but she probably had the dubious distinction of being the least sparkling woman in the room. Hers was a steady beauty, calm and accepting. Not flashy, not fast. In fact, the more one studied her, the more out of place the widow seemed. A dove in a flock of peacocks.

"How are you feeling, Esmerelda?" Lady Willoughby asked.

"Refreshed. This afternoon I discovered body parts of which I was unaware."

Lady Willoughby smiled. "Riding will do that to you."

"And falling." Roth wasn't smiling.

"Yes, well, my first time on a horse was definitely not stellar," Calliope said.

"You did very well. That was not the problem," Roth said.

Lady Willoughby looked uncomfortable. A waltz struck up and she turned to Roth, a questioning look in her eye.

He bowed over her hand and led her to the floor. Calliope looked at James. He was staring after them speculatively. She nudged him in the ribs and he smiled.

"You need not resort to physical violence, I'd be delighted to partner you."

He swept her onto the floor and she laughed. His eyes twinkled. They were usually the color of obsidian. Tonight they were black velvet.

He held her tightly as they spun among the couples. They didn't touch another body in their dance. Dancing with James meant there were no collisions, no mishaps running into another couple.

He trailed his left hand down her waist to her hip. Every place he touched was left tingling. She could feel the heat from his body everywhere, permeating through her from her legs to her hips. From her waist to her chest, in her cheeks and eyelids.

She looked into his eyes. He had laughed with her as if they were old friends this afternoon. Had worried over her when she had fallen. Had carefully carried her back to the house. Had stayed with her while she slept. The beast had turned into a knight somewhere along the way.

Throughout the dance they never broke eye contact. Never spoke. His eyes held forbidden promises. He smelled rich and warm.

The music ended, but still they maintained their position. His warm hands, her trembling limbs.

People pressed around them, exiting the floor, and he finally turned and led her to the terrace, one hand still caressing her waist.

She didn't look away. She didn't hesitate.

People were milling outside. He kept moving, heading into the garden. The crescent moon shed little light, but she could see his every movement. The focused saunter of his legs, the coiled strength in his arms. And then he pulled her into his arms.

Her mind registered a fragrant smell. They were somewhere in the rose garden.

The night was chilly but he was so warm, and so was she. He kissed her throat, trailing kisses down the bare expanse of her chest. Her head tilted back.

His kisses worked up to her jawline, then to her ear. He tugged on one lobe with his lips and heat spiraled through her. He returned his attention to her mouth, gently at first, then deepening the kiss, awakening a deep, unfamiliar ache. Her hands wound around his neck, her fingers stroking the nape, wrapping in his thick hair.

She was fully pressed against him but strained to get closer.

He swept her up and laid her down on a bench. She barely registered the cold stone. One hand cupped the back of her head while he continued to kiss her. His other hand was on her ankle, working its way up. The back of her knee. Her garter. Her thigh. Slowly inching farther up.

She gasped. He caught the sound with his mouth and she found herself kissing him hungrily, demanding more. More of everything.

He lifted her so she was straddling him, much as they were the day in the coach. Her dress bunched around them. His trousers were undone and heat pressed to heat. Calliope's entire body was on fire and her head felt heavy. He pulled her toward him and the moonlight glinted in his eyes.

This was what the actresses discussed in titters backstage. What she had never understood. Feelings and emotions she had never experienced.

Longing poured through her, making her voice husky. "James."

The bushes rustled. "Stop complaining. The plan went perfectly."

James rose and twirled them around the hedges so quickly she nearly gasped again. His quick movements flung her dress out and back down, covering her.

"What was that?" a voice said.

"Stop changing the subject. Complaining, am I? You're wasting precious time and you didn't finish your job."

"I did exactly as instructed."

"No, you didn't. She's inside, dancing."

The voices were muffled but it was a woman arguing with a man. Calliope tried to peer through the hedge but James pulled her back against his chest. It was still warm.

"I did as instructed. You take it up with him if you're dissatisfied."

"What about the other task, did you finish that?"

"I don't take orders from you. But if you aren't

careful, I'll start giving them." Calliope shuddered at the meaning in the hushed male voice.

"Just you remember. She needs to be out of the way."

"I know my position. You'd do well to remember yours."

One set of light feet beat a hasty retreat, but the heavier set didn't move.

Calliope could feel James's muscles tense. He was ready if the intruder turned the corner. After a moment the man headed down the same path the woman had taken, a path that led to the lake.

James waited another minute before loosening his grip. Calliope shivered and he absently ran his hands along her bare arms. "I'm going to take you back to the house."

Calliope's insides were shaking from both thwarted desire and fear. "Who were they?"

"I don't know, the voices were too muffled." He frowned. "I'm going to have a look around."

"James, I'm worried. Please take Roth with you."

He hesitated but nodded. "I'll have a word with him when we return to the ballroom."

James stood and set her on her feet. All of his clothing was in place, somehow. Calliope hoped she looked half as composed.

They stepped back into the pathway and exited the garden. Calliope breathed a sigh of relief when they stepped onto the terrace. They started for the ballroom doors. The festivities were still in high swing.

There was little doubt: The man and woman had been talking about her. Now they had three suspects to search for. Maybe she could convince James to let her search through Lady—

A female shriek broke through the merriment. "Oh, my God!"

The chirping of crickets and bullfrogs ceased. The ballroom stilled and then emptied as people crammed through the doors vying to see who and what caused the commotion. James and Calliope were already running toward the sound.

"The lake."

James nodded and kept running, dragging Calliope behind him. She stumbled and he slowed the pace. She could hear some of the other men catching up to them. They broke into the clearing around the lake.

James and Calliope were two of the first to arrive. Tanner, the groom, dashed in from one side of the clearing, lantern held high, and Pettigrew appeared from the other side. Neither had come from the direction of the house or stables.

Lady Willoughby was standing by the lake. Roth was standing next to her. A body was floating face down in the water.

Pettigrew looked slightly flustered. "Tanner, wade in and retrieve the person."

Roth had made no move to retrieve the body. Calliope had thought him a fairly take-charge individual. Odd.

People started pushing against her back as they tried to move closer.

"A body!"

"Who is it?"

"Is the person alive?"

"What happened?"

"Who screamed?"

"Who did it?"

"Did what, what happened?"

Questions and comments darted around the group, which was getting larger by the second.

Tanner slipped into the water. She saw him try to hide a shudder at the temperature. He waded over to the body, fortunately close to shore, and tugged on the shirt until he was back at the water's edge.

A stable boy assisted him in lifting the inert form and dragging it ashore. Tanner quickly exited the crowd. Probably to find a hot bath and some dry clothes.

Calliope spared the groom little thought as the moon glinted off the water and onto the body. Dread and fear coiled in her.

The body was dressed in rich clothes. Blond hair was matted to the man's skull.

She started praying.

Chapter 12

~~~∽∞∽~~~

Pettigrew reached down and turned the body over. A letter opener protruded from the chest. "It's Ternberry."

"Ternberry!"

"Move, I can't see."

"Ronald Ternberry!"

"I thought he left."

"Is he alive?"

"What's going on?"

"Gentlemen, please escort the ladies indoors." Pettigrew's voice was tight and agitated.

Guests in the rear were pushing forward, trying to peek through the spectators in front. A few of the men started herding the bewildered crowd toward the house. It took a few minutes of commotion before the crowd began to move.

James bent and whispered in Calliope's ear. "Stay with Lady Willoughby. We will follow in a few minutes."

Calliope nodded. Lady Willoughby had turned and was walking toward the house, a straggler behind the swarm. Calliope kept a few paces behind.

Lady Willoughby's stride was short, her shoulders hunched forward. She tripped twice. Calliope didn't feel very relaxed either. Ternberry's twisted features would star in her nightmares.

They reached the house and joined the other ladies and a number of the gentlemen in the salon. Lady Pettigrew was fluttering. The servants were dashing around serving brandy and tea. One gentleman started to light a cigar. He stopped en route and surprise lit his face. He hastily tucked the unlit cigar away, finally remembering where he was. The atmosphere was tense.

Calliope continued to follow Lady Willoughby until she stopped short of a group of women. She looked unsurprised to find Calliope on her heels. Penelope Flanders was regaling the group with details.

"Grotesque. I tell you, it was as if he were the devil laughing, his mouth stuck in a twisted line. His eyes bulging. I can't believe my smelling salts are missing." Penelope fanned herself. "I don't know what I shall do. The parties won't be the same without dear Ternberry."

She wiped a nonexistent tear. "I do hope Flanders makes us leave tonight. Back to town, where it's safe." Penelope's eyes were lit with anticipation, even as she affected a shudder. Whoever made it back to London first would have the juiciest piece of gossip this season.

Lady Pettigrew fretted at the table, unsure whether to be pleased or nervous that her party would be on everyone's tongues.

Lady Willoughby's eyes narrowed, but she ignored Lady Flanders, who continued trying to fuel the hysteria in the room. "Esmerelda, do you know what the men are planning to do? I saw Lord Angelford speaking with you."

"Other than contacting the constable, I don't know. I think it would be a mistake for the party to attempt the roads at this time of night. Too many opportunities for a broken wheel."

Penelope moaned. "Oh, no, we are trapped. Perhaps that is what the murderer is after. She will kill us all."

A couple of ladies gasped and one fainted on the blue velvet settee. Lady Pettigrew looked like she was choking.

"How do you know the murderer is a female?" Calliope asked.

Penelope raised a brow. "He was killed with a lady's letter opener."

How did she know? Calliope had been close to the body and it had been hard to see even from her vantage point. "A man could have stolen it."

The rest of the room had become silent and intent on their conversation. A couple of the men murmured their assent.

"Stolen? How?" Penelope postured for the audience.

"I suppose the way people normally steal. Pick it up and take it," Calliope responded.

Penelope tapped her chin. "And maybe that person is trying to make it appear like a man took it in order to cover her tracks." She looked pointedly at Calliope. Calliope forced her mouth closed. It took effort.

Lady Willoughby shook her head in disgust. Penelope turned on her. "Didn't you find the body? What were you doing there?"

Roth walked into the room. "That's enough." He looked at Penelope in displeasure.

"Now that you are here, of course it is." Penelope smiled but wisely took a step back into the crowd.

Lord Pettigrew huffed into the room, the rest of the men trailing at his heels. "The constable was summoned and is on his way. If everyone could please go to his or her room I am sure this unfortunate incident will be resolved. The constable may need to talk to some of you."

A few of the guests hurried from the room, others reluctantly followed.

Pettigrew looked at Lady Flanders pointedly. "Your presence is unnecessary."

She smiled and dithered until Flanders walked into the room. "Good night, all. Do let me know if I can be of assistance."

Since her husband was present, Penelope no doubt figured she would get the details later.

Lady Willoughby started to follow her. Roth caught her and whispered something. A frightened look passed over her features, but she nodded. They walked to Pettigrew's side to wait.

Calliope assumed she would be asked to remain, but James escorted her upstairs.

"This is not how I envisioned our evening to end." He tucked a loose tendril behind her ear. "Keep your door locked. I might be a while, there's no telling how long the constable will remain."

He gave her a kiss on the forehead and was gone.

Calliope stood in the middle of the room. What to do? She pulled her knotted fingers from her dress. She wished she had a sketchpad to keep her fingers busy and her mind occupied.

The clock ticked.

Perhaps a short nap would help. She haphazardly disrobed and climbed into bed, placing a newly lit candle on the nightstand. The smooth sheets smelled clean, but they were freezing. Betsy must have forgotten a warm brick in the excitement. Calliope's teeth chattered. She tried moving around to warm the covers, but it didn't help.

Poor Ternberry. Forever cold.

Like her father.

She stared at the ceiling as the seconds ticked past. Then the minutes, then the hours. Booted feet clomped down the hallway and one pair stopped in front of her door. A key scraped the lock.

James stepped inside and shut the door. The nearly extinguished candle cast him almost into the shadows.

"Are we going to search tonight?" Calliope asked. She scooted until she was sitting against the headboard.

He shook his head. "Most people will be in their rooms. The ones who prefer to spend the night elsewhere are too risky. We don't know which room they'll choose."

"Who is still downstairs?"

"The constable just left. Pettigrew, Roth, Flanders and a couple of the others are retiring now."

"Was anything discovered?"

"Not yet. As expected, no one has claimed the letter opener."

"Lady Flanders said it was a woman's letter opener."

James mulled the information. "A few of the men were discussing it. Penelope has ears for gossip. Did she say anything else?"

"She tried accusing me and then Lady Willoughby of the murder."

"What did you say?"

"Roth interrupted before I could counter. He is strung tightly tonight."

James sighed and sat down. "Both of us worked with Ternberry. I wasn't fond of the man, but can't say I wanted him dead."

"Would Roth?"

James shook his head in the negative and stood. "No, Roth liked to tease Ternberry, but I don't recall any bad blood. Roth can be cold-blooded but this isn't his style."

"What about Pettigrew?"

He began pacing. "Pettigrew worked with us as

well. I would be unsurprised to find the letter opener belongs to his wife. It would be easy enough to steal on a weekend such as this."

James leaned his head back and put his hands in his trouser pockets. "I should have known. Should have put someone on Ternberry this morning. Thought I could wait until we were back in London."

"How would you have known?"

His face was flushed. "First Stephen, now Ternberry. I was so scared tonight. I saw the blond hair and . . ." James shuddered. "The worst thing is the relief after seeing it wasn't Stephen. I actually felt relief it was Ternberry."

Calliope threw back the covers and closed the distance between them. She wrapped her arms around him. "Me too."

He hugged her tightly and then looked into her eyes. He let her go and walked to the decanter of brandy. He poured a finger, capped the bottle, uncapped the bottle and poured a bit more. He swirled it in the glass without taking a sip.

"Did Lady Willoughby go to the lake by herself?" Calliope asked.

"That is what she claims."

"And Roth was the first one to arrive?"

"That is what he claims."

"Odd, I didn't take Lady Willoughby as the fast type."

"She's not. I have no clue as to what she is doing here, in fact. She may be a widow, but she is a respectable widow. Never heard a single piece of gossip attached to her," James said.

"What do you suppose happened at the lake?"

"With Roth and Lady Willoughby? Or with Ternberry?"

"You think Roth and Lady Willoughby were there together?" Calliope asked.

"Yes. I'm as surprised as you."

"What were they doing?"

James gave a half smile. "They claim they weren't together, remember?"

Calliope laughed. It felt odd, but good. She perched on the arm of the sitting chair and curled her cold toes under her nightgown. "What about Ternberry? Did you learn anything from his . . . from the body?"

"Ternberry wasn't dead long. His face wasn't bloated."

Calliope shivered. "What does Ternberry have to do with this? What does he have to do with my . . . father?"

"Other than being part of Salisbury's last mission? I don't know. Ternberry wasn't a member of our inner circle. He was always a bit on the outside. We were surprised when Holt chose him as secretary."

"Who was Ternberry close to?"

"No one on our list. Roth probably interacted with him more than anyone besides Holt. But Holt isn't close to anyone. He can't afford to be, in his position."

"Must be lonely."

"Maybe that's why he chose Ternberry."

"Ternberry came back to meet someone tonight, didn't he?"

"All signs lead to him meeting the person who stabbed him. He wasn't taken by surprise; there was no evidence of a struggle and he was stabbed from the front. He didn't announce his return to Pettigrew or anyone else in the house, that anyone will admit."

Calliope mulled this information but the Salisbury connection kept intruding.

"What . . . when did you meet my father?"

"He took Stephen and me under his wing when we finished Oxford."

"What was it like? Working with him, I mean."

"He was very intelligent. Very dedicated. Never did anything half measure. I see a lot of him in you. He earned all of our respect and loyalty."

"That's why you were so angry last night when we were speaking of him."

James nodded. His eyes softened as he looked at her. "We'll sort the mess when we find Stephen." He seemed to consider his words and then nodded to himself, as if emphasizing the *when* in the statement.

The old feelings for her father resurfaced, but not as strongly this time. She felt a little better, wound a little less tightly than usual. "All right. I agree."

His shoulders relaxed a bit.

"We should talk to Ternberry's servants," Calliope said.

The clock struck five.

"We can discuss our plans in the morning."

"It's nearly dawn. This is the morning."

James grimaced. "I know. It will be a long day."

"Are we going to stay here for the day?"

"No, I think we should return to London quickly. I don't think there is much to uncover here."

Calliope nodded and padded over to the bed, snuggling into the covers, which were beginning to cool again.

James took a deep breath and exhaled slowly. He put the full glass of brandy on the table.

He grabbed the blanket, which was folded on the settee, and shook it.

Calliope bit her lip. "James, why don't you sleep here?"

He stilled and looked at her.

"Just to sleep," she added quickly.

He didn't move for a long moment. He started undressing and her breath caught. Couldn't he sleep in his eveningwear?

He left his undershirt and trousers on and slipped in beside her. Her heart was racing so fast it nearly popped out of her chest and smacked against the wall.

The bed, which had seemed ample before, now felt tiny. She didn't dare move or she'd be plastered against him. She spent a few fretful moments trying to decide how to sleep.

What position to lie in? She settled on her side near the edge of the bed. What to do if he turned toward her?

The feelings he had stirred in the garden returned. She had never expected anything remotely like what she had experienced for the brief moments on the bench. No wonder the women whispered and giggled. Calliope had thought them mad.

She peeked over her shoulder, but he was still lying on his back, one knee in the air. His breathing was even.

He was asleep!

The rotter.

Chapter 13

A number of guests had wandered downstairs dressed for an early morning ride to examine the scene at the lake. Many couples had already left for London, eager to be among the first to town with the news of Ternberry's death. James found Calliope waiting near the front entrance conversing with Lady Willoughby. Rogers and Betsy had finished loading the baggage and would follow behind them.

After saying their farewells, he helped Calliope into the carriage.

The coach bumped and swayed as his driver negotiated the ruts that had become more rough and dangerous with the spring rains. They had been on the road for more than five minutes and Calliope sat quietly, fiddling with her hands and staring out the window. James kept silent waiting for her to compose herself.

She finally turned toward him. "Thank you."

He raised an eyebrow. "For what?"

She shook her head and said, "Just thank you."

He nodded, and she sagged against the cushions.

"I need to get to the theater. I'm worried about my family."

"Will they leave?"

She paused and then slumped fully into the seat. "No. Both of my adoptive parents are performing this evening, and regardless of threats, they would never leave the show."

She absently moved her fingers across her brow. "They're unaware of the potential danger. I'm frightened for their safety. They may be caught unawares."

James reached over and patted her knee. "They will be fine. I have men watching the theater. When we get back to the city, I'll see what they have to report."

James had stationed a man at the theater as soon as he had learned of her ties there. The connection between Calliope and Salisbury was still too strange to be a coincidence. There were twists and links in the puzzle and everything seemed to point to Calliope.

"We'll return to Stephen's townhouse for the night and have another look through his files and belongings."

The effort would probably be pointless. They had searched thoroughly before. But she must have felt a bit better because she shifted her position and relaxed her shoulders.

James figured it was as good a time as any to catch up on missed sleep. Leaning back, he allowed his eyes to close. Calliope squirmed, attempting to make herself more comfortable against the plush seat. He cracked open an eye, watching her shift positions. After several minutes of fidgeting, he leaned forward, plucked her off the seat and deposited her next to him.

"What are you—"

Her mild shriek was cut off as he wrapped her in his arms.

Calliope's mind went blank. She was nestled against him, and he had never once opened his eyes. For some reason, that irritated her.

She tried escaping by pulling toward the opposite seat. His arm was like a vise. But other than tightening his arm, he didn't move.

His head lay against the seat. She peered around at him. She had been feeling out of sorts ever since finding herself curled against his side this morning. "My lord, I really don't think this is dignified."

He gave no indication of having heard her.

"My lord?"

Nothing.

"Angelford?"

Silence.

"James!"

One eye opened.

"Don't you think I should return to my own seat?"

"Shh, get some rest. You didn't sleep last night any more than I."

For some reason, that made her feel infinitely better. She was exhausted. And it was more comfortable on this side of the carriage. Yes, if he was going to get the better side of the coach, it was only fair that he share. She closed her eyes and her head lolled onto his shoulder. The motion of the carriage was soothing. Warm and cozy dreams enveloped her and the nightmares ceased for once.

It was a brilliant summer day and she was strolling in a meadow. Flowers were blooming as far as the eye could see. James came toward her, a bright blue flower in his hand. She took it and inhaled the heavenly fragrance. It was like that spicy scent that clung to him. Strange, for a flower to smell that way.

But it was a beautiful bloom and the scent was manly, much better than the common fragrance of roses. He looked down at her with tenderness and bent his head. She would delude herself no longer. This was what she had been yearning for; every part of her said this was right. Her body thrummed and her breath caught as he leaned closer.

She sighed happily.

Unexpectedly, he jerked away.

"No!"

Calliope jolted awake as James moved his shoulder. He looked down at her. "No, what?"

The coach had stopped.

"Uh, nothing, just, uh, I was surprised we were there already."

How incredibly stupid.

He stared at her for a second and then exited the coach. He held up a hand to help her down. The return to London was a jolt to her system. An ending almost. Quickly moving toward the door, she saw that her burly footmen were still in place. Thank goodness.

She frowned.

She had ceased to consider James the enemy and started thinking of him as her savior. Around the same time she had stopped thinking of him as Angelford.

More Angelford, less James. Now that they were back in London, that would be best.

They entered the library and he walked to her favorite chair. For once that was fine with Calliope. She sprawled on the brocade settee and shut her eyes.

"I thought we were going to search through Stephen's things."

She opened an eye to see him staring at her superciliously. "Right. I'm just resting my eyes. How about ten minutes from now?"

He shook his head and she swore a smile flitted across his features.

"Fine, we'll do it now instead."

A smile lit his eyes.

Calliope looked at the magnificent bookcases and sighed.

* * *

Twenty minutes later she was still sighing.
James felt frustrated himself. Not only was he certain the object they were searching for was here in
this room, but his response to Calliope was reaching a fever pitch.

She had removed her wig, and her soft curls caressed her shoulders.

He shook his head, trying to concentrate on the
task at hand, and spied a walking stick resting
against the wall. He picked up the smart mahogany and gold cane, recognizing it from the
night she tried to brain him with it.

"A slight step up from the one you abandoned
at the Killroys' ball."

She looked up from a stack of papers and eyed
the cane. "Did you find my cane at the Killroys'?"

"Yes. Imagine my surprise when you sailed
back into the ballroom, graceful as can be.

Calliope flushed. "I don't know what caused
me to forget it."

"I thought we had determined you missed me."

She looked disgruntled. "You are a menace."

James smiled. "Do you need to use a cane at all?"

"Not often, just sometimes when I get tired—it
makes it easier to move around."

She walked over and reluctantly plucked the
stick from his hand. Her eyes were intense. "My
mother left this with me. It was the last time I saw
her. She thought she had enough time to run back
into the burning house."

Sadness and pain darkened her face. The expression tore at him.

"Why did she run back?"

"She tried to save the documents my father left with her. I've always blamed him for her death."

She said it nonchalantly. They could have been discussing the weather, but her eyes were anything but calm.

"You've saved the cane all these years."

"Yes, I generally keep it close at hand, although I don't use it. It's a reminder."

"Maybe it would ease the pain if you started thinking of the cane as just another object."

She was silent for a long minute.

James wasn't sure what to do or say; the lost look on her face was making him crazy. He was about to take the offending object away from her when she became a whirlwind of motion.

She struck a fencing pose. A rather good fencing pose.

Astonishment pierced him. "You fence?"

"I was once a pirate at the Adelphi when one of the actors fell ill. I practiced other stances after that. It is rather a fun hobby."

A pirate? "How many other roles have you played?"

She shrugged and jabbed toward his stomach with the blunt end of the cane. "I've filled in as needed. Small roles. Chorus parts, mainly. If one of the stars falls ill, an understudy steps in and sometimes I assume the smaller part. It's actually rather fun. Performing is quite exhilarating. One doesn't get noticed much in the chorus, so no stage fright."

Calliope was thrusting and parrying across the

room. She lifted her left leg at the knee, balancing on her right leg. The cane was gripped in her right hand and perched horizontally over her head. Two fingers on her left hand were pointed upward at the end of the cane. She then dropped the raised fingers to her right wrist and thrust her left hand and the cane away from each other in diagonal directions.

"What posture is that?" He was considered an expert swordsman, but he had never seen that particular move.

She looked at him in surprise. "I don't know. An extra who returned from the Far East taught me that maneuver." She coughed discreetly. "Well, not exactly taught, but I secretly watched him practice enough times to learn."

James was intrigued. He moved toward her. "Do it again."

She repeated the movement.

He studied the move, trying to think of ways to incorporate the technique. "Shouldn't the sword be pointed more at an angle for better entry?"

She sent him a dark look as he came closer. "Look here, I know what I saw."

Calliope jabbed him in the side with the cane to emphasize her point. He scowled and pushed it aside. She twisted the handle to yank it back and it made a clicking noise.

"What the—" James stared down at his midsection.

Calliope followed his gaze and gasped when she saw bright red blossoming across his stark white shirt. The cane dropped to her side and she rushed to him. "My god, James, your shirt!"

James frowned at the cane and picked up the end. A sharp blade protruded from its tip. Calliope gasped and lifted his shirt. Blood seeped from the wound.

"Stand still. You're hurt," she said, blanching as she inspected the wound.

"Luckily the bloody thing was too far away to do major damage. But I'd be most appreciative if you could stop trying to kill me with that thing."

She gave him a worried look. "Sit and don't move. I'll have Grimmond call for the doctor."

"Relax, I was teasing. It's just a scratch. I've endured worse during fencing practice."

"Apply pressure here, and sit down so you won't pass out and bleed all over Stephen's carpet," she replied tartly, and left the room quickly to find a clean shirt and medicinal supplies.

James remained stoic as she cleansed the area around the wound, but Calliope grimaced, fearful she was hurting him. For a lord of the realm he was in superb shape. His broad chest was tanned and lightly brushed with hair. How would it feel to run her fingers across the planes of his muscular chest and back?

Her hands paused. Cleaning and applying ointment to the area was an intimate act of a lover or wife.

Calliope felt a light blush and continued working. She bandaged the gash and assisted him with his shirt. He grumbled about flesh wounds.

Calliope plunked down on the settee and inspected the cane. She turned it to the left and the blade retracted. She turned it to the right and it protruded.

"I should have been using this long ago."

James said something unintelligible.

She leaped from the seat, struck a pose and twisted left. It retracted. Right. Protruded. Left. Right. Left. Right. She giggled. "I feel like a real pirate now."

"Calliope, will you please sit down?"

Now that the cane had lost some of its hold on her, she didn't want to put it down. The connection to her father was still present, but it felt different somehow.

She sighed. The blade was out. One twist left and it was in. She decided to make sure it wouldn't do any unintentional damage and twisted left again, hoping to lock it in place. To her surprise, the handle twisted open.

"What is this?" She peered into the hole. There was something wedged inside. She gingerly slipped two fingers inside and pulled out a wrapped object. Handing it to James, Calliope searched for anything else. She gave the cane another twist, but it appeared to only have the three settings.

Satisfied the cane was closed, she set it down and looked up at James's shocked expression.

"What is wrong? Does your wound hurt?"

He sat in stunned silence staring at the object in his hand.

Calliope peered at it. It was a ring. The ring looked vaguely familiar.

James just shook his head. "This can't be."

"This can't be what?"

He held out his hand to her and she plucked the ring from his palm and noticed the image of a bird engraved in the gold.

"This is what we've been searching for, isn't it?"

He nodded, a wry grin spreading across his face.

"Stephen must have found it and made an imprint."

The grin slipped from his features. "The cane belonged to Salisbury." It wasn't a question.

The pain spread through her again. "Yes, he left it with my mother. That is why she made sure it survived the fire. The papers were destroyed with her."

Calliope felt a reassuring grip on her shoulder.

"Salisbury must have assumed the cane and papers perished in the blaze with the two of you. Possibly whoever set the fire thought so as well."

She glanced up at him, startled out of her reverie. "What do you mean, whoever set the fire?"

He was gazing at her in a cautious manner. "It's too coincidental and the timing was too close to Salisbury's own assassination."

Had her heart stopped? Calliope took a few deep, steadying breaths.

"Are you implying that my father really did cause my mother's death?"

"Absolutely not. Believe me, Salisbury blamed himself enough for both of you. One had only to see him to know it. Someone murdered them both." He rubbed her hands. "I need to call on a friend of mine. He knows all sorts of interesting things and may be able to tell us about this ring."

"All right, let's go."

"No. He is a cautious fellow and doesn't like unfamiliar faces. It will only take a few hours. I'll be back shortly."

Calliope let him leave without her. She had used enough contacts when researching caricatures to know how skittish people could be with their information.

She walked aimlessly around the townhouse. The servants were keeping to themselves. Ever since the new footmen had arrived, they had been strangely quiet. Almost fearful. The atmosphere was driving her mad.

She plopped onto the sofa and thought about what James had said. It was hard not to blame her father. She had been blaming him for so long that it was hard to break the habit.

She vividly remembered the night when she had lost everything in her world and had approached Lady Salisbury for assistance. Yes, now that James had dredged up old memories, Lady Salisbury had definitely appeared scared. There had been fervor in her eyes and fear.

Calliope wondered what it had been like for the woman. Lillian Minton was Salisbury's lifelong mistress. Everyone knew he had no intention of giving her up, and no intention of marrying.

It was something that had always troubled Calliope. It was an accepted fact that Salisbury would never marry another because of his love for her mother. Therefore, why hadn't her father married her mother? Was it societal restraints or something else? It was the unanswerable question that haunted her.

Calliope backed away from the thought. She closed her eyes and tried to conjure more pleasant thoughts.

A few hours passed before the front door opened and James entered the room, looking more energetic and healthy than when he had left.

"It's a Falcon ring," James said.

She waited patiently for him to explain and was fortunately not disappointed.

"There was a secret society formed to depose Bonaparte. The members worked behind the scenes and received no aid from the government. Only a handful of men have these rings, and I'm fairly certain neither Stephen nor your father possessed one."

"What was the name of the society?"

"There was no official name, though 'the Falcons' stuck because of the insignia. Their rings identified them. The general populace knew nothing of the group. In fact, most people in the government still are unaware of them. Hell, I thought it myth."

He was silent. She could almost hear his brain chugging away.

"My source was aware of only one member of the society." He paused for a long moment and then said, "Holt."

"Lord Holt." Her thoughts whirred. "What does his son have to do with this whole situation? And why is his birth certificate wrong?"

James again hesitated. "If I'm right about when Holt was married, then it would point to his only son and heir being illegitimate."

She gasped. "Then he couldn't inherit."

"A powerful incentive to make sure no one found out."

"And Ternberry had the certificate."

James's mouth was grim. "Yes."

"We should search their offices. At least Ternberry's, since he definitely won't be there."

"It's not that easy."

"Pffft, I saw how easily you broke into Pettigrew's rooms. Let's go."

She could see in his face that he wanted to go.

"I'll go alone."

"Oh, no. I'm coming with you or else I'll find a way to do it on my own."

He started to shake his head, but then paused. "Yes. You have the right." He surveyed her from head to toe. "Do you have anything more suitable to wear?"

Calliope didn't give him time to change his mind. She raced up the steps and into her room. Pulling out her old trunk, she found an old costume from a play where she'd been an extra chimney sweep. Changing quickly, she grabbed a black cap and ran back down the stairs and into the study.

A brief stunned moment passed as he viewed her black breeches and shirt. "Absolutely not. Go back and change this instant."

A mutinous look slid into place and she temporarily forgot her tenuous position. "This is the perfect outfit. No one will recognize me, and if they do, I can simply say it is a foil for your odd ways."

His brows rose, but he turned and strode out the door. She grabbed her black cape to cover her garments and ran after him. He called up the carriage and they stepped in. James did nothing to hide his irritation.

She twisted her hair and shoved it into the boy's cap. "How will we know if Holt is out?"

"He's out. But rest assured, if we decide to search his townhouse we'll make sure before venturing in."

James exchanged words with his driver. The carriage stopped only a few blocks down the street. Looking around one last time to be certain no one was watching, he grabbed Calliope, and they darted into an alley. Someone moved out of the shadows. She immediately recognized the man, and James instructed him to ready "Number Three." James's regular carriage rolled down the street. A diversion.

Number Three turned out to be an old hackney. It was hitched to a pair of unremarkable brown mares. She cast him a questioning glance but he continued to rattle off instructions to the driver. Jenkins, the driver, disappeared into the darkness, then reappeared a few minutes later, winded, but dressed in common garments. He had replaced the resplendent livery worn by Angelford servants.

"Let's go."

Calliope climbed into the carriage and settled herself on the faded but surprisingly comfortable seat. James hauled himself in and sat across from her. They moved down the drive and set off for Ternberry's, on the other side of Mayfair. James drew the curtains and darkness enveloped them.

"I will turn you over my knee if you leave my side. Understand?"

A protest rose in her throat. She swallowed it when she realized how tightly wound he was. The air was charged. She nodded and then realized he couldn't see her. "Yes."

They remained silent until the coach slowed.

"I told Jenkins to stop down the street. We will walk the rest of the way. Ready?"

She grabbed his outstretched hand. It felt right.

James secured her cape and threw a greatcoat around his shoulders. It must have been inside the carriage. Calliope started to wonder how frequent an occurrence these types of trips were for him. No one would mistake them for Lord and Lady now.

Lord and Miss, she amended.

They approached Ternberry's house from the rear, crossing through a number of yards to reach it.

There were only a few windows in the back. Ternberry must not have been too fond of the light.

The house was dark.

James already had a tool out and was fiddling with one of the windows. The clasp released and he crawled inside. A minute later he reached down and pulled her in. He lit a small lamp by the desk.

Ternberry's study was a mess.

"Someone's already been here," James said.

"Are you sure? His room at Pettigrew's looked the same."

He nodded. "Yes, but he ordered things in a clockwise manner. Look at those papers on the desk."

Calliope looked at the desk. They did look a bit perfect in their scatter.

"What do you want to do?"

"Let's take a look anyway. Something may have been missed."

"Do you think Ternberry returned to town during the weekend at the Pettigrews'?" Calliope asked, reading and discarding paper after paper.

"I think so. But I'm not sure. I will have Finn ask some questions of the staff tomorrow."

"How did he return to the Pettigrews' estate?"

"More importantly, why did he return to the Pettigrews' estate?"

"And was anyone with him? Or did he meet someone there?"

"Try to find the papers we found at the party. I suspect if they were here they are gone, but it's worth it to try."

An hour later found them no closer to the papers or any other evidence. Calliope was sitting on the floor. She laid on her back, trying to stretch.

"Are your muscles still sore?"

"A little."

"I'll give you a massage later to loosen them." James was poking around the desk. He had found three secret drawers and was looking for more. Nothing important had been inside any of them.

Her heart quickened. She turned toward him. "I think that sounds—"

Something was jammed under the desk.

"Yes?"

She scurried to her knees and peered under the desk.

"Did you find something?" He strode around the desk and sat on his heels next to her.

"There's something lodged here. Hold on. Got it." She retrieved it with two fingers.

A half imprint stood out in red. Half of a falcon ring print.

"A further indication that the ring is important. Should we head over to Holt's now?" Calliope asked.

"Yes. We can return here later."

He blew out the lamp and they crawled back through the window. James latched it and they headed for the carriage.

"Are you sure he's out?"

"I told you we would make sure before going through his smallclothes."

She bit back a smile.

The hackney was in the same place. James nodded at the driver but they walked past. Holt's residence was nearby; it was easier and less suspicious to walk.

James had a firm grip on her hand. It was warm and comforting.

"What do you think we'll find?"

"I don't think we'll find much, actually. Holt is

a pro. If he doesn't want something found, chances are it won't be."

"Then should we even bother?"

"Yes. People make mistakes. And if our suspicions are correct, then he is playing a deep game."

Holt's townhouse loomed in front of them and Calliope's pulse quickened.

The house was dark. They skirted the back and stopped at a window overlooking a well-tended English garden.

James jiggled the window and it moved slightly.

"Sloppy. That's unusual." He looked slightly perturbed. "I hadn't actually thought this would open."

Calliope looked down and saw fresh footprints carved into the damp soil. "Someone has been here recently."

He looked down and swore softly. "We're leaving. Now."

"Wait, what about his office? What about the ring?"

He shot her a dangerous look. "Not tonight."

James grabbed her hand again and started walking so swiftly she had to run to keep up.

They moved up the street toward the coach, which had moved to the other end. Jenkins looked nervous. "Milord, I have a nasty feeling about tonight."

"So do I, Jenkins, let's get home."

James tossed Calliope into the carriage and vaulted in after her.

She didn't mutter a protest. Her senses had started screaming as well.

The coach sped down the street. It wasn't a great distance to travel to James's residence and Calliope suddenly wanted to be safely ensconced in his extravagant house.

A screech of hooves grated through the coach's walls.

A shot rang out, and the carriage careened out of control.

Chapter 14

⌒◯◯⌒

Calliope grasped air as she was flung toward the coach's floor. She girded herself for the bruising impact but was caught roughly by James. He pulled her against him and braced them both against the sides of the coach.

He swore fluently and Calliope clutched his arm as they rocketed pell-mell around a corner. It was apparent the animals were running unchecked. Buildings streaked past and shouts echoed in the night. Calliope prayed Jenkins would regain control of the frightened beasts before they neared the theater district.

Her prayers went unanswered. They raced down the Strand and past the Opera House.

A woman's shrill scream pierced the night. Angry shouts followed.

James tried to open the trapdoor but something was blocking it. Cold ran through Calliope as she realized that Jenkins's heavy form was probably the culprit.

James opened a box hidden in the squabs and thrust a small gun in her hand, then placed two other pistols on the seat. He yelled over the noise from the wheels and the shouts from pedestrians outside, "They're loaded. Use the smaller one only if they get close."

Not waiting for a reply, he threw the coach window open and crawled through. She gaped at his retreating backside as the coach lurched precariously.

Calliope held her breath until she knew he had safely reached the driver's box. Snapping to attention, she repositioned herself, propping her legs against the seat across from her. Calliope heard the horses' angry snorts as James attempted to get the frightened creatures under control.

She stuck her head out the window to call to him. A pole whirled past and she pulled her head in so fast that she bumped it against the top of the window frame.

How had he climbed out without getting hit?

Being more circumspect, she again peered upward out the window. She detected the slumped-over form of Jenkins. She prayed fervently that he was only slightly injured. Straining a glance behind the coach, Calliope spotted two riders approaching at a fast clip.

Shots rang out again and she whipped her head inside. How many guns did the assailants have?

She tucked the smaller gun in her breeches and picked up one of the other pistols. Keeping a tight grip, she leaned out the window, cocked the hammer and squeezed the trigger. One of the riders ducked but continued to give chase. She fired the other, with the same result. Her ears rang from the report.

Her hands shook as she tried to reload the gun. Under the best of circumstances it required a steady hand to pour the powder down the barrel, but in a wildly swaying vehicle, it was nearly impossible.

The contents jiggled as the carriage tossed on the rutted road. She shoved the powder case toward the muzzle. Powder spilled onto the carriage floor. Muttering in frustration, she tried again. The coach lurched. She pinched her fingers together around the case in a bone-crushing grip. Another carriage jerk caused her cap to slip over her left eye. Hair loosened from its constraints, chunks of curls came tumbling out, further obscuring her view. Calliope elbowed the offending hair back.

A violent pitch caused her bad leg to give out and, losing her precarious balance, she fell against the left side of the coach. Still concentrating on the powder, so close to the hole, she poured it in. Finally. She grabbed a paper wad and a ball and pounded them down the shaft.

Meanwhile, it seemed James had managed to get the old town coach and four horses under some semblance of control and the seat wasn't wobbling as much. The team continued moving at a breakneck pace, weaving around obstacles and taking sharp turns. She stuck her head out the window, took aim and blindly fired.

The two riders slowed and moved to either side of the street. James circled Trafalgar Square and the coach headed back down Whitehall.

She ducked back into the carriage as they hit a bump in the road. It tossed her to the side and her valuable bag of powder poured uselessly to the floor. Damn, and damn again.

Her only alternative was to join James and see if she could be of assistance. Checking that the small gun was secure in her breeches, she grasped both sides of the window frame and hauled herself halfway out on her backside as she had seen him do. Sitting in the frame, she reached for the top of the carriage and was nearly tossed out as they hit a furrow in the road.

She felt the gun slip from her waistband and grabbed it just in time to keep it from falling to the ground. She sent silent thanks that she had worn breeches. James cursed loudly as Calliope stretched toward the driver's seat. He reached around to pull her up and over Jenkins like a sack of flour. The horses balked at the loosened reins and Calliope could do nothing but hold on for dear life as James hauled her into the seat.

"What are you doing, woman? Are you trying to kill yourself? Come to think of it, I could kill you myself." He didn't look her way, but his face was drawn in harsh, intense lines.

"I thought I might help. I know you're trying to outrun those riders."

"Well, you could have shot them. That would have helped."

"I tried. Three times."

"More times would've been helpful. From inside the carriage. I can't see any way for you to reload up here."

"Uh, yes. You see, that was the crux of the problem—"

A shot rang out over their heads.

"Damn it, get down."

He pushed her to the floor and hunched over the reins as they sped past the Admiralty.

Coming up here hadn't been her brightest idea. More shots rang out and she heard a hiss from James. It was lucky the horses were back under control, because he was now holding them with only his right hand. For the second time that night he was covered in red.

Calliope gasped and rose to assist, but he pushed her down with his injured left arm and urged the horses on.

"It's fine. I need to find a distraction and I don't need it to be you."

The sticky smell of blood overpowered the London air.

She looked at Jenkins's head, bouncing near her. A bullet had nicked him on the side of his skull. Blood was flowing from the wound. She tore two pieces off her shirt and held one tightly against the wound while binding the other to hold it in place. Looking up at James, she ignored his command and reached up and unfurled his neckcloth in one swift tug. She was very glad he favored simple styles. Calliope knew her head was in the line of fire but she pushed her fear aside. She tried to open his shirt but he shook his head.

"If you aren't going to listen to me, then just bind the wound and get back down."

She quickly complied and he shoved her to the floor. "Grab Jenkins and hold tight."

They were close to the Government Offices and nearing the Houses of Parliament. Before hitting the floor, she had seen the rows of empty vendor stalls by the square. He was going to ram them. Calliope held on to Jenkins and prayed.

The horses were balking, but a second before they reached the stalls, James gave a sharp left jerk on the reins and urged them on. The tired beasts responded and turned. The rear of the carriage skidded outward, hitting the stalls and sending wood and materials into the air. Calliope managed to hold on to both Jenkins and herself. Terrified that James had slipped off the side, she glanced up, but he was confidently spurring the horses forward. Blood pounded in her ears.

She looked back at the carnage. Stalls and beams were strewn across the street. The riders couldn't pass. She breathed an audible sigh of relief.

He gave her a sharp look. "We aren't home yet."

She grabbed the small gun and looked around, but the tired horses carried them the short distance to James's townhouse without further incident.

A small army of servants appeared and carried off Jenkins. Finn mumbled under his breath about his employer taking off without him.

"Finn, take care of Jenkins, post guards and get someone to rub down the horses." He pointed at Calliope. "Follow me."

Calliope shadowed him to the study. "What about your wound?"

"It's merely a nick. Bullet passed through."

Templeton appeared in the doorway, anxiety on his usually calm face.

Calliope inspected James's blood-soaked shirt for the second time that day. "Templeton, please get us hot water, towels and bandages."

Templeton, who was staring at his master's shirt, didn't question her right to attend his master or give directives. He ran from the room.

"Damn it, I said it's just a nick. And give me that gun before you shoot yourself."

"I know what you said," she said soothingly, and placed the gun on the table. "Now please remove your shirt so I can attend to the scratch."

His brows drew together in a fierce scowl but he said nothing.

Templeton returned so quickly that Calliope wondered where he hid the bandages. She took the supplies from the butler and thanked him.

James sat, eyes closed. He crossed his arms and pain flashed across his brow. She put her hands on her hips. "Honestly, you're acting like a child. Now take off your shirt."

He glared at her as she moved toward him. If he wasn't going to take it off, then she would.

Calliope could have sworn he growled at her, but he acceded to her command and removed the blood-soaked shirt. She carefully checked his torso for other wounds, even peering under the patch covering the stab wound. She had seen his chest earlier in the day, but the intimacy of the act still moved her.

She snapped to attention, concentrating on the task at hand. Dipping a towel in water, she cleansed the colorful mess on his arm. The bullet had taken a fair chunk out of the side. A nick indeed!

After she bandaged the wound, she sat back on her heels.

Templeton, who had been anxiously hovering during the entire ordeal, relaxed. "I will be in the kitchen, ma'am. Please pull the cord if you or my lord require anything." He exited the study and closed the door behind him.

Calliope studied James as he stared at the ceiling. His eyes were dark and remote. What was he thinking? She had prodded the wound and knew it had hurt, but as earlier, he remained detached and distant.

"Are you all right?"

He refocused on her, an intense look on his face. "What the bloody hell did you think you were doing, climbing out of the coach?"

"I—I—I thought I could help." His stormy look had reduced her to stammering.

"It would have helped if you had stayed inside the carriage."

Her chin went up a notch. "Jenkins might've died."

"Yes, and so might've you." He heaved a breath and leaned back against the sofa. "As it so happens I would not have pulled that maneuver had you been inside the carriage."

She brightened perceptibly.

"But don't ever do it again." His aristocratic mien was back in place and she wanted to smack him. She balled her hands into fists instead.

"You can't return home tonight," he said.

"I know."

He nodded and closed his eyes.

A wave of pent-up emotion washed through Calliope and she fought a hysterical giggle. She lost. One eye peeked open and he looked at her. He repeated her earlier question. "Are *you* all right?"

Another shrill giggle bubbled out and this time his other eye snapped open.

Hysteria whipped through her and it must have shown, because he swept her onto his lap, disregarding any pain in his left arm.

"You're safe. Let it go."

His gentle words were her undoing. She buried her head against his neck and let the tremors sweep through her. The fear uncoiled within and she held on to him tightly, tears running down her cheeks unheeded. The stress that had been building since the beginning of the masquerade burst forth, as if waiting for just this moment to be released.

James ran his fingers down her back and stroked her hair with his left hand, comforting her as if she were a child, and whispering soft, incoherent words against her hair. He was using his injured arm to comfort her and that made her cry even harder.

Calliope couldn't seem to stop. James was murmuring about stressful campaigns, battle-hardened men reduced to tears, her needing this release.

Calliope finally reached the sniffling stage, feeling infinetely better than she had in a long time. And safe. Nothing harmful could happen as long as he continued to hold her this way. James pulled her head back and smoothed her hair away from her face. She knew her eyes were bloodshot and her face was mottled,, but James's eyes were the same mesmerizing black velvet as the night of the Killroys' and Pettigrew's balls. Energy sparked between them and it sent a shiver down her spine.

James twirled a ringlet of her hair around his finger, then curved his hand gently around the back of her head, slowly drawing her toward him, allowing her time to settle back against his shoulder or pull away. The gentle caress and the intensity in his eyes were her undoing. She lifted her left hand and traced a path from his cheek to his silk collar. She heard his sudden intake of breath and her eyes searched and held his for a long moment. This man had somehow lodged himself into her being. His eyes mirrored her own need and a rush of excitement pulsed through her veins.

His lips touched hers like a feather. Then another mere brush. The gentle pressure on her head ceased and he looked into her eyes once more. He was allowing her time to make her decision, and once made, there would be no interruptions. Her heart made the choice. She relinquished her rigid control, shed all guises and gave in to the dream. "Make me whole, James."

Her words loosened a dam within him, as he stroked the back of her neck and claimed her lips in a searing kiss. Calliope felt a sunburst in her stomach and she kissed him back with a longing she didn't know she possessed.

It was heavenly, his spicy cologne, the feel of his lips against hers. He leaned into her and laid her against the sofa's armrest.

He kissed her over and over like a starving man who hadn't eaten a meal in days. Calliope felt the same way. Her hands delved beneath the edges of his white broadcloth, stroking the heated skin and exploring the hard-muscled planes she had observed earlier. He groaned.

Suddenly her shirt was unbuttoned and his hands slipped inside her chemise. He didn't stop kissing her as he lightly rubbed his thumb over her left nipple. Everything blurred and little red and gold lights burst in her vision. She leaned her head back as he trailed kisses down her neck, over her breasts to her stomach. Her breeches had somehow come undone. Then they were gone. His hands and mouth were everywhere. Dear lord, his mouth was everywhere.

She gave in to the pleasure and arched on the sofa as her body reveled in the new sensations he stirred. He quickly removed the rest of her clothes and his. She gasped when she looked at him naked before her, all hard muscles and strong taut planes. Gone was the aristocrat, and in his place was her fantasy. And for one night he was hers.

His eyes seared her as he touched her with his hands. The inferno raged as he stroked her again and again, reaching his head down to pull first one nipple and then the other between his lips. Half the staff could have appeared beside the couch and she wouldn't have cared. The pleasure was so intense she thought she might explode.

His eyes were molten and she wondered how she could have ever thought him cold. He continued the assault on her senses until she was damp and aching. She needed him to fill the missing piece.

"You're beautiful. Beyond my wildest imaginings." He suddenly changed course and kissed her lips again, deeply, at the same time lifting her hips. She gripped the back of his head and kissed him hard, whispering against his mouth for him to hurry. She couldn't remember ever needing anything so badly. He eased inside her and discomfort overrode the pleasure as she tried to adjust to the foreign sensation. He looked into her eyes, a question appearing in their depths, but she gave a tentative wiggle and they darkened. He continued to gaze at her, stroking her between their bodies until her wiggles became frenzied and the discomfort was forgotten.

Then he began to move. She lost all rational thought as the room lit on fire. A crescendo was building inside her unlike anything she'd experienced. Her body moved with a will of its own, pulling James closer, and matching him eagerly stroke for stroke. She cried out his name and heard hers echoed before losing all thought to the overwhelming waves of passion.

The grandfather clock in the hall struck three. He had been stabbed and shot, and he was feeling better than he could remember. James almost smiled.

What was it about her that made him feel? Feel everything: anger, passion, tenderness, jealousy. Vulnerability.

She was lying on top of him, long legs akimbo. James lifted a lock of honeyed hair off his chest and rubbed it beneath his nose and over his lips. The silky strands were a pleasant tickle. Lilacs. She always smelled so good. He replaced the lock and smoothed her hair from her face. Calliope sighed and snuggled closer. An overwhelming protectiveness stirred within him. It wasn't the first time he had felt this way around her, but the enormity of it rocked him.

They had much to discuss. She had a number of questions to answer. But the pleasant lethargy was too nice to spoil, so he lay staring at the ceiling, allowing his mind to connect the pieces of the puzzle. Calliope wiggled into a more comfortable position and settled in for a lengthy doze.

No woman had spent the night in the townhouse since his father's death. But Calliope looked right. There was no place he would rather have her be.

There would be plenty of time to talk in the morning.

* * *

Calliope woke feeling better than she could remember. She was more than a little tired. James had awakened her twice during the night. Once to carry her up to bed and the other time to . . . She couldn't stop the blush staining her cheeks. The heavy red and navy curtains above her were plush and exotic. Like something brought back from the Crusades long ago. Calliope looked around at the mahogany furniture and rich dark colors. They suited their owner. The pillow next to hers carried a deep indentation that indicated it hadn't been abandoned much earlier. However, James was nowhere to be seen.

She rose and searched for her clothes. Spotting only a deep violet gown lying across an armchair, she picked it up, running her fingers down the silk. A surge of jealousy swept through her. Whose gown was it? It was designed in an older, classic style.

Having no desire to walk unclothed through his household, she reluctantly put it on. Thankfully it was an easy gown to fasten, and she was able to do it without assistance.

On the dresser lay a beautiful silver brush set, which she used to comb her hair into some semblance of order. A matching violet ribbon lay next to the brush.

Negotiating the hallway, she found a staircase leading to the first floor. She headed for the study, made a wrong turn into the drawing room and then backtracked to find Templeton standing in the hall.

"I heard you come down, miss. His lordship is in his study. Please follow me, it's right this way."

There was a deferential note in Templeton's voice. And if she didn't know better, she would say there was a more engaging manner in the way he addressed her.

He led her to the study, bowed and took his leave. She could have sworn there was a lighter hitch to his step.

Calliope entered the firelit room and found James staring at a ledger on his desk, his glasses perched on his nose. He stood when he heard her enter and removed the glasses. The heated look in his eyes warmed her to her toes as he approached.

"I hope you don't mind wearing my mother's old gown. Even though it is a bit outdated, I thought it might be a bit more fashionable and comfortable than your breeches."

His mother's gown? Calliope felt her cheeks heat and cast her eyes downward. "Thank you." She suddenly felt shy.

He led her to the sofa and chairs that were grouped near the blazing fire. The same sofa that . . .

"Would you care for some tea? Biscuits? Something more substantial?"

Calliope shook her head and sat next to him on the sofa. He waved off Templeton, who shut the door behind him.

"Well, then, I have a question for you. How did a virgin become a courtesan and manage to remain a virgin?"

Panic flowed through her and she looked to the door for escape.

"What game were you and Stephen playing?"

Calliope pulled herself together and stammered an answer. "W-we were just waiting. He was giving me time to adjust."

James looked unconvinced.

She tried again. "You know what a gentleman Stephen is."

He cocked an eyebrow. "Can't say that I do."

"Well, he is. He was allowing me to adjust to my new role." Calliope panicked and forced herself to continue the charade. It wasn't time to tell him. Not yet, not when he was looking at her with such heat.

"Well, I'm not Stephen. And I want you."

"I, uh, that is—"

"Money, protection, security for life. I can give you all you desire."

The look he gave her promised just that. It made her sizzle, but visions of her mother anxiously waiting for Salisbury to appear each night danced through her head. There had always been the uncertainty and sometimes the disappointment.

"I am quite sure you don't know what I desire."

"I know enough." He tucked a strand of hair behind her ear and let his hand trail down the back of her neck.

The room was getting warmer by the minute and if she wasn't careful she'd find herself blissfully entwined and begging for all he offered. Time to change the subject. "How shall we proceed today, my lord? Do you know who was chasing us last night?"

"Back to 'my lord' and business, are we? Pity. I could think of plenty of stimulating things we could do with the day. I suppose what I have in mind will have to wait until this evening."

Calliope tried to breathe normally and ignore his comments, even as her traitorous body responded to the look in his eyes.

"My men have been out all night making inquiries. We'll have an answer soon. Meanwhile, we'll stop by your townhouse so you can change." His eyes turned mischievous. "Then we can take some air. You are looking a trifle overset."

James bundled her into his coach and they set off for Stephen's townhouse. She hid beneath a large bonnet, another piece from his mother's closet, in case they encountered anyone while entering or exiting the coach. They reached the residence and James talked to his two men while she changed.

The violet dress winked at her as she set it down. It was only then that she remembered her forgotten breeches and shirt. Throwing on a light tan day dress, her wig and makeup, she rushed downstairs as quickly as possible. She could hear the men talking.

"Two blokes tried entering last night. One man stood in the shadows watching the whole time. Couldn't make out any features but he set my teeth on edge. We got the two lackwits but weren't able to nab the third man."

"Good work. I'll talk to them later. Stay here just in case."

"Right-o."

James caught sight of Calliope and walked toward her. The two men bowed awkwardly and left the room.

"Are you ready? I thought we might drive by Holt's and then walk down the Strand, since we didn't bring the curricle."

Calliope nodded. A walk sounded good. Brisk fresh air, lots of people, limited personal conversation.

They got into the coach and drove briskly until Holt's house came into view. It looked empty. Oddly, there appeared to be no activity inside or out.

"Let's continue. I'll make a social call later and see what he's about. I sent Finn to Ternberry's to talk to the servants. Hopefully we can piece this mess together."

They reached the Strand, parked and exited the coach. The driver would rendezvous with them on the other side.

"It's a beautiful day to be out. I have frequently wondered how the pasty ladies get by without being in the sun."

She relaxed into his small talk and soon found herself enjoying the gorgeous day and being with him.

A man sullenly walked by and Calliope instantly recognized him as George Cruikshank, Robert's brother. George was also a caricaturist. He was a staunch moralist, the opposite of Robert in personality and decorum. George knew nothing of Thomas Landes's identity, of whom he would disapprove mightily. The two brothers were as different as night and day.

A small crowd was gathered outside a shop. The ladies were tittering. As James and Calliope neared the window, one of the ladies caught sight of them and giggled behind her hand. The group looked their way and hurried off in the other direction.

James frowned. Calliope was bemused. She glanced down at her gown and touched her wig, trying to figure out what was amiss.

James's frown turned to a scowl as they neared the shop. "I should have known."

Calliope looked up at his stormy visage and then to the area that had been vacated. Large windows lined the shop and prints were hanging in the windows. They had reached Ackermann's.

Calliope gasped, a cold knot forming in her stomach. Since teaming with James she had been too involved to keep track of the caricatures she had given Robert. Her vendetta with the marquess had slipped by the wayside. James had charmed her with his intelligence, friendship and caring.

Calliope did some quick arithmetic.

Why today? Why today of all days?

Calliope instinctively placed a restraining hand on James's arm. He gripped it and pulled her along with him.

Her last drawing of James adorned the center window.

"Damn and blast it, I'd like to get my hands around that malicious artist's neck."

Calliope swallowed, trying to keep her throat from closing.

James was furious, and for good reason. This illustration was her coup de grâce, the one that had spoken from her hurt feelings. The moment at the Killroys' ball when she had thought he was poking fun at her by offering the beautiful flower. Of course, with a new perspective that moment seemed different. She had found it convenient to place the blame for the entire night at his feet. But it was far too late. The damage was done. The illustration was visible for all Londoners to see.

"Maybe the artist made a mistake."

"Right. And the other drawings of me showed that the artist had fallen hopelessly in love," he drawled.

Not a good sign. A tightening sense of dismay enveloped her. "Possibly."

James shook his head. "Do not defend the man, Cal. He is vindictive."

Had he just called her Cal? She was finding it hard to breathe.

"I mean, look at the position he has placed me in. I am offering a flower to that governess in mockery while a crowd of my peers dances and laughs. And look at what I am doing with my hands. I will kill him, I promise."

Calliope swallowed, but there was no moisture in her throat.

He continued his tirade without response from her, still examining the picture with an odd contemplative quality to his voice. "It's odd where Landes gets his ideas. I've never been one to frequent parties. In fact, I only started going because of— Oh, never mind." James smoothed over whatever he was going to say. "Besides, I'd never offer anything pretty to a lady of the ton. It would be quite out of character—"

He stopped abruptly and frowned.

The frown deepened and Calliope felt moisture gather down her back, just as it had the night of the Killroys' ball.

"Should we keep walking, my lord?"

"My lord?" His look was penetrating and Calliope's legs readied for flight.

"I think it's time we get back. After all, you are going to Holt's and I need to get ready for the Ordines' ball and there are so many things to do between now and then. I should really stop by and tell my family that I'm well. Do you think we might stop there on the way back?" Calliope knew she was babbling but she couldn't seem to stop. Especially when she saw the cold light appear in his eyes.

"You are the only woman I have ever offered a flower to. And no one was there to witness it."

"Oh, really, my lord. There must be dozens of women for whom you buy flowers."

He shook his head, anger replacing the shock. "Not a single one."

"Well, I do believe I might have mentioned it to Lady Simpson, and you know how she has the tendency to talk." Calliope couldn't stop herself. One part of her had stepped away and was looking at the remaining part in horror.

"No, I don't believe you ever saw Lady Simpson

again. But soon afterward there was quite an un-flattering rendition of your confrontation with her done by this same artist. I started following *his* work after it appeared I had become his primary target."

"Then he must have been at the Killroys' party."

"Yes, I do believe you are right."

Calliope fought the tears and desire to flee as she stared at him mutely, pain in her heart.

"Why, Calliope? What did I do to earn your scorn?"

A tear slipped down her cheek. "You were the epitome of a haughty aristocrat. And I was just another piece of dirt on your way to the ball."

His face was still angry but he wiped the tear away with his thumb. "Didn't you run into that with others? The ton is full of such people. Why me?"

Her voice cracked. "Because you were such an arrogant ass. You always riled me. Lady Simpson fired me because of our final interchange." And the reactions he always caused had unnerved her.

"What if I told you that you were the reason I went to all those dull parties?" His face softened a notch.

Calliope shook her head. "No, you thought I was dowdy and beneath your notice. You only took interest in me after you thought I was flashy and loose."

James's face tightened back in anger. "You have a real cruel streak, Calliope Minton. Thomas Landes is one of the more vicious caricaturists. Let's go.

You will remain in your townhouse while I seek out Holt."

Calliope was drained, her emotions too raw to argue, so she allowed him to lead her to the carriage waiting at the end of the street.

The ride home was tense and silent. She couldn't remember ever feeling as miserable.

They walked to the door.

"I don't want you stepping a foot outside this house. Understood?" James said it as he was turning around to go back to the carriage.

"My lord. You must come inside." One of the footmen made an urgent motion toward the hall.

James frowned, but the uncharacteristic, jerky motions of the footman must have convinced him because he followed.

"Upstairs, quickly."

Something was wrong. Calliope ran to keep pace with the two men as they vaulted up the stairs.

They reached her room and the footman opened the door. Suddenly Calliope didn't want to look in, afraid that a loved one's still body might be inside.

The sharp intake of breath from James caused her to look around him.

Stephen was lying prone on her bed, white as death.

Chapter 15

❦

"**S**tephen!" Calliope said as they rushed to his side.

Stephen was haggard, his face damp with unhealthy perspiration. He didn't acknowledge Calliope's cry; his lashes lay still on his cheek. James nudged her aside and ran fingers around Stephen's face. Stephen's heartbeat was strong and his chest rose normally.

"He's alive. Where has he been?"

"A street urchin brought him in a hack, my lord. She made certain he was brought in, then she took off before we could detain her. Slippery little thing. And the driver couldn't tell us anything."

James looked down at Calliope and saw tears running down her cheeks. She looked as if her life depended on Stephen waking up and speaking.

"Have you called a doctor?" he asked one of the footmen.

"No, milord, he arrived minutes before you returned. I wasn't sure if that was what you would want, what with everyone thinking he was dead and all."

James nodded. "Good."

Calliope looked at him, aghast. "James, we must call a doctor. Look at him. He's at death's door."

"Stephen's heartbeat is steady. Quite frankly, I'm more concerned that whoever did this to him will try to finish the job if they know he is alive."

Calliope stood and poked him in the chest, punctuating her words. "I can't believe you are going to let him lie here unattended. We don't know the extent of his injuries and if he catches fever, he may die."

"An hour or two should not matter." He turned to see Grimmond in the doorway holding blankets. "Grimmond, cover him and have the lads warm bricks. Have Cook prepare broth that can be spooned down his throat when he awakens." James looked into Calliope's eyes. "I need to talk to Holt first and determine his involvement in this whole affair. Then we will call a doctor. Holt has contacts everywhere and I don't know any medical man who wouldn't be inclined to talk to him if pressured. Believe me, Stephen would want it this way."

"Fine, then leave."

She dismissed him and went back to tending her patient. She made soothing noises and spread her fingers across Stephen's brow. She had betrayed him and was now acting as if their roles were reversed. James felt like shaking her. He remembered his words to her outside.

"She is not to leave this house," he ordered the footmen.

He saw her body tighten, but she made no comment as James headed for the door.

There was no use staying here and trying to appeal to her. His time would be better used questioning Holt. James knew when he had been abandoned.

Calliope's emotions caught up with her for the second time, and she allowed them to spill. What a watering pot she was becoming. When she had spotted Stephen, it was like having an old friend return in the middle of a crisis. He was her lifeline. But all she really wanted was for James to return. Foolish of her.

Seeing that caricature had brought reality back like a slap in the face. James was the Marquess of Angelford, nobleman and lover. Not Mr. James Trenton, friend and suitor.

And what was this about her being cruel? She wasn't cruel. She was just . . . She just gave what she got. They deserved it.

She hated the nobility. Didn't she?

Sleep. Maybe it would bring a new perspective. She would definitely feel better after a nap.

Calliope made Stephen comfortable and drew up a small armchair and quilt.

She wished Deirdre were here. She needed her

sister's advice and comfort. But Deirdre wasn't there, so Calliope sank into the soft fabric and laid her head against the cushions.

When had things gone so wrong? When had life become so complicated?

Calliope stared at the ceiling, too tired to sleep. Why had she created so many illustrations of James? Probably because she was already half in love before she knew him.

Being in constant proximity to him these past few days had only made her fall the other half of the way. And fall hard.

Tears slipped silently down her cheeks. Yes, she admitted to herself, she was in love with James Trenton, the Marquess of Angelford. And it hurt. He was not for her. He would never be for her.

She had proven inept in proper society when allowing her real personality to show. She wasn't cut out for their circles. The Killroys' ball—what a travesty. It had been quite an awful experience to live through, but she had rendered a bucketful of marketable caricatures. And she had retained her dignity.

Thank goodness for Terrence. If he hadn't lent her his carriage she would have been forced to walk the entire way home that night. And walking home would have been . . .

Calliope bolted straight up. Terrence's card. The ornate one with the seal that had slipped from his pocket. She had dismissed it as the seal of his father's baronetcy. No wonder the falcon ring design had seemed familiar. She had seen its like before.

From where had Terrence gotten the seal? Calliope jumped off the seat, wiped her cheeks and hurried to change. She had to question Terrence and she had better dress as Margaret Stafford.

With renewed energy, Calliope changed into an outdated outfit and grabbed her father's cane. If anything untoward should happen, it would be a useful weapon. Not that Terrence was in the least threatening. No, he had probably unknowingly picked the card up. Calliope just needed to find out from whom he had gotten it.

She checked Stephen, satisfied he was breathing comfortably and pleased he had regained some color. The errand would take little time and he would be safely guarded. Servants were frequently checking on his progress. As she hurried to the door, she remembered James's orders to the footmen. They wouldn't allow her to leave. They would heed James's directives.

She headed for the study. She would be able to climb out the first-floor window without difficulty. Oddly she was not interrupted on the way. Once there, she opened the window, hiked her skirts and shimmied into the bushes, pulling the cane and her reticule behind her. She sprinted around the side of the house and edged her way to the street. It was broad daylight. She hurried before anyone from the house spotted her.

No alarm was sounded as she hailed a hackney rambling down the street. Unfortunately, there would be no one to accompany her.

As a result of her research she knew Terrence's rented house was in a less prosperous district of town. She had kept tabs on a number of people in the ton. But what would she use as her excuse for going to his house? It was unseemly for an unaccompanied woman to meet with an unmarried gentleman at his residence.

The hackney pulled up to a charming but shabby old building twenty minutes later. Calliope paid the driver and used her cane to maneuver up the drive. She was suddenly glad she had brought it with her. Her leg had started aching a bit last night and it had gotten progressively worse with the stress of the day.

Calliope knocked on the door and was surprised when Terrence opened it seconds later.

"Miss Stafford, wh-what are you doing here?"

His eyes were wide and his mouth was slightly open.

"I hope I am not intruding, Mr. Smith, but I wished to speak with you."

He hesitated, but finally said, "No, do come in. I hope you won't think me rude, but I'm expecting company soon."

"Thank you, I won't stay long."

He showed her into the surprisingly modern drawing room.

"Please sit. Would you like tea?"

"No, please do not trouble yourself. I was in the neighborhood and just wanted to thank you for what you did the night of the Killroys' ball. It was such a nice gesture."

Pink stained his cheeks. "Well, it was the least I could do after what that—that—woman did."

Calliope allowed a graceful blush to stain her

cheeks and ducked her head shyly. "It was most kind of you to provide your carriage."

"Are you doing well, Miss Stafford? Have you found other employment?"

"Oh, indeed I have! I have a lovely job working in a barrister's office not too far from here. It is quite a wonderful place to work."

A genuine smile lit his face. "I am glad to hear it."

"Actually, that is the second reason for my visit. I was hoping you could tell me who designed that beautiful eagle seal that I saw on one of your cards the night of the ball. The barrister for whom I work uses an eagle as his trademark and I would love to have calling cards created as a gift for hiring me with so few references."

Terrence shifted in his seat. "Well, as it happens I don't believe it is an eagle. And I am not sure where that seal was purchased. The card was given to me by a . . . friend."

Calliope leaned forward in her chair. "If you tell me who your friend is, perhaps I could ask him." She threw an extra dash of feminine helplessness and appeal into her entreaty.

Terrence suddenly straightened. "I say, Miss Stafford, I think I could ask around and see if I can find a similar type of seal. Maybe one with a true eagle emblem."

She chewed on her lip. "I did so hope to give it to my employer soon."

"I will find it! I promise. What is the name of your barrister's office?"

"Yes, Miss Stafford, tell him the name of the office."

Calliope jumped at the sound of the unexpected voice. It was cold and silky. She shivered and turned in her chair.

Terrence jumped to his feet. "You're early, my lord."

"Yes, and it is fortuitous, I see."

A startled look appeared on Terrence's face and Calliope saw the intruder. A tall, distinguished man with dark hair shot with strands of silver was standing in the drawing room doorway, a coat elegantly draped over his arm.

A wave of apprehension spread through her. A rustle in the hallway alerted her to the presence of another. A second man appeared, this one much stockier in stature. The look in the second man's beady eyes chilled her. Her entire body screamed danger.

"Miss Stafford, is it? I'm glad you're here. It makes things so much easier, you see."

Terrence stared at them, openmouthed. "Did you know Miss Stafford was coming today? What does she have to do with this?"

"A great many things, I'm afraid." The earl uttered the words and the short man rubbed his pudgy hands together in anticipation. Calliope took several short breaths to calm herself.

"I don't understand." Terrence remained stupefied.

The earl merely smiled. "Yes, I expected no less of you, Terrence. What did you find out about Angelford?"

Terrence anxiously looked at Calliope, but the earl motioned him on.

"He was roaming the streets today with his light-skirt. I trailed them to the Strand. They didn't stay for long. They returned to Chalmers's townhouse, and he left shortly thereafter. Unaccompanied."

Calliope could hear her own heart beating madly. Why in heaven's name had she come here alone? And without informing anyone of her whereabouts?

"Good. Angelford will be cooped up there for hours. He is like a dog sniffing out a bone. He won't leave Holt's until he is assured of his innocence. Or his guilt." A sly smile appeared. "Hopefully the latter."

Terrence glanced nervously back at Calliope. "Why are you discussing this in front of her?"

"Oh, she won't talk. My associate here will make sure of that."

Calliope rose to her feet and the earl arched an eyebrow. "And where do you think you're going, *Calliope*?"

Her breath caught.

Terrence frowned. "Her name is Margaret."

The earl sent a condescending look in Terrence's direction. "That is why I let you trail Angelford. You would have too difficult a time keeping up with his woman."

Terrence looked thoroughly confused. It showed in every muscle of his body. "I told you, the woman is at her house."

"Would you like to tell him or should I?"

Calliope sent him an angry look and mustered her temper. "No, my lord, I would not deny you the chance."

"Feisty little thing. I see why he keeps you around. I thought I was rid of you after the Killroys' ball. A couple of well-meaning hints in Lady Simpson's ear . . ." He smiled and shrugged.

So her firing had nothing to do with James after all. Calliope balled her hands.

"Are you implying that Miss Stafford is that Esmerelda woman?" Terrence was naïve and a bit slow at times, but not stupid.

"Actually, there is no Miss Stafford. There is no Esmerelda either. I have no idea how many other guises she has taken, but this is Miss Calliope Minton, daughter of the Viscount Salisbury."

"And I assume you are the man who killed him."

The earl cocked an eyebrow at her. "That credit will fall to Holt, not to me."

"I don't know why you did it. I barely know who you are. But it was you."

The earl produced an unpleasant laugh. "My dear, you wound me to the core. Nevertheless, Holt will take the blame for your father's untimely death and your dear lover will die proving it."

A surge of fear shot through Calliope, but she tried to maintain her composure. "How exactly is that going to happen?"

Terrence was looking at the earl as if he were the Hydra, sporting multiple heads. "See here, what is this about dying and murdering? I don't want anything to do with that. You said I could court Lucinda and marry her if I fulfilled my end of the bargain."

"Keep your mouth shut and stop blubbering, you twit."

"Lucinda?" The pieces began to assemble.

"He's her uncle and guardian. Lucinda listens to him, she'll eventually begin to know the real me."

"Oh, Terrence," Calliope said sadly. He looked miserable and her heart went out to him, but she focused on the scowling earl. "Terrence was just supposed to keep tabs on James, wasn't he? He knows nothing about any of this."

"Now that he does, however, we will need to rearrange our bargain."

Terrence looked terrified and Calliope didn't blame him.

"Miss Minton, tell me where the ring is."

"A ring? That is what this is all about?" she asked innocently.

The earl was not amused. "Where is it?"

"Did my father take it from you? Is that why you killed him?"

"It is my ring and I want it back."

"And our townhouse . . . you set the fire to destroy the evidence, didn't you?"

"Give it to me."

Calliope gave him a superior look. "By now James has shown Holt the ring. It will only be a matter of time before they find you."

The earl gave her a withering look. "I doubt that, my dear, but if so it will be of no interest to you."

The stocky man ambled forward. He had crooked teeth, a hooked nose and an extremely pockmarked face. "Shall I take care of both of them now?" His eyes didn't touch on Terrence, he was totally focused on Calliope.

"We don't want to worry our young helper, Curdle. He is still our friend, after all. Come, Terrence, tie up Miss Minton, here, and then we'll talk."

Terrence looked at Calliope but she gave a firm shake of her head. It would do no good to argue. Save that for later.

In fascinated horror Calliope watched as the stocky man moved forward, but Terrence had obviously read his intentions correctly because he reached out and gripped Calliope's arm.

Curdle yanked her away and roughly pushed Terrence back. Her body instinctively recoiled and she struggled.

Curdle laughed unpleasantly.

They tied a cord around her arms and legs and she was helpless to move. His fetid breath brushed her brow. She spat in his face and he backhanded her and stuffed a wad of cloth in her mouth. He grabbed the top of her dress and callously ran his hands over the material.

"Enough, Curdle," ordered the earl. "There will be time for that later."

After some argument, Curdle shoved her in a small, dark storage room. Terrence was barely able to throw the cane in after her before Curdle slammed the door. She could hear them arguing on the other side.

"I'll stay with the filly. Never know who might be visiting."

"You can have your sport later. She's not going anywhere. I need you to head over to Holt's. If Angelford is there, kill them both. Terrence and I will be waiting for your return."

A shuffle of footsteps echoed down the hall.

"Where are the papers, Terrence?"

"They are in a safe place." The frightened note in Terrence's voice was audible through the door.

"I want them. Where are they?"

"I—I won't give them to you. I want to know what is going on. What are you going to do with Miss Stafford—er, Miss Minton?"

Calliope heard a loud thump and the sound of a heavy object hitting the floor.

The door opened and the earl stood tall in the doorway. "Sorry, my dear. But I don't believe you have any more information for me. And unfortunately for you, you have too much information. But not to worry, you won't die alone. Terrence, here, will be with you. And your dear James will join you shortly after he gives me the ring."

He gave her an almost fatherly smile. "Goodbye, my dear. Your antics were amusing to watch. It's a shame we couldn't get along more companionably."

She shrieked at him through the cloth that was tied over her mouth, as he closed the door and she was once more thrust in the dark. Why hadn't he put a bullet through her?

At the moment she didn't care; she was still alive. Calliope wondered what had happened to Terrence. Poor misguided Terrence. Lucinda Fredericks would be the death of him after all.

Calliope worked her hands, trying to free the ropes. It was useless, they were wrapped too tightly, but as she struggled, her left hand brushed her cane and a small ray of hope bloomed. Calliope shuffled the cane's head back to her hands. A little more. Just a little more. The handle was in her fingers. Twisting it was another matter. She couldn't get her wrists far enough apart to turn the knob. She needed more leverage.

She sat for a second before the idea came. She moved the cane as quickly as she could until she was sitting on the handle. Grabbing the rod with both hands, she twisted. The joyous sound of a click registered in Calliope's ears.

She moved the cane around and positioned the blade between her tightly coiled wrists. She started sawing at the cord and nicked a finger. She stopped for a second to reposition when she smelled smoke.

The terror paralyzed her. Fire. She could smell the pungent fumes. Now she knew why the earl had not returned. Instinct kicked into motion and she began furiously sawing at the cords, heedless of the pain radiating from the nicks and cuts to her hands, wrists and arms. Smoke filtered under the door and she screamed into the cloth.

James walked swiftly down the street. He was off his usual stride, too emotionally wound to saunter as usual. He had told the driver to meet him at Holt's. He couldn't stay in the carriage one second longer. He was almost there.

Hurt and anger raged through him. Stephen

had obviously known Calliope was the caricaturist. It would explain the political cartoons: Stephen could have easily filled Calliope in on the events at Parliament. It would also explain Stephen's comical reaction when James had shown him the illustration at White's. What a good laugh they must have had at his expense. No, that couldn't be right; Stephen had been surprised. Stephen hadn't known Calliope caricatured James.

But James should have known. All the pieces had been in front of him, but he had never entertained the notion that Landes was a woman. His thoughts muddled together. The stakes of the game were too high and he needed to sort his personal feelings from his professional ones.

What had happened last night? He was thoroughly confused by her.

James maintained the brisk pace. She had never been intimate with Stephen. That was obvious. But why? Was this a part of her caricature scheme? It made sense. It was a good way to get entrée into society. And it would explain why she had been a lady's companion before. But how had she gotten involved with Stephen? That was an especially intriguing question since she was personally tied to Salisbury.

He was going to have answers before he wrung her neck. No, he was going to take her upstairs as soon as he got her to his townhouse. Then he would wring her neck.

Of course, her answers probably would not be

what he wanted to hear. She had looked at Stephen like the sun rose and set with him. Perhaps now that he was back she would become his mistress in truth. There was nothing standing in their way.

He didn't care if Stephen was his best friend. The thought of her with another left a bitter taste. He didn't know when he had become so possessive, but the feeling wouldn't leave.

A hackney barreled past and stopped a short distance ahead. Finn jumped out and ran toward him.

"She's gone, my lord."

"What do you mean, she's gone?"

"She escaped through the study window while everyone was busy."

"One of the footmen is in my carriage down the street. Tell him to take your hack to the Adelphi Theatre. She is probably visiting her family. Grab my carriage and wait for me here, I'll only be a few minutes."

Finn nodded and hurried off. The more James thought about the situation, the less he was sure she was at the Adelphi. Why wouldn't she have taken one of the footmen? He cursed when he remembered giving the instructions that she couldn't leave the premises. It had been highhanded of him, but he had done so for her safety.

Why did loved ones always disobey?

James stopped cold.

A vision of her in her dowdy garb standing up to the ton harpies was followed by one of her at Madame Giselle's, defiant in her shift. Her laugh-

ter learning to ride, her bravery in the coach during the chase through London, the passionate
look on her face last night . . . the images coalesced into one thought.

He forced his right foot to take a step. Then his
left.

He was in love with her. Now that he acknowledged the emotion, it was apparent to him that
such had been the case for a long time. He
couldn't remember ever being as personally interested in a woman before.

It should have been obvious when he looked
at the caricature earlier. He had no interest in
the ladies of the ton. He abhorred the philander-
ing of the wives and the insipidness of the debutantes. He disliked the games, the gossip, the
insincerity.

All along he had known this was where it
would lead. Had felt it the first night he laid eyes
on her. She was the instrument of his father's re-
venge. James would lose the woman he loved in
payment for his mother's death.

He was scared. He freely admitted it. It was the
reason he had studiously avoided falling into love
after seeing his father's downfall. What would it
be like to watch the woman he loved leave him?
James squelched the thought before it took hold.
He was nearing Holt's walkway and he willed
himself to proceed up the drive instead of turning
around to scour the city for Calliope.

The butler ushered him into the study and Holt
dispensed with the formalities. "I know why you

are here. There isn't much time. My spies tell me movement is afoot. You are close. That much is apparent, if the underworld is scuffling about. You should head out of town for the night, and take your ladybird with you."

James resisted the urge to correct Holt for calling Calliope his ladybird.

"Why should I leave? I'd prefer they come after me so I can end this."

"You don't know with whom or with what you are dealing."

"Yes, I know. It's one of the Falcons. One of them went rogue."

"Yes." Holt showed no surprise at James's knowledge.

"Where is your ring, Holt?"

Holt produced it from a hidden pocket in his coat. It was nearly identical to the one in Salisbury's cane.

"We found the missing ring."

Holt's eyes gleamed. "Where is it?"

James pulled it out of his pocket and handed it to him.

"Oh, dear. I wish Stephen had entrusted me with this weeks ago."

"He probably didn't know if you were involved."

"Yes. But now it may be too late. This is an internal matter and it must be kept that way. Few people know about the Falcon rings and the society."

James nodded at the ring. "Whose ring is this?"

"The Earl of Flanders."

James digested that startling piece of information. "Do you know who is working with him?"

"I have been keeping tabs on all of you lately. Flanders has been keeping company with some pretty low types. He's also been seen slipping in and out of Terrence Smith's house for the past few months. No doubt Flanders promised his ward's hand in marriage or some such nonsense."

James felt like someone had punched him in the stomach. He suddenly knew Calliope's destination. "Where is Smith's house?"

Holt looked askance but rattled off the direction.

"It is too bad Stephen is not here to help," Holt said.

Another strong feeling pounded through James. "You should leave, Holt. Go now with someone you trust. You are in danger, someone is trying to frame you. We found a phony birth certificate for your son, Edmund."

Holt sent him an odd look, but nodded.

James ran out the door and into the waiting carriage, giving the directions to Finn.

They took off toward the other side of town. He cursed every rut that slowed them down and yelled at other carriages to move from their path. They were taking too long to reach her.

Excruciating minutes later, they pulled up to an already smoking house. She was inside, he could feel it. Fear as he'd never known thrust him from the carriage and inside the human furnace.

Calliope could barely feel her hands, they were so bloody and battered. But she felt the final snap of the cord and pulled them apart. She ripped off the gag and, grasping the blade with both hands, began cutting the cord binding her feet. She made quick work of it and stumbled to the door. She clasped the hot handle and opened the door. A dense gray fog filled the passageway and she could see flames down the hallway.

Finn was standing over Terrence's inert form.

Where had he come from?

"Finn!" She tried to scream, but her smoke-filled lungs only produced a weak sound. He turned and saw her. Relief crossed his features and he motioned for her to follow. They navigated the staircase and made their way to the front yard, where Finn deposited Terrence.

"What are you doing here? Where's James?"

Finn was moving back toward the door. He didn't answer.

"James is inside?"

A fear unlike anything Calliope had experienced swallowed her whole. She had thought she had no strength left, but blood pumped through her veins as she chased after Finn. They reached the porch stairs when a loud crack sounded and the second-floor supports began to give way.

"No!"

Finn grabbed her and hauled her away from the porch. "You can't do him any good, miss, if you get yourself killed going in there."

Calliope tried to push through him, but Finn was an immovable object.

She kicked him in the shin, used his surprise to push him off the porch and then raced through the front door. Vivid memories of her mother running inside their townhouse returned with painful clarity. Calliope felt sick and terror consumed her, but her foremost thought was finding James.

"James! James! Where are you?"

There was no answer. The entire back of the house was engulfed in flames. Sparks singed her hair and face. Seeing a shape ahead, Calliope dropped to the floor and crawled on hands and knees to the back hallway. James was pinned between a beam and the floor. He was trying to move the obstruction.

"What the hell are you doing? Get out of here before the ceiling collapses," he shouted.

It wasn't exactly the welcome she had been hoping for, but she ignored his orders, panting as she tried to lift the beam. It was heavy. Falling cinders and scorching heat blasted her. Her bloody handprints stained the wood.

"If you don't move your bloody arse towards the door, I will kill you myself."

"If you could carry out that threat we wouldn't be here right now."

His eyes tried.

She bent her knees and heaved. Nothing. Suddenly Finn was next to her helping to lift the beam. The splinters of a crushed chair littered the floor around James. She grabbed one of the chair legs and used it as a lever under the beam. Finn grunted; she pushed. One more inch . . .

He was free.

James scooted out from under the beam and rose unsteadily to his feet. He nodded at Finn, who ran toward the door. James pressed her forward and she stumbled. Scooping her up, he hobbled as fast as he could.

Planks were falling everywhere and the opening of the door was surrounded by flames. James pulled her head against his chest and leaped through.

Chapter 16

Calliope closed her eyes as they dove through the burning doorway. James twisted in the air and took the brunt of the impact as she landed on top of him.

Together they collapsed on the grass, entwined and panting for air.

"How did you find me, James?"

"So that I could kill you." He coughed, his brows drawn together.

Calliope looked into his pain-filled eyes and fell in love with him all over again. She smoothed a lock of hair from his eyes and ran her fingers down his cheek. "*How* did you find me; not why."

He grunted. "It was something Holt said."

"Holt knew I was here?"

"No, but he said the Earl of Flanders was often seen visiting Terrence Smith."

"You know about Flanders, then?"

A cinder landed on his torn shirt. "Yes."

Finn interrupted. "Do you think we might move away from the house?"

She scrambled to her feet and James followed. James limped a few steps before bending over. His hacking coughs inspired a similar reaction in her.

After a few minutes of bone-jarring coughs, her throat was raw but her lungs were clear. Satisfied that she was still intact, Calliope grabbed the cane from the ground. The handle was slick with blood where she touched it.

James was still bent over when she offered it to him. He took one look at the handle and grabbed her hands.

"Are you hurt anywhere else?"

He checked her hands, ignoring her head shake. "Who did this?"

"I did it while trying to escape." Calliope pointed at the cane. "Cut them on the blade."

An icy mask fell over his features. "And your ripped dress?"

She had never seen him so angry. Calliope looked down at her hands. There were deep cuts oozing blood and she'd probably have some scars. But they still worked and that was all she was worried about at the moment.

James tore his cravat in two and wrapped the pieces carefully around her palms. He then picked up his discarded jacket and placed it around her shoulders.

Neighbors gathered around the edges of the property to watch the edifice burn. They were muttering among themselves, concerned about their adjoining properties.

"You'd think people would have used stone to build after the Great Fire."

"One can never be too careful."

Some kindhearted soul had begun a bucket brigade to extinguish the flames, but it was a futile attempt. The building would be a total loss.

Finn dumped Terrence's unconscious form into the carriage. His body sprawled across one seat. James lifted Calliope into the coach so she didn't have to use her hands. As soon as he sat down, he pulled her onto his lap. She rested against his shoulder and he laid his cheek on her hair. She felt better than she had all day.

"Why did he start a fire?" James asked.

"It had to be the papers Flanders asked about. Terrence wouldn't tell him where they were hidden. Destroying the whole house, with us in it, was the most efficient way to accomplish all of his goals." She shuddered. "But how did Holt know Flanders was the villain?"

"He recognized Flanders's ring. Apparently each ring is unique and Holt knows the markings on all of them."

She kept silent for a minute.

"We need to fetch a doctor for both Terrence and Stephen. Is it safe to send for one now?"

James nodded against her head. "Hopefully Stephen is awake and I can tell you both my plan."

They reached the townhouse and James lifted her gently from the carriage. He spoke to Finn, who nodded and then continued down the street.

James and Calliope walked unsteadily to the door. No one greeted them and the door remained closed.

James opened it. "Where are the footmen?"

They walked slowly into the hallway. The two beefy footmen weren't at their posts.

Something exploded in the backyard. They ran to the windows and saw Stephen's carriage house ablaze. All of the servants were working to extinguish it.

James pulled out his pistol and pushed her behind him. "I should have had Finn take you someplace safer. I thought we had time."

The shrieks of the horses and yells of the servants trying to extinguish the blaze reverberated through the otherwise empty house.

"I want you to go back to the street and hail a hackney," he whispered.

"No. We have to see if Stephen is still upstairs. I'm not leaving without you," she whispered back. She wasn't going to budge.

He narrowed his eyes. "Stay behind me."

Their footfalls registered on the marble floor with each step.

There wasn't a servant in sight.

The stairs rose into the distant shadows. Each step increased her anxiety. Calliope's nerves were frayed by the time they neared her door.

James reached for the handle but it was flung aside. A flash of movement from the corner of her eye was the only warning she had before a rough hand twisted her arm from behind.

"Move inside, my lord." Curdle's oily voice and fetid odor coated Calliope's skin.

Flanders stood inside the doorway. "My, my . . . your survival skills are amazing, my dear. Glad you two could join my little party. Where is Terrence?"

"He's safe," James said.

"We shall see. I don't think Terrence has enough survival skills to last long."

Calliope looked to the bed. Stephen's eyes were burning holes into Flanders's expensively tailored coat. His complexion was still pale, but he was conscious. Curdle shoved her forward, positioning himself with his back to the corner.

"Stephen, are you all right?"

"I've had better days. You two don't look so well either."

Calliope gave him a weak smile and tried to edge away from the gun's barrel.

"Don't you worry, my sweet. You will be the last to go. I have plans for you." The whispered voice repulsively caressed her ear as he ran the gun down her side. "I thought I'd lost my chance, but the fates are kind today."

James's eyes were murderous as he moved toward them, but he stopped when the hammer cocked at Calliope's side.

"The good Mr. Chalmers has deigned to grace our presence once again," Flanders said. "You were lucky you had such a faithful watcher Chalmers, or else we would have had you days ago."

Stephen frowned in obvious confusion, but said nothing.

"But you finally made a mistake, Chalmers," Flanders said with relish. "At our meeting I noticed your expression when you saw Holt's ring. I knew then that you had mine or at the very least knew where to find it. You found Salisbury just before he died; it made sense you recovered it, even though I didn't find it on him myself."

"Why did you need it back?" Calliope's interruption caused Flanders to shift his attention to her. James was inching toward Stephen and he needed more time.

"I needed that ring back so I wouldn't be implicated. The ring identifies me as plainly as my face."

"Implicated in killing my father? Why did you do it?"

"The bloody bastard was investigating us, his own team, and he was too close to finding the truth."

"The truth that you were working with Bonaparte, not against him?"

Flanders stared at her, mouth gone slack. James and Stephen both turned to her as well.

Calliope continued. "If the group's sole purpose was to work against Bonaparte and the members started cannibalizing each other, then it was because some of you were working for the general."

Stephen nodded at her. "Our intelligence sources detected a resurgence of correspondence and suspicious movement among Napoleon's staunch supporters. We knew the Old Guard was assembling and that plans for Napoleon's escape from Elba were being hatched."

"A contingent of us was sent to Austria to work out the particulars at the Congress of Vienna prior to Wellington's arrival," James said, "Meanwhile, Stephen, Merriweather, Roth, Holt and Salisbury were working in Brussels and France gleaning information from informants. Shortly after Wellington's arrival at the conference, it was announced that Napoleon had, in fact, escaped from Elba and was returning to France. What I want to know is, what were you doing there?"

Flanders narrowed his eyes. "It matters not, as it is." He snorted. "Funny how you have figured that out, yet you have no idea who is really behind the whole thing."

"You killed my father," Calliope said.

"I was second in command, and I did the dirty work. But I wasn't the one responsible for the organization."

Flanders emitted a strange noise, like he was trying to say more, but his mouth caught in a sickening position as he slumped to the floor, his pistol dropping harmlessly beside him.

"No, you weren't," a new voice agreed.

Calliope stared at the stiletto protruding from the inert form on the ground, then slowly moved her gaze to the silhouette in the doorway. Lord Holt strode nonchalantly into the room, gun cocked and poised.

Curdle's gun was still pressed firmly against her side, although the weight of the little man was shifting. He was obviously trying to decide what to do.

Holt stared at the man behind Calliope. "Curdle, correct?"

He must have jerked his head in the affirmative, because he didn't make a sound.

Holt smiled. "Good. I think we can work out a deal between us. I know what you want. You can have her and be well compensated for your time."

Calliope was unaware of what was happening behind her, but whatever it was, Holt seemed satisfied.

James and Stephen were preparing to move, their faces tense with concentration.

"Tut, boys. At this range Curdle can't miss killing Miss Minton if you persist on playing the heroes."

Curdle grasped Calliope's hair, yanking her head back. Pain radiated through her skull. They stopped.

Holt slipped into the blue padded armchair near the door. His actions were casual, but he kept his gun trained on James. Another pistol was tucked into his waistband.

"Thank you for gathering together. It saves me a lot of trouble."

"I was going to expose you. The invisible power behind the French conspiracy," James gritted.

"Naughty boy, you didn't tell me Stephen was alive. But it was a fact that one of my spies remedied. Without that small slip, you had me convinced I was in the clear."

"You had a Falcon ring, and I would never suspect you of being a follower. You could only be the leader of such an organization. Furthermore, you are the only one who could have pulled any of this off. No one else had the contacts. And you never had to soil your own hands; all you had to do was appoint spies to key positions as diplomats and agents. If anything went wrong, they would take the blame. You were the perfect double agent with the perfect motive—the illegitimacy of your son. I should have killed you earlier."

"Yes, perhaps you should have."

"Who found your son's real birth certificate?"

"The French, obviously, and then Flanders stumbled upon it. Of course, he was ecstatic when he found it. He figured he had something on me should his ring ever be found. And then the ring was found. I made sure you, Angelford, were out of the way and flashed the ring to Stephen at his debrief, hoping he would discover Flanders, and that one would kill the other. Flanders was greedy, but not an idiot. He had Curdle, here, plant Edmund's real birth certificate on Ternberry in order to show me he was serious with his threats. Ternberry, the poor fool, came to me the minute he found it, a huge mistake on his part."

"Why kill Ternberry at Pettigrew's?"

"I didn't attend the party; no one could connect me to the event. There were plenty of people present on whom to cast blame. Flanders, Pettigrew, the two of you, even Roth, if I had desired to try that tack."

"Why did Ternberry return to the party?"

"I informed him that I wished to confront the

villains, and he agreed to accompany me. Poor fool. Always did have an inflated opinion of himself."

"So, all this time you and Flanders have been trying to frame each other. How trite."

"No, Flanders was trying to frame me. I was trying to kill him." Holt shrugged. "Looks like I won."

Calliope broke in. "I thought you and my father were friends."

"We were, my dear. We were the very best of friends. Unfortunately, the French found Edmund's damn birth certificate. Used it against me. When your father started investigating the intercepted messages between our camp and the French, I had to make a choice."

"A choice?" Calliope's voice came out strangled. "A choice as to whether to murder your friend?"

"Edmund would have been ruined, all our lands dispersed to some country bumpkin of a cousin. Edmund couldn't be made to suffer for Salisbury's persistence." Holt gripped the gun tightly.

"His persistence to identify the traitors? You're crazy."

"No, I am merely living within the limits of the nobility. I would think you, with all of your guises, always living on the fringe of society, would understand."

Calliope stood motionless.

Holt smirked at her in amusement. "You, Angelford, and Chalmers have been blessed by great fortune. I thought Curdle here would have done you all in long ago. Chalmers somehow survived the beating by Flanders's men and drowning in the Thames and Angelford survived being shot by my highwaymen. And you, my dear, have survived not one but two fires. A pity you didn't die long ago with your lovely mother."

"You bastard. My mother did nothing to you."

"Flanders always liked fires a bit too much. Seemed to think they hid all his mistakes. She had evidence that was damning—his ring. But it seemed to have survived the fire. How was that?"

She said nothing.

"It doesn't make a difference in the end." He sneered and rose. "Now, then, what should we do, my dear? You have been a thorn in my side and caused me no end of trouble."

Calliope saw a flash and rose on her toes to block Curdle's view of the doorway. He jabbed her hard in the spine. She winced, but spoke quickly to keep all attention on her. "You betrayed your nation, you abused your position of trust and you masterminded the deaths of friends. I think maybe you should run."

It worked; Holt swung his gun toward her. "Really? How quaint. And why is that?"

A voice laced with contempt spoke from the doorway. "Because you're one step behind, old man."

Holt turned his gun toward the voice. There was an explosion.

A look of shock was etched in Holt's face as his body jerked to the carpet. His gun fell to the floor a few feet in front of him.

Calliope looked to the door. The tendrils of smoke swirled around Roth's handsome face.

"Curdle, is it?" Roth kept a second gun trained on the foul-breathed man.

"Get out of my way. Me and the lady here are leaving."

Roth cocked an eyebrow. "Really? And how do you propose to get past me?"

"I'll kill her if you don't let me through."

"Then it will just be you, Chalmers, Angelford and me. Not a pleasant scenario for you, I think."

"I'll take my chances."

Stephen inched across the bed, moving closer to Holt's gun. James crept toward her.

Curdle must have noticed the movements, because he pushed her toward the doorway and whipped the gun from her back, firing at Roth. Click. Misfire.

There was a moment of silence and then pandemonium. Calliope fell forward. James hurdled toward her as Stephen dove for Flanders's discarded gun.

James grabbed her arm and yanked her diagonally. Calliope saw Curdle drop and pull the knife from Flanders's back. Two shots were fired.

She landed in a heap on top of James.

"Callie? Are you hit?" Stephen rushed over and separated them.

It was hard to tell. There was blood splattered and splotched all over her clothes, but most of it had been from her hands, hadn't it?

James started prodding her in the side.

"Ouch! Stop that."

Relief crossed his features. "If you can yell at me, you're fine."

Curdle lay in a heap on the floor. She didn't know who had shot him, and she didn't care.

Stephen gave her a squeeze. Everything hurt, including reassuring squeezes.

Roth was poking through Holt's clothes. Finn entered the room and Roth looked up and nodded. Finn gave her a concerned look. "Everyone unhurt?"

Calliope nodded.

Roth smiled. "Good. But you look awful," he said to Calliope. "I'll summon a doctor." He ducked out of the room.

"Where did he come from?" Calliope asked.

Finn answered. "Said he followed Holt here. I met him at the front gate. He didn't seem surprised at the hubbub."

"I shared my suspicions with him at Pettigrew's after we found Ternberry. I didn't get a chance to update him today. I'm just glad he appears to be a step ahead, as usual," James said, running a hand through his hair.

Curdle's legs disappeared from the doorway as Finn dragged him out. Flanders and Holt still littered the floor.

James touched Calliope's hand. "Let's go downstairs."

She stepped over Holt and walked out the door.

Chapter 17

~~~⌒⌒⌒~~~

A few hours later, Calliope huddled on one side of the sofa drinking tea. James sat behind the desk and Stephen was relaxed on the other side of the sofa. Stephen was already looking remarkably better. The doctor had checked them all over and advised plenty of rest and laudanum after he had tried to bleed Calliope and nearly been torn apart by both men. James had been tight-lipped, but she had discovered his mother had been bled for days before succumbing to a lung disease.

They had filled Stephen in on everything that had happened while he was missing. Everything that he needed to know, at least. Stephen had sent for Deirdre and Robert and they were seated across from the sofa alternating between mothering and chastising her.

"I can't believe you didn't tell us Stephen was missing."

"We could have helped, if you had just let us know."

"Do you know how worried we've been?"

"What were you thinking of, taking off with Angelford—no offense to you, my lord—and not informing us of what was going on?"

"Mother is going to flay me alive, and you too, when she finds out."

"You could have told us of your relationship with Angelford. We've been worried sick that you had developed a *tendre*—no offense, my lord—and were going to end up quite hurt from it all." Calliope silently acknowledged the truth of Robert's statement.

Deirdre shoved a scone into Calliope's hands and unsteadily poured more tea into her cup. "Well, you are coming home with me, and that's that. How long will it take you to pack?"

"Really, Dee, everything is fine. Stephen said—"

"No, I insist. I will bring reinforcements if you don't comply."

"Deirdre, Calliope can stay here. I don't think—"

"Stephen, you can't be serious. There are *bloodstains* on the carpet. Bloodstains from dead bodies!" Deirdre was almost shrieking.

"She doesn't have to stay in that room. She can have any room she desires. It's her decision, Deirdre. She hasn't said she wants to end our arrangement."

"I have to agree with Deirdre, Stephen,"

Robert said. "Your relationship and this arrangement can be sorted out later." He cast a quick look at James. Calliope hadn't had the chance to tell Robert or Deirdre that James knew about the caricatures.

Calliope tried to rectify the slip. "Oh, by the way, he already—"

"You are in no shape to argue anything. Kidnappings, chases, fires, murders. Whatever is this world coming to?" Robert rolled right over Calliope's statement, intent on winning the battle with Stephen.

Calliope went back to sipping her tea and listening to them argue. It didn't matter if the whole tale came out now or later.

From his chair across the room, James watched the four of them clustered together arguing. Like a family, relaxed, friendly and comforting, kindred spirits bickering at each other and then smoothing ruffled feathers. He felt like an outsider. He didn't belong.

Stephen had said she could have any of the rooms she desired. *Any* included his. She hadn't said no.

The room was suddenly oppressive. He needed air. No, he needed a smoke. He rooted through the desk for the cheroot he had seen when searching earlier in the week. He seized it and racked his brain for the last time he had smoked one.

The Killroys' ball.

James stood abruptly. The movement interrupted their squabbling. Four pairs of eyes stared at him.

"I'm going out for a second."

He left the room quickly and headed out the front door.

He lit the cheroot and leaned against the stone. Fresh air. Well, fresh London air, at least. He inhaled and the smooth smoke caressed his throat.

The door opened and Stephen poked his head out. "You all right?"

"Yes, go back inside with the others. I'll be in soon."

Stephen frowned but didn't argue and the door was shut once more.

James couldn't sort his emotions or think straight. Being outside didn't help. Smoking didn't help. Maybe a scotch would help.

It was time for him to leave.

He started down the walk and then stopped. His coat was inside the foyer. He could grab it and leave without anyone being the wiser.

James didn't like the sudden creeping thought that said he was being a coward. He just didn't want to interrupt their reunion. That was all.

He opened the door and stepped inside. His coat was on the table. The staff was still in an uproar and things were scattered to and fro.

James snatched his coat. He wasn't going to look in the study.

The door was partially opened.

He looked.

"Oh, Stephen, thank you. I can't tell you how much this means to me."

Calliope was hugging Stephen hard. James could see tears running down her face.

Something broke in his chest.

He didn't belong here.

James blindly found his way out of the town-house and into his carriage. He needed a scotch—a big glass of it.

"Oh, Stephen, thank you. I can't tell you how much this means to me." Love and sadness coursed inside her. The first paragraph of the first letter was all she had needed to turn into a watering pot.

"Well, you can thank Robert too. It was a joint effort. Poor boy braved the stews of London to get these for you."

"Can't say it was a pleasant experience," Robert said.

Calliope looked at him quizzically. "Why did you have to go to the stews for my father's letters?"

"Our plans went awry when everything else went awry." Stephen shook his head. "Poor Robert was convinced Pamela, Lady Salisbury, was a fire-breathing dragon with a forked tail. And I was gone. He believed you when you said I'd left. I have always been one to up and disappear."

Robert snorted. "We'll see next time."

Stephen smiled and ignored him. "And as it turns out, Pamela volunteered the letters."

A carriage clicked familiarly down the street. James had left. He hadn't said goodbye. Calliope's heart constricted and she looked at Robert. "I'm not sure there will be a next time. I have some thinking to do."

The three of them looked at her as one.

"Oh, don't look at me like that. I'm fine. It's just I'm not sure my heart is in the caricature business any longer."

"Never say that, my dear, you are too talented. Perhaps you just need a different subject." Robert cast her a knowing glance. Calliope just shook her head, unable to respond.

Deirdre jumped up. "I think we should be going. I'll be back to help you pack in a few hours."

Deirdre had always been able to read Calliope's moods. She had probably heard the carriage leaving and correctly assessed the situation.

"Thanks, Dee. Tell everyone I'm fine and I'll see them tonight."

Deirdre gave her a big hug. "Come, Robert, let's be off."

Robert sent Calliope a concerned look, but she waved him off and he followed Deirdre out the door.

Calliope turned to Stephen. "What's going to happen to Lady Flanders? She was the one we overheard in the Pettigrews' rose garden, arguing with Curdle."

Stephen brushed a hand through his hair. "Roth is taking care of her. We don't know how deep a hand she had in the whole affair. Depending on the outcome, prison, maybe being shipped across the Atlantic. She may have targeted only you, or she may have been aware of all of Flanders's schemes. Roth will find out."

"Stephen, I have to ask. Why didn't you tell me you knew my father?"

Stephen hesitated. "I thought I had plenty of

time to broach the subject. Robert told me you believed your father abandoned you."

"Yes."

"Robert approached me with your masquerade plans. He was privy to just enough information to know I'd been involved with your father. When he presented the idea of helping you out, I immediately accepted." Stephen smiled. "Had I known earlier that you were alive, I would have figured some way to approach you before."

Calliope squeezed his hand.

"After learning that you thought Salisbury had abandoned you, I convinced Robert you were mistaken. We devised a plan to share some of his letters with you. Something to convince you of his love."

"Why didn't you just tell me?"

"You had spent years convincing yourself otherwise. Again, I thought I had time. Time to make it easier for you." Stephen shook his head. "As to the other, the only way to get his letters was to approach his mother. We had to tiptoe around Lady Salisbury, so as to not give away our plans. Pamela isn't a bad person, but she was always too protective and possessive when it came to her only child. She was frightened of you and your mother, and your relationship with her son."

Calliope nodded. "I finally figured that out."

Stephen looked at her cautiously. "She gave the letters freely. And she wrote one of her own. I don't know what it says, but it's at the bottom of the pile."

"What a mess."

Stephen looked cheerful. "Yes, relationships of-ten are."

"How would you know?"

Stephen squeezed her hand. "So I've heard." He paused. "By the way, do you know who brought me here?"

"No. The footmen were unable to question her. She slipped away too quickly."

"Hmmmm."

"You were lucky she found you."

"And I'd like to thank her. But first I have to find her."

"What are you going to do?"

"I suppose I can take the footmen around London and see if they spot her, but that doesn't seem very efficient."

Calliope patted his hand. "I'm sure you will fig-ure it out. I could try to put a sketch together from their descriptions."

He nodded. "Speaking of drawings, what are you going to do about James?"

Calliope looked down at her feet. They were swinging guiltily. "I don't know what you mean."

"Sure you do."

"I don't know."

Stephen shook his head in a mocking fashion. "Such indecisiveness from the girl who always has a battle plan."

"Leave me be, Stephen."

He nudged her in the side. "You're perfect for each other. You need each other to chase the shad-ows away."

She didn't answer and he finally gave in. "I will

take my leave too. It strikes me that there are a few things I need to do."

The look of anticipation on Stephen's face didn't bode well. "I'll see you tonight," he said. He gave her one last squeeze and left.

What would she do? Calliope had no idea.

She stared at the pile of letters. She picked the pile up and went to the desk.

Calliope sifted through the letters and then smoothed the one from Lady Salisbury.

It was short but to the point.

Miss Minton,

Please understand that I tried to do all I could for my son. In hindsight I probably smothered him. But then, I was never what you would call a good mother. I wanted him all to myself. The night I turned you away has haunted me. My son mourned your death, and died without knowing his daughter was still alive. It is the worst thing I have ever done.

I have followed your progress for these long years since my son's death. Watching you, wondering if I should approach you. Maybe someday I shall discover the nerve.

Until then, I give you my most sincere apologies, for whatever they are worth. Please accept these letters with my blessing.

Sincerely,
Pamela Salisbury

Calliope had forgiven her father and Lady Salisbury. She had forgiven them before she had been presented with proof of her father's love and her grandmother's remorse. She felt lighthearted for the first time in a very long while.

Calliope stared at the pile of unread letters. Later, when she was alone, she would read each of them and cry for what might have been. Right now she just wanted to savor the precious feeling of being loved.

She opened her writing desk and carefully placed the letters inside.

Years ago she had thought she had plenty of time to speak with her father. And Stephen had thought he had plenty of time to speak with her about her father. Time wasn't something to trifle with.

An eagerness to see James coursed through her. She wanted to share her good news; she wanted to share her feelings and to explain her drawings.

Stephen was right. She needed to decide what to do about James and take action. She couldn't wait, she couldn't count on time.

Some of her unfinished sketches and practice papers were lying in the drawer. Stuffed there out of James's sight during their searches.

Calliope picked up the top one and smiled.

She would take over some of her sketches. Call a truce between Thomas Landes and the marquess. Maybe get him to understand why she had acted the way she had. It was very important to make him understand.

Calliope bundled the papers and grabbed her pelisse.

James stared broodingly at the fireplace.

Damn, he should have known better than to become emotionally involved.

He had only himself to blame. He had witnessed his father consumed by love, despair and finally death. James just hadn't been wise enough to keep his own heart out of the fire.

And now that fire would blaze on someone else's hearth.

"Hullo, James. Thought I'd let myself in."

"And you can let yourself back out, Stephen," James growled.

"What has you so crotchety?"

"None of your concern."

"I came to talk about Calliope."

"What about her?"

"What happened between the two of you?"

James looked at him. "Why, do you want to marry her?"

Stephen frowned and raised his voice. "No, James, what are you—"

James narrowed his eyes and raised his voice as well. "That makes sense. Why would anyone have to marry her? You don't have to worry about her state anymore. She is happily broken in. She can even become your real mistress now."

Something fell in the hallway, but James barely heard it.

Stephen moved so quickly and unexpectedly

that James found himself pinned against the wall. "I swear, James, if I didn't feel sympathy for your situation, I would beat the living hell out of you."

Stephen gave him another shove. James didn't fight back and Stephen released him. "All you have to do is look at her caricatures."

"Yes, they are quite flattering of me. It seems you both want your pound of flesh."

Stephen narrowed his eyes. "I'd like to feed your words to you right now, but I'm sure you will be eating them soon enough."

Stephen headed for the door. It was already slightly ajar. He turned around as he reached it. "You'll find they taste like crow."

"Good evening, Templeton."

"Good evening, miss. May I say, you're looking well this evening."

Calliope knew she still looked frightful, but she gave him a warm smile. Templeton took her coat and moved toward James's study.

"Oh, I think I will just come with you, Templeton. Now that I'm here, I'm in a bit of a hurry to state my business."

A dash of a smile may have flitted across the butler's impassive face, but she couldn't be sure.

"I don't think he'd mind, miss. However, Mr. Chalmers is with him now, so I need to announce you first."

Calliope nodded and followed him, clutching the sketches to her chest. Having Stephen there might bolster her courage. Yes, his presence would be to her advantage.

Light streamed from the room. Someone had forgotten to shut the door. Loud voices issued from inside.

"Why would anyone have to marry her? You don't have to worry about her state anymore. She is happily broken in. She can even become your real mistress now."

Calliope froze.

Templeton had just reached the door, and he stopped as well.

He turned to her, horror and sympathy etched on his face.

She was speechless.

How could she have followed in her mother's footsteps? How had she let this happen?

The sketches slipped from her fingers.

"I—I—"

Calliope turned and ran. Her screeching demons chasing behind.

James reached for the decanter. If he was going to be like his father, he might as well act the part. His mission was to get foxed.

A knock interrupted his progress.

"What is it?"

Templeton entered and cleared his throat. There was an unusually disapproving look upon his face.

"Miss Minton was here while you were speaking with Mr. Chalmers."

"What did she want?"

"I believe she wanted to speak to you."

"Then why didn't you announce her?"

"Well, my lord, I suppose I felt I owed her dignity that much."

James frowned. "Speak English, Templeton."

"It was unfortunate that she overheard part of your conversation."

James stilled. "Which part?"

"Something about 'breaking in' and marriage."

James swore violently.

Templeton approached and handed him a pile of papers. "She left these and her coat behind."

"Thank you, Templeton."

Templeton let himself out at the dismissal.

Gideon stretched out his paws as James sat down next to him in front of the fireplace. James set the papers down and eyed his glass. He ignored it and reluctantly picked up the first drawing.

Stephen looked silly in a picture at the opera. The next one featured Stephen walking in the park with an overly exaggerated grin and carefree air. The sketches of Stephen had been done with an inordinate amount of fondness. There were drawings of Robert and Deirdre and of the four of them plotting and cooking up schemes, literally. All were done with affection and fraternal love.

James tightened his lips, unwilling to see anything unusual in the emotions brushing the pages. He lifted the next one. It was one of the drawings Calliope had done of him. He was splayed across a garden bench staring at the sky, watching Hercules fight the Hydra. Hercules looked to be losing.

James studied the sketch for a long time. Passion burst from the image. Not with the familial love of the previous sketches, but with a flurry of jumbled feelings. A thoughtful expression adorned his face in the sketch, as if he were learning something from the battle. Jagged wounds cut across both Hercules and the Hydra, and one fallen head from the Hydra lay on the ground, carelessly tossed there by Hercules.

His mind had known what his heart had refused to believe. Her drawings of him had always been personal.

When she had been lying in his arms outside the burning house, he had felt as if his world were complete. She had stroked his cheek. She had promised him with her eyes. Her beautiful scent had enveloped him through the smoke. How had he felt? Powerful.

Now? Now he felt defeated. Alone. Weak. Yes, he felt weak. Why had he ever thought love made one weak?

Love was powerful, and he had allowed his father's problems to interfere with the only woman he had ever cherished.

His head fell onto the back of the sofa. "Calliope, I'm so sorry."

Chapter 18

Calliope stared out her window. She hadn't moved in hours. She was stiff. Both in body and soul.

She had been an automaton when Robert and Deirdre had come to collect her personal belongings from Stephen's townhouse. She hadn't seen Stephen since he had given her the letters and she was glad. She didn't know what she would say to him.

Robert and Deirdre had tried to cheer her up, but she had seen the worried looks pass between them. And when she had finally returned to the Daly's home the same worried glances had passed between the other members of her family. She had claimed exhaustion from the day's events. Her family had relented and left her alone, hoping that a good night's rest would restore her spirit.

She was truly exhausted, and if she had been able to sleep a wink maybe she would have felt better. But it was hard to imagine her spirit returning even with a full night's rest. Everything seemed so bleak.

Daybreak came and people woke to their morning routines. Vendors assembled their products; servants drowsily began their employers' tasks. She noticed a man in the distance walking purposefully up the street. She recognized his gait and followed his progress. He had probably come to pound in the last nail.

A commotion ensued downstairs and a short time later her door creaked opened. "Calliope?" The unusually hesitant voice came forth.

She remained motionless as she felt him step behind her.

"Please turn around." His voice was soft.

She shook her head sadly as she looked through her shadowed curtains at the milieu carrying on their daily lives. Her heart cracked as she spied a nicely dressed woman tweak the bonnet of a little girl standing by her side.

"Please go."

"I came to apologize. I know you were in my townhouse last night."

"You said nothing that wasn't the truth."

"Of course it wasn't the truth. I was angry and in pain."

Calliope looked down at her bandaged hands—working hands, not a lady's hands.

She looked over her shoulder. He was shrouded in the early morning shadows.

She turned back to the street. "My lord, we are from different worlds, you and I. You are a marquess, a peer of the realm, and I am a . . . well . . ." She let her voice trail. "Who knows what I am?"

"Who cares what worlds we are from?"

"Everyone cares, James."

"No, not everyone does. My friends care only for my happiness, and I care not a whit for the opinions of my peers. You should know that by now. You fit with me. That's all I care about."

"What do you mean?"

"I want you to come back with me."

"Why?"

"Because I need you."

Something bittersweet broke and coursed through her. She felt a sudden connection with her mother. At last Calliope understood her mother's decision to remain with the man she loved no matter the situation.

Calliope turned sadly and placed a hand on his cheek. "I love you, James, but I can't be with you."

"You love me?" It was barely a whisper. "Then why not?"

Calliope turned back to the window, unable to face him. "I didn't like playing the role. I loved my mother, and I am beginning to understand the choices she made, but those were her choices, and it is something I just can't do right now."

"What?" His voice was confused, but something registered, because his voice softened as he said, "I can't say I like making a muddle of this, but I have never been in love before and haven't had the practice."

Her heart stopped and she looked at him. "What did you say?"

"I'm asking you to let me prove it to you."

Had he just said he loved her?

"I've kept myself shut away from that emotion for so long, Cal. It may take me a while to rub the rust off, but it's something I desperately desire. Even if it takes forever to get it right."

James pulled a blue and purple flower from his jacket. It was a single beautiful bloom like the one from the Killroys' ball. Her hands automatically reached for it as he held it between them. She noticed the petals were somewhat crumpled from being stuffed in his coat and the edge of the stalk was sandy. Just like them.

She fleetingly wondered whose garden he had robbed.

It didn't matter. Calliope understood the gesture. "Yes."

And as she stepped toward him her arm brushed the curtain. A ray of sunshine streaked through the window and pooled at their feet. James stepped into the light and pulled her into his arms.

Epilogue

Calliope opened the morning paper.

A cartoon with the caption. *Marrying the Marquess* was prominently displayed. A mad wedding was depicted. Acrobatic folk hanging from the rafters, outraged matrons sitting next to women of questionable virtue, naïve debutantes being chased by bewigged actors. Roth and Stephen winking at scantily dressed opera girls.

In the center, untouched by all of the chaos surrounding them, the handsome groom gazed lovingly at the radiant bride. A single beautiful bloom was held tenderly in her hand.

Calliope smiled and let the paper float to the desk amid her ink and paper.

"Goodbye, Thomas Landes, and thank you."

You can never have too much romance, especially when you can choose from these riveting November releases from Avon Books . . .

DUKE OF SIN by Adele Ashworth
An Avon Romantic Treasure

When someone threatens to expose Vivian Rael-Lamont to scandal, she will do anything to preserve her hard-won privacy and peace. But her only hope is an original signed copy of a Shakespearean play owned by the mysterious William Raleigh, Duke of Trent. He is the Duke of Sin, and he is Vivian's only hope . . . and soon, her only temptation.

THE THRILL OF IT ALL by Christie Ridgway
An Avon Contemporary Romance

Try as Felicity Charm might to reinvent her background, the truth will come calling unless she sorts out her nutsoid family—and fast. But first she'll meet Michael Magee, an extreme thrill-seeker who's just as caught up in the antics of the Charm family as Felicity is. He's wrong for her in every single way, but get the two of them together and everything's oh-so right.

CHEROKEE WARRIORS: THE CAPTIVE by Genell Dellin
An Avon Romance

When her headstrong younger brother disappears, Raney is frantic that his life is in danger, so she insists on joining Creed Sixkiller, a man she cannot forget, in a search for the boy. On the trail it becomes all too clear that she still loves him, but Sixkiller is a man who has not yet learned how to forgive. And yet, when he has Raney in his arms, he is willing to try . . .

DARK WARRIOR by Donna Fletcher
An Avon Romance

He calls himself Michael, the Dark One, and he has come to rescue Mary from her abduction by a fearsome warrior. Though they travel through dangerous unknown territory in search of safety, Mary finds she feels safe in Michael's care. But in a moment of vulnerability, can she reach out and know that she—and her future—will be safe in his arms as well?

REL 1004

Avon Romances—
the best in exceptional authors
and unforgettable novels!